the Werewolf queen

BRANDI ELLEDGE

WHEEL OF CROWNS
BOOK ONE

Printed by Aelurus Publishing, January 2019

Cover design by Molly Phipps

ISBN 13: 978-1-912775-07-1

www.aeluruspublishing.com

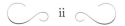

This one is for God who loves me even though I'm sometimes undeserving and for my family who is my biggest blessing.

acknowledgements

It takes a support group to get a book finished — big shout out to Brooke Forshey and Sarah Kirby for giving me their input. Thanks to a fantastic but a brutally honest mom that'll give me pointers on the field and cheer me on from the sidelines. Dad – I would love to give you a shout out, but you brought nothing to the table other than your witty banter. Better luck next time.

Much gratitude to my publisher, Jeff Collyer, for taking a chance and making all of this happen and to my editor, Rebecca Jaycox, for her invaluable skills.

And last but not least thank you to a fantastic husband and two precious kids who have encouraged me with every stroke of the keyboard.

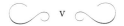

chapter one

This was it, what every teenager dreamed of. The last week of school. Everyone always said, "One day you will miss this," but I had a feeling those people were delusional or perhaps sentimental jocks. Little Reef High School would soon be an end of a chapter in my life, and that thought alone made me ecstatic. After parking my beat-up Nova in the designated lot for seniors, I marched to my first class of the morning—supernatural history—like a girl on a mission. Five days and done.

The building before me was relatively tiny, as far as schools go. Two levels and eight rooms, not including the cafeteria, gym, or library, was all there was to my school. I guess, historically speaking, the aesthetics were cool. The bricks making up the school were the first ever to be laid in this small town, so to say the building was old was an understatement. Yeah, the building was cool, as was the small town I'd known my whole life. I loved living on the Palmetto State coast. Sand, beaches, and the sun were my friend. What totally sucked about my town were the kids who attended the school—a school for supernaturals. Our school catered to witches, warlocks, and similar beings.

Our town had no werewolves, vampires, and definitely no humans. A long time ago, some old geezer put a magic spell over our town repelling humans.

Jolene, my best friend—Jo for short—met me as I was going up the stone steps leading to my current Hell. Jo had to come in early this morning to do some research in the library, such a closet nerd. She rocked her usual gothic attire, and I smiled at how I knew the pair of us appeared together. Me with my white-blonde hair hanging to my hips, tan skin, and sporting a bright yellow sundress, and her with her pale skin, jet black hair cropped in a bob that was shorter in the back with the front pieces touching her shoulders, and wearing Lara Croft *Tomb Raider* attire. She was the yin to my yang.

"Dude! It's hot as balls out here," she said, as her heavy boots clonked up the stairs.

"Thirty-five more hours and we never have to come here again, unless we decide to toilet paper the grounds at night," I said more for myself than her. A last-minute pep talk before the bell rang. I hated this place.

"Sadie, don't let your anger get the best of you on this glorious morning. Stay classy, friend."

Why, hello Confucius. Sometimes—no most of time—it sucked to have a friend who was psychic. Jo was a walking fortune cookie. She would give little clues or hints, but she never just outright revealed what was about to go down. I hated surprises almost as much as I hated the boy we were about to pass.

Timothy sat on some benches outside of the school with his loser friends. His auburn hair was perfectly coiffed. His blue eyes glared at Jo. He was one of the richest boys in school, but when he realized that money wouldn't get him everything, like a date with Jo, he turned psycho on the psychic. He had made her life a living hell this last four years.

He said loud enough for everyone to hear, "Look! It's Morticia Addams."

My mouth opened, but Jo lightly touched my wrist. This must be what she'd predicted. Well, I would show her. I could be classy when I wanted to be.

We started to move past him when he said, "I heard her mother slit her wrists as soon as she took one look at Jo."

Class was overrated. "Timmy, what's up, bud? I'm super impressed that you just said a whole sentence without your voice squeaking. Puberty must have finally happened for you." I bluntly stared at his crotch. "Well, maybe not all the way. At least from what I hear in the girl's locker room. But don't be ashamed. It's all good. Well, you know, as good as it'll probably get."

His cheeks turned crimson as his friends laughed at him. As we walked past him, I could feel him glaring at our backs.

Jo pulled me into the school. "Dude, I warned you."

I just shrugged. "Moms should be a no-no subject. He pressed a button, and class flew out the window. Sorry."

She sighed. "Don't apologize when you don't mean it."

"Um? I'm sorry that I'm not sorry."

She was shaking her head at me as we entered our first class of the day. Lucky for us, Timmy wasn't in this one. It would give him time to lick his wounds and me time to cool down. He shouldn't have brought up her mom and he knew that. Jo's mom was a psychic, too, but she had let the voices control her, and in the end, she went crazy.

Mr. Borrow, also known as Mr. Boring, hiked up his pants way past his navel, because why not? His glasses were sliding down, so he pushed them back up his chubby face. "All right class, since we only have a week left today, we're going to talk about the future." He glanced at Jo, and she gave him a stiff nod. What the hell?

She caught me looking at her. "Pay attention."

Mr. Boring pulled down a map of the world. "As we've discussed, a thousand years ago there was a battle amongst the supernatural community. This battle was between the Lux and the Degenerates. We've lightly skimmed over what each group represents, but today I would like to go more in depth. I would like to discuss the different factions and who are the leaders of these factions. Now, we're lucky our town hosts mostly witches and variations of witches, like our mind readers and healers, but out there," he said, tapping the map, "are all kinds of supernaturals, including vampires and werewolves."

I felt myself nodding off. It was way too early in the morning to listen to his monotone voice talking about some dead people or overgrown dogs. Pain radiated in my shin, causing my eyes to water.

"Did you just kick me with those big ass boots?" I snarled.

Jo pointed a finger at me. "Pay attention."

Jeez. Since when was Jo concerned with my learning? She should have been on me our freshman year, not the last week of our senior one. Girl had issues.

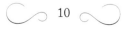

I glared at her as Mr. Boring continued, "These two groups, the Lux and the Degenerates, came into play when the supernatural community was divided. Some factions saw that Earth would be destroyed if there weren't rules. Some didn't want to play by the rules."

David, a cute, but nerdy kid who had social anxiety issues with everyone but teachers, pushed his glasses back up his nose. "Like, don't eat the humans?"

Mr. Boring nodded. "Yes, David. But also, Earth needed to be able to sustain all living creatures, and that would be hard to do if the land was torched. Some supernatural factions didn't care if they ruined the land and made it barren because they didn't need food to survive." He tapped the map again with a stout finger. "There are forty-nine portals all over the world. Can someone tell me how many keys there are that will open and close these portals?"

Jo raised her eyebrows at me. Did she expect me to answer his question? I gave her my best hell-if-I-know look, earning me an eye roll.

David, sweet, sweet nerdy David, piped up, "Seven, Mr. Borrow."

"Yes, David, seven keys will open these portals. Now, I know that I'm jumping around a bit, but try to stay focused."

Was he looking at me? What was happening today? I sat up straighter in my seat.

"There was a meeting," Mr. Boring continued. "The supernaturals that didn't want any harm to come to earth or its inhabitants, like humans, decided that they would send the debauched, wicked miscreants, also known as the

Degenerates, through the portals to different planes. This was a good plan. The bad guys who wanted to harm earth would now be cast from it. All the nobles, also known as the Lux, had to control and keep the seven keys safe."

Jo mumbled, as she stared off into space, "Not all that were cast from earth are bad. Need to fix that."

Um, okay? I silently wondered if she ate any more of those brownies recently.

Becky raised a hand. "I understand the Degenerates are the bad guys, but they're bad because?"

This time I kicked Jo. "At least I'm paying more attention than Becky."

Mr. Boring smiled kindly at Becky. Go figure. "Most of the Degenerates were and are made up of demons, ghouls, rogue vampires, and were-creatures. They are bad because they don't care about anyone but themselves. Now, most of them were dragged through the portals by the powerful Lux. Of course, the Lux couldn't round all of them up, but over the span of forty years, they did their best. The Degenerates the Lux missed were either too powerful to be dragged through the portal, or they went into hiding. Recently, some powerful Degenerates have come out of hiding, forming small armies to go after the Lux."

"But there's not enough Degenerates on earth to worry about, right?" David asked.

Mr. Boring grimaced. "Normally, no, but the seven keys have recently gone missing, and there is talk that the Degenerates are opening the portals to let the cruelest supernaturals back over."

Color me intrigued. I raised my hand. "Mr. Bori… um, Borrow, how were the keys lost in the first place? I mean, if the Lux were so powerful that they could drag the Degenerates to different planes, how did they misplace the keys?"

Mr. Boring clapped his hands and Jo smiled. "Good question, Sadie!" He turned on his projector. "Someone dim the lights. The seven keys were distributed amongst the most powerful supernaturals." A photo of a handsome, older gentleman graced the screen. He had silvery hair, and there was a certain light about him. "This is the Fae king. He was given a key to watch and protect, and he did that until his grandson stole it from him. Supposedly, his grandson was trying to prove his love for his girlfriend." A second image replaced the first. It was of a young boy with spiky brown hair. "This was a young vampire who had a heart of gold, which is a rarity in the vampire community. Because he was strong and noble, he was entrusted with a key. Big mistake. He was too young, and his mighty strength wasn't enough. The rogue vampires circled him like sharks around a baby seal. He was dead within twenty-four hours after being entrusted with the key. No one knows where the key is now."

"That's intense," I whispered to Jo. She just put a finger up to her lips, telling me to be quiet. The way she was acting, you would think she foresaw a pop quiz at the end of class.

The next picture popped up of a striking, middle-aged guy with dark red hair and blue eyes. "This is the Zombie King; he got the title because he is a necromancer. He held the key for a time before he married the Vampire

Queen. She killed him for his lack of ambition when it came to ruling the world, and she took the third key."

A guy with long, stringy black hair and a hawkish nose flashed onto the screen. He was dressed in all black and had a serious, contemplative expression on his face. "This, class, was Devon. He was the ruler of the warlocks and witches. Everyone loved him for his kindness, and the whole community was in shock when his brother, Merek, killed him for the fourth key."

Mr. Boring hit a button on the remote, switching the image. This time we all stared at a young girl who looked very ordinary. "This was a psychic who was killed in her sleep by Merek's son, Cecil, for the fifth key."

"You would have thought she would have seen that coming," I murmured this time, dodging the kick Jo had intended to land. "Ha! See? I'm not a psychic, but I saw that coming."

"The sixth key was stolen from the Werewolf King," Mr. Boring continued. The image changed once again to a stunning man. He had a rugged look about him with his long, brown hair and blue-green eyes. "This was the Werewolf King. After a long search, he found his one true mate, and most of the supernatural community knew they could not steal the key from him, so they killed his mate instead. He followed his mate into the afterlife. A demon is rumored to have the key now."

"This is super depressing," I said out loud, causing several students to laugh.

"Yes, it is Sadie." Mr. Boring nodded. "And the last key, the seventh key, no one knows who has or had it. There's a rumor that a soothsayer had it at one point or another.

There's also a rumor that the same soothsayer has enlisted the most powerful Lux to find those keys. As a school comprised of Lux, we can only hope the soothsayer knows what he or she is doing."

Mr. Boring turned the projector off, and a kid jumped up to turn on the lights. Of course, it was David. Mr. Boring sought me out. His eyes narrowed with laser beam focus. "Sadie, did I answer your question?"

"Yeah, the Lux lost the keys because of love. At some point, they trusted the wrong people or fell in love, and in the end, it killed them."

Mr. Boring rubbed his forehead. I was pretty sure that wasn't the answer he was looking for. "We've spent all semester learning about our individual powers. I told Principal Waylon that we should have been preparing all of you for what could possibly come to our doorstep, but he said the chances of that were slim to none but now…" He cleared his throat. "A war is coming folks— one between the Lux and the Degenerates. It's imperative that the Lux find the seven missing or stolen keys and do a better job of guarding them this time. Maybe fate will call on one of you to save earth and all of us. In that case, remember the key players. Any questions?"

We had sixty seconds left of class, and I glared at my classmates, daring anyone to raise their hands. I sighed in relief, as no one asked a question, including the ass kisser. I would hate to have to harm sweet David, but a girl had to do what a girl had to do.

The bell rang, signaling it was time for the next class. I hopped up and moved towards the door before Mr. Boring decided to tell us one more thing. He stared at me in an overly concerned way. Either someone had stuck something to my back, or unbeknownst to me, I was failing his class. Here's to hoping I was wearing a "kick me" sign. I so couldn't afford to fail his class.

chapter two

$\mathcal{I}$t was lunchtime, and I was sitting with Jo in our little unspoken claimed spot next to the windows. She was playing with the potluck Monday cafeteria food but not eating. Strange. Jo was always eating or thinking about eating. "Why are you acting so weird?"

"Dude. I'm always weird, and you're just now noticing," she said, without her usual enthusiasm.

"Fine, why are you acting weirder than usual? What's up?"

Her blue eyes went blank for a second before she returned her focus to me. "You do have powers. They are just not awake."

What was she talking about? I was the only one at this school with no powers. Zilch. None. Nada. The only reason they allowed me to attend was because my family had pretty impressive magic, and everyone still held out hope for me. Plus, my older brother, Austin, graduated two years ago, and he made sure they'd allowed me into the school.

I batted my eyelashes at her. "Aww. My Disney-loving friend. Are you saying I'm like *Sleeping Beauty*?"

My best friend rolled her eyes. Jo's love for Disney movies was borderline cray-cray and kind of funny, considering she was always channeling her inner Johnny Cash. Her wardrobe consisted of all shades of black.

"No, Sadie, I'm not saying that. Why do you try to romanticize everything?" In a sarcastic tone, she added, "I can picture you now, sitting at a spinning wheel, waiting for some hot hunk to rescue you. Let's be realistic, though. As hyper as you are, I find it hard to believe that anyone could put you in a deep slumber. Well, except for that one time you got all jacked up on Pepsi and Skittles and came crashing down from the sugar high. Besides, if you were going to be a Disney character, it wouldn't be that one. She was way too sweet and shy. You're more like that Tangled chick with the frying pan."

"You know what would help tone down the weird factor? If you would stop watching so many Disney movies. Just saying. But back to the original point, what exactly are you trying to get at, Jo?"

Jo's beautiful face turned into a scowl. "The majority of us are born with powers. Some, like your hot brother and me, have kick-butt powers, and some, like that conniving heifer Stacy, have mediocre powers, right?"

I nodded. "She's a wall-crawler. Seriously? How the hell is that helpful?"

"Truth!" Then Jo's face turned serious as she looked down at her boots. "I guess what I'm saying is, your powers are dormant... sleeping if you will. Quit worrying about why you haven't come into your powers yet, just remember all good things come in time."

Of course, she knew that my non-existent powers were a thorn in my side. She probably saw a lot more than I wanted her to. "What do you mean, they're sleeping? Jo, you obviously know something."

She glanced away from me. Damn her!

"Sadie, you know if I tell you the things I've seen, I might alter your future. Set you on a different path. I can't do that to you. All I can say is you are in for one hell of a ride and it begins tonight."

Then the chick had the audacity to wink at me. She started to get up from the table, and I grabbed her arm, pulling her roughly back down beside me. "Wait, that's it? You can't say something that dramatic and then just saunter off. Come on. Seriously?"

At the touch of my hand on her arm, her eyes glazed over as she stared off into space like she had done since we were kids, and I knew she was seeing something I couldn't. I waved a hand in front of her face. "Hello. Come back to earth."

She finally shook herself out of whatever vision she just had. "Sorry, where were we?" She tapped her chin lightly. "Oh, yeah. Happy Birthday. My early present to you is when in doubt, turn left. No joke. Don't hesitate. When you get to that moment when you're like, 'Which way do I go?' just remember your sweet, intelligent, and way above average ride-or-die home girl told you to go freaking left."

I was still processing her words when she jumped up from the table, making sure to evade me this time. I yelled at her retreating back, "Directions? That's what you give me? I held your hair for hours the night you lost the battle with Tennessee whiskey, and this is what I get. Freaking directions!"

She held up her middle finger as she continued out of the lunchroom.

Once I realized that was all I was going to get out of her, I stood up and stretched before heading down the hall towards my next class. I walked in and dropped my bag right next to Jo.

"Seriously, we have almost every class together. It's not like you can escape me."

In typical Jo fashion, she changed the subject. "There is poor Michael. That boy has been in love with you since day one." I looked over at Michael and his small group of friends filing in. "Why haven't you given him a shot? Or any of the guys here for that matter?"

"Oh, wait. Is this where we pretend that you don't know the answer to that question?" At her death glare, I laughed. "So touchy today. Hmm. Let's see, first there isn't that much to choose from, and second, even though Michael is cute, he isn't…"

Jo's eyebrows arched. "Swoon-worthy? A pulse-racer? A panty-dropper?"

"Yeah, something like that."

Jo nodded. "I agree. You should wait for your soulmate."

"You're ridiculous. There is no such thing as a soulmate."

I thought of something I had been wanting to ask her for some time. "Can you see your future?"

She gnawed on her bottom lip, coated with a dark purple lipstick. "I don't get to pick and choose what I get to see, and for some reason, I don't get that much about my future."

"Guess that puts us on level ground, huh?"

Michael chose the seat right in front of me. He was cute with his cropped blond hair and brown eyes but positively not swoon-worthy. "Hey, ladies."

Aww and such a gentleman. "Hey, Michael. How's it going?"

"Good." He took his books out of his bag. "I'm so excited for your party tonight."

I almost groaned. I forgot about the birthday party Jo was throwing me. "Yep, it's going to be a killer."

"So, I was wondering if—"

A loud clapping sound had Michael turning in his seat to face forward.

"Class, please don't think just because this is the last week of school, you can goof off. Turn to page three hundred and twenty-three and start studying. There will be a quiz on this passage tomorrow," Mrs. Jennings, our short, plump literature teacher said.

I had never liked that woman until right now. She helped me dodge a bullet in the form of Michael, and because of that, this one time, I would do what she asked without giving her too much lip.

I started reading the passage, but my mind drifted back to what Mr. Boring had said about the keys. Two hours ago, I'd been thinking about graduating and maybe seeing the world, or at least a small part of it. I'd always wanted to go on an adventure, and I'd never really paid attention to when the grown-ups talked about an upcoming battle that never seemed to be close. In my mind, it was something that would never reach us, but from the way Mr. Borrow talked, it could destroy all of us. If powerful

supernatural kings and queens couldn't keep the keys safe,
then there was absolutely nothing I could do about it.

Jo and I shared rent on a two-bedroom trailer on the outskirts of town. We were roomies for many reasons. Jo was an orphan by the time she was three years old, and I, unfortunately, never had the chance to meet my mom, but Jo and I had heard stories of our moms. They had been best friends since they were little girls just like us. When Jo had nowhere else to go, my grandmother didn't hesitate to take the toddler into her home. My dad was a heartbroken widower trying to cope with raising two children on his own, or he would have taken Jo in himself. Regardless, we grew up like sisters, instead of friends. Over the years, we noticed the older Jo got, the more visions she experienced. At the age of sixteen, it got to be too much for her to live in town, where she might accidentally bump into someone. She'd begged my grandmother to let her live in the country, so of course, I'd begged my dad to let me move in with her. Living in a supernatural community, no one batted an eye at two sixteen-year-old girls moving into the country to live by themselves.

To get to our place, you drove about twenty minutes from town, and then you just kept driving until you felt like you couldn't drive anymore. Then you took a couple right turns and bam; there was our seen-better-days pink trailer. Jo said our home put the trash in trailer. I thought it was homey with its white shutters, and our porch that was almost bigger than the trailer. I planted all kinds of different perennials around the trailer to cover the ugly underpinning. I tried to tell her it wasn't what you got, but how you kept it, but she just bounced her eyes at me, as if she wasn't buying what I was selling. Heifer.

What Jo did appreciate was that mentally she had been in a better state since we'd moved to the middle of nowhere. No one lived on Sugar Mountain but us. The visions still came, but not like they did when she was around the constant hum of others. One would think being around other supernaturals she would fit in, but that wasn't the case. She had been picked on since she was little by people who made Timmy look like chump change. Since she was old enough to talk, she started freaking people out with her power to see the future, especially when what most people assumed were ramblings turned into premonitions. No one liked knowing their affairs or misdeeds would be known to Jo, and unfortunately, when she was little, she had no filter. Come to think of it... she had no filter now. Over the years, she had become something of a recluse and being her bestie, I'd decided that her enemies were my enemies. Screw them.

I'd always thought her powers were freaking amazeballs, but she strongly disagreed with my sentiment. Jo swore knowing what would happen before it did was nothing but a burden. We seemed to balance each other out. I was always griping about my non-existing powers, and she was always jealous of my quiet mind, as she called it. In my defense, it was hard not to complain. Coming from a family of powerful supes, every single one of them had some nifty trick up their sleeve. My brother had several powers, the coolest, in my opinion, was that he could teleport. Well, the coolest power of his that I knew about. He was so weird when it came to talking about his powers.

Our father could read minds. Talk about a power that came back to bite me more times than once. Me and my brother never got away with anything. My sweet mama, God rest her soul, had the gift of healing. When my mom was seven months pregnant, she was in a terrible accident. Someone ran her off the road, causing her car to flip off of a small bridge. After she pulled herself out of the car, she immediately went into labor. I was born very weak an hour later, and she knew I wasn't going to survive. My mom, in a blind panic, healed me with everything she had, saving nothing for her own internal injuries. At that moment, she had chosen me over herself. No one talked about her because it always sent dad into a tailspin of depression. Even as a child, if I ever just wondered about her, I could tell it upset dad. Once I got older, I learned not to project my thoughts so loudly, where he wasn't picking up everything running through my head.

Missing my mom wasn't the only thing I was depressed about. It was sometimes tiring to grow up around my family and a best friend who had amazing, vast powers, and I was over here with what—the title of Scrabble champion? They had never looked down on me, but I couldn't help but feel like an outsider. A dud. Honestly, at this point, I would take whatever power came my way as long as it came. Even if it was something lame like that hoochie Stacy's powers. Then again, I didn't know about that. Wallcrawler! How freaking lame.

As soon as I entered my bedroom, I picked up the silver-handled bristle brush off my dresser that had belonged to my mother. It was one of the few things I had of hers, along with a small picture I kept beside the antique brush. It was my little shrine to a woman who I didn't remember but wished that I could. I ran a finger over the frame, studying my mother's image. Her eyes were a brilliant green the color of grass. She had high cheekbones and full, ruby red lips slightly turned up at the corners like she had a juicy secret, but she would never tell. Dad said I was the spitting image of her, except she had honey blonde hair, whereas mine was white as snow. I placed the hairbrush back on the dresser with one last touch. When I got a little down and out, holidays or birthdays like today, that was when I missed her the most. Maybe something fantastic would happen tonight.

According to my own personal psychic, who didn't cost me $4.99 a minute and was a helluva lot more accurate, tonight was going to be one hell of a ride. I walked towards my tiny closet with excitement. Might as well dress to impress. I grabbed one of my favorite summer dresses that was the same color as my eyes, jade green. Plus, it was short and sexy.

A pain hit my stomach, making me bend over. The dress fell from my hands as my head started spinning.

What was happening? Trying to make it to my bed, I stumbled over the rug on the floor of my bedroom. Good lord, why was this trailer so hot? I could barely breathe. Everything blurred. I lay there for a while trying to get my bearings.

How much time had passed? Minutes? Hours? At some point, I saw a panicked Jo keeling beside me on the floor where I had collapsed. Her mouth was moving, but I had no clue what she was saying. The moment her hand grabbed mine, something happened to me that had never happened before.

chapter four

Jo held my hand as I witnessed a scene. She was the one who had visions, not me. How I was privy to something that had happened in the past was beyond me. How did I even know that it was in the past? Maybe I was having a seizure of some sort and was hallucinating. Two young men began to speak to one another, and I squeezed Jo's hand with what little strength I had. Did she see this, too?

"Brother, I have just been informed by the pack's soothsayer that the one who will help you find the key to win the war will be coming into her powers soon."

A man, who appeared around twenty, grabbed the back of the office chair with enough pressure to bend the metal under his bare hands. His coal black hair curled a little at the ends. His aquamarine eyes met his brother's dark blue ones over a large conference table in some sort of office.

They were brothers? Two brothers never looked more different. Both were more than six feet tall with mouth-watering physiques. But that was where the similarities ended. The blond was almost beautiful with his fair hair, blue eyes, and angelic face. He gave the impression he could be trusted. There was something about him that made me want to smile. The other one was ruggedly handsome with his disheveled black hair and five o'clock shadow on his strong, square jaw. He was the most attractive man I'd ever seen, and yet there was something about him—something dark and dominant that should have made me feel afraid, but instead I felt intrigued.

I knew I wasn't just witnessing a scene, but I was gaining knowledge. Even though this dark stranger was extremely young, he was a leader over something. I didn't know how I knew that.

The tall, dark, and hot stranger glanced over at his brother. "Jamison, Ariana is positive that the help we need is awakening soon?"

Jamison's easy smile turned into a full-blown grin. "Yes. She is positive, and she is adamant that you be the one to go on the mission, or the key will slip through our fingers." The dark stranger released the chair and walked over to the wet bar. He poured himself two fingers of Johnny Black. Jamison sat down in one of the chairs and threw his feet onto the large mahogany table. "So, Brother, what is the plan?"

The young man set his now empty glass down. "The plan is to win this war no matter what, and if the soothsayer says we must have this creature, then we will take him or her. Are you in, James?"

Jamison stood up slowly, with a rakish smile on his face. "Are you kidding? I would not miss this adventure for the world." The blond angel wiggled his eyebrows up and down. "I've been preparing for the trip to the coast since Ariana called."

Ariana must be the soothsayer. Everything was connecting.

The dark stranger regarded his younger brother with pure disgust. "You are way too happy. You must know something I don't."

Jamison laughed. "Don't be so paranoid."

The handsome boy shook his head. "I cannot believe we are related." To be fair, it was hard for me to believe it, too.

There was something about him—maybe it was in the way he moved, but I felt a magnetic pull to him. Michael might not have been swoon-worthy, but this boy didn't have that problem. Forget swooning. With one of his smoldering looks, a girl could pass the hell out.

Both boys grabbed their expensive looking coats and went to a private plane, heading to a destination that had a key. Whether they were Lux or Degenerates, I couldn't be certain.

chapter five

Sweat poured off of me, and I couldn't decide if I was hot or cold. I felt someone gently shaking me, but I was so exhausted I just wanted to sleep forever. Why wouldn't they leave me alone?

"Baby, wake up."

I tried to roll over, but I hurt everywhere. "Dad, is that you? Just give me five more minutes." I felt the edge of my twin bed dip dangerously low with an added weight. I pried my eyes open. "I think I ate something bad. I don't feel so good."

His eyes roamed over me in concern. "Jo came and got me from the shop as soon as your body quit shaking. She knew you were going to be okay, but she was still scared."

"What exactly happened to me? Do you think it's viral? Some kind of stomach bug." I attempted to push him away from me. "Maybe you shouldn't be sitting so close to me."

"Since when have I ever got sick?"

True. I had never seen him or my brother sick. I studied my dad. My hero. He was a big man, with thinning blond hair and warm brown eyes filled with concern and something else.

"Sweetheart, there is something that I want to talk to you about. I've been waiting until the time is right, and according to your friend, the time is now. On a side note, that girl's manners are atrocious."

I didn't have the energy to laugh, but I did pat his beefy hand. "Dad, you know just as good as me that you wouldn't change Jo for anything in the world. You love her like a daughter."

He snorted. "That might be true, but her running into my shop and screaming in front of customers, 'Oh, big daddy, shit just got real, yo', did make me want to strangle her."

That was fair. I groaned as I tried to sit up. Dad owned a mechanic shop right in the middle of town. I could see he was still in his work clothes, covered with grease and looking more than a little frazzled around the edges.

"Sorry that she got you from work, Dad."

Dad squeezed my hand before clearing his throat. "Sadie, I know that we don't talk a lot about your mama." He took a couple of seconds to control the emotions leaking from his voice. "But you know that she was best friends with Jo's mom, and they had talked about the baby she carried—you. Your mama trusted that woman just as you trust Jo and because of that, she said I would never have to worry about you when your powers came to you, but you're my baby, and it's my right to worry. No matter how old you get, you're still my baby." He ran a huge, calloused hand over his tired face. "That's why tomorrow morning, I want you to immediately start training with your brother to learn how to use your powers. His flight was delayed, or he would have been here for your party."

Wait! What powers? "But I'm a dud."

Dad chuckled. "My darling girl, even if you had no powers, you could never be a dud. Shoot, you've had me wrapped around your pinky since you were a babe." He laid an envelope on my bed and stood to walk out of my bedroom. I picked up the creamy envelope and just stared at it. Dad's voice trembled with emotion when he said from the doorway, "I've got to go get cleaned up for the birthday girl's big party tonight. Go ahead and open it up. If you have any questions, we can talk after your party."

I knew how much it hurt him to think about my mom. If I did have questions, I wasn't sure I could ask him. Somewhere in the distance, I could hear him starting his old pickup truck. As it rumbled to life, I tore into my mama's letter.

Baby Girl, my best friend, Hannah, can catch glimpses of the future, and she told me that I would one day have to choose between my life and another. She also told me I would never get to watch you grow up. That was a hard pill to swallow. When Hannah broke the news to me, I wanted to leave you and your brother a letter for when the time was right. I'm assuming the time is now. You see, sweet girl, Hannah knew what my decision would be, and since she knew I wouldn't get to witness your journey first hand, she told me of what your life will be like. My girl will be powerful once she comes to age. That's good and bad. She showed me that with a power like yours, there will be many that will come after you and try to make you their slave, using your power for their good. My dear friend has allowed me so many glances into the future that I feel like I was really there. With that being said, I am proud of what you will accomplish. Don't tell your brother of this letter.

When your brother is ready, he has his own letter that his father will give him, if he hasn't already given it to him. I love you, baby girl. My little Sadie, you're a rarity, a one-of-a-kind power manipulator. Always do good with your powers. I'll be watching over you.

Love, Mama

I let the note slowly fall to the floor, as I threw the blankets off of me. So many emotions flooded me at once. Grief washed over me as my heart squeezed with love. A mother that I never met, but who'd loved me dearly, was giving me advice from the grave. My eyes became blurry as I stood up on shaky legs and made my way to the kitchen. I was in desperate need of coffee. There sat Jo in one of the mismatched vinyl kitchen chairs. "I'm guessing you knew?"

"Well, duh. Seeing stuff is kinda my thing." She gave me a sheepish look. "You mad at me?"

"Miss all knowing, if I was mad at you, wouldn't you know it?" I went to the cupboard and got down two mugs. After pouring us both some coffee, I handed one cup to Jo and slipped into a chair, facing her.

She took a slow sip of coffee. "So, you want to talk about it?"

"I don't know what I want to do, Jo. I thought I was a dud, and now I find out I've got like the best power ever, but the catch is hordes of bad guys will probably come after me."

"I'm assuming my mother told your mother something?"

"Yep."

"It's more than just the obvious." Jo pushed her short hair behind her ears. "Sadie, you've been marked as a key player. Your destiny is to find an object that will help save the earth. Others know this, so of course someone will try to kill you, and those trying to befriend you to use you."

"Kill me? No. I'm good. Thanks." My hands shook around the coffee cup. "I don't know what you've seen, but I'm just an eighteen-year-old girl that didn't even plan to go to college. Who in their right mind would mark me to save the world? I mean, what kind of idiot—"

"Shh!" Jo's eyes were round as saucers. "You never know if she is listening. I've personally seen her help you with information in the future. If you piss her off, she might not help you later on. We don't want to change fate."

"Um, you're freaking me out right now."

"Good. You should be. This shit's serious."

I gave her a steady look. "I'm a part-time waitress at Bubba's, for Pete's sake. Marked by fate or not, I am no match against killers. Against Degenerates. In case your psychic powers haven't given you a clue yet, I'm not prepared for all of this."

Jo's beautiful face scowled at me. "Well, this is the hand you've been dealt so—"

"Just roll with the punches, right?"

Jo got up and came around the table. She reached out to lay a hand on my shoulder. "Everything's going to be—Sadie?" As soon as she made contact with my skin, I saw... myself in a battlefield with bodies all around me and a bloody sword in my hand. Jo flung herself away from me. "Holy crap, Sadie!"

I looked up at Jo. "What? What was that?"

Jo sighed. "You just siphoned off of me."

"And what exactly does that mean?"

"It's extremely complicated, but the gist is your power enables you to leach off of other supernaturals' powers, basically."

My hands shook as I yelled, "So I saw the future? You're telling me I was on a freakin' battlefield?" No, absolutely not. Nope. Not happening.

Jo studied me like I was a mythical creature, her eyes rounded and her mouth slack with shock. "Wow, I knew what you were to become, but, man, it's still freaky."

I screamed at her, "You're freaked out? You didn't just see yourself on a battlefield with blood on your hands!"

Jo wiped her palms on her jean shorts and sat back down in her chair. "Well, it could be worse. You could have seen yourself dead on a battlefield." I just glared at her. "Listen, you've got to take a crash course, because we don't want everyone coming to your party tonight to be as equally freaked as I am. I'm the only one allowed to be called crazy. It's a title I'm proud of, and I think I wear it well. Plus, you might decide to leave this one-horse town one day, and you know the law. Non-supernatural beings cannot know that we exist. If they ever find out about us, then it upsets the natural balance of things, and it's punishable by death."

"I'm not going to the party. I can't."

"Yeah, that's not going to work for me. You have to go, or it'll set you on a different path."

Ugh. "Tell me what I need to do."

"You're going to have to start putting up a wall when you're around your family, me, and everyone in this town. That way you don't siphon off their powers. Imagine placing one brick on top of another until there is a barrier on every side of you."

I put my head on the table. At least I had a power. I made a mental agreement with myself not to panic. This power could be viewed as a gift. I just had to look at that glass as half-full. "Okay, I can try to do that, and what else?"

Jo resumed pacing back and forth in our tiny kitchen. "Until you know the extent of your powers and you're more equipped to handle them, maybe you should try and refrain from touching anyone."

I looked up at her. "Is there a good side to this?"

"Yes. You can use other supes' powers to benefit you when you need them to. But not all supernaturals. Some will be off limits to you. I'm not really sure why, but I know it has nothing to do with them being too powerful. It's more like some supernaturals don't have an aura or at least one that you can see. I haven't seen everything, so it's kind of hard to explain."

"Well, that's not reassuring, now is it? So, the ones that I will be able to siphon off of—wait, how do I even siphon off someone?"

Jo gave me a nervous look. "I don't know how much I can say. Just... look for the aura surrounding the supernatural being. Then imagine calling their aura into your own body. Because you siphon off of others, you can feel their powers when they are around you, and from what I've seen when you're in immediate danger, that will help you. Kind of a heads up to watch your back."

"I guess I need to get through the night. Once my brother arrives tomorrow, we can work on figuring out my power together."

Jo looked down at her clasped hands. "I'm starting to cross a fine line of what I should and should not say." She tapped a finger on her temple. "You know how this works. It's like a static filled switchboard that never turns off. I can't seem to figure out the right frequency. I know that's why my mom went crazy."

I started to reach for her hand but caught myself just in time. She said no touching or I'd siphon. This might be harder than I'd thought. "Jo, you're the smartest person I know. You'll get the hang of this. I promise I won't let you go crazy."

She gave me a half smile. "Maybe I'm already headed there. Regardless, there's things I have wanted to tell you for so long, but I know without a shadow of doubt, it could alter your future. I can't say much more but trust me when I tell you, you will learn how to use your powers, and you will have the best teacher."

My brother was pretty impressive. "I've got one last question. Before I passed out, I had a vision. Do you think it was me siphoning off of you, or do you think I was wigging out?"

"What was it about?"

"Two hot guys—"

"Let me stop you right there, sister." Jo held up a hand. "How hot were they? Like, make your ovaries scream?"

Was she avoiding the question? "Yeah and then some," I answered truthfully, as I thought of the dark stranger.

"Descriptions? And what was the vision about?"

"If I tell you about my vision, and you know who they are, will you tell me?"

She started biting her bottom lip, and I knew she had no intention of sharing info with me. I gave her a small smile before I walked out of the kitchen. Jo was still asking questions, but I was no longer listening. This time I flipped her the bird. How do you like me now? I could hear her laughter as I walked down the narrow hallway. She couldn't answer my questions, and if I was being fair, I understood. She said she would alter my fate, and who was I to mess with fate? Didn't mean I wasn't frustrated. I went back to my bedroom and flopped on my bed. I didn't want Jo to see my frustration. After all, none of this was her fault. Apparently, the grass wasn't always greener on the other side. I got what I'd always wanted, but now trouble might be on the horizon.

chapter six

When Jo and I arrived at the town hall, the place was already packed with family and friends. Even that conniving Stacy was there. Who invited the wall-crawler? Fortunately for me, the first person we ran into was my grandmother, who I affectionately called Granny. This woman was so terrific in every way; I was convinced that those that didn't have a Granny got the short end of the stick. Her gnarled hands went to grab me up into a warm hug but Jo intercepted her. If Granny thought that was funny, she didn't say anything. I'd eventually tell her what was going on if Jo didn't beat me to it. But not tonight. Tonight was for celebrating. White as snow hair was pinned up in a bun on top of her head, highlighting her green eyes. Granny had dressed up for the occasion. Usually, she was in baggy sweatpants and a slogan T-shirt. Yesterday's read, "BLINK…if you want me." Most grandmothers channeled their inner Jackie Kennedy or Martha Stewart. Mine channeled her inner thug.

She let go of Jo and whispered to us both, "There is young blood over by the punch bowl. He has been asking for you, Sadie, and he is drop dead gorgeous. Like phat!

For the first time in forty years, I think I felt something in my who-ha. It was like wazzzap!"

"Granny!"

She patted her hair. "What, child? I might be old, but I'm still a woman."

Once again, Granny didn't have her glasses on. If there was a hot boy in this town, I would have scouted him out a long time ago, and Jo would have stalked him. She was the best stalker ever. I was sure her psychic skills helped. Granny leaned in close to Jo, whispering something in her ear, when Dad walked over to us, smiling. "I'm so glad all my favorite girls are having a good time."

My smile fell from my face as he put a hand on my shoulder. Oh no. Something funny was happening. I concentrated on the man in front of me and was shocked when I saw what must be his aura. It was beautiful. I reached out to touch the light pink swirl and grinned when it curled around my hand. I dropped my hand in embarrassment after I realized what I had been doing. "Dad, your back is acting up again. Why don't you go have a seat?" Everybody looked at me, eyes rounding in shock.

Then Dad gave a false laugh. "Hmm, that's interesting. It's not annoying when I'm the one wielding the mind reading powers, but I'm not so sure how to feel about being on the other end."

Jeez, I had been here less than five minutes, and I'd already forgotten about my dang walls I was supposed to be building, even around my own family.

Granny was a healer, just like my mama was. She laid a hand on Dad's back, and he let out a hiss. After a couple of minutes, he smiled fondly at her. "Thanks, I was in quite a bit of pain." Granny pinched him hard on the arm. "Ouch! What the heck was that for?"

"That was for not coming to me when you first started hurting. How many times have I told you not to be so stubborn, Russell?"

Jo shook her head at all of us. "I can't tell you why, but trust me when I say we don't want anyone here knowing you came into your powers, so build your walls constantly. Go mingle, birthday girl." She snagged my dad's arm. "I need to talk to you for a second."

They headed across the open space towards the foyer. Call me suspicious, but I was about to go and eavesdrop on that convo.

Granny stepped in front of me, blocking my path. "Shoo. Go find the punch bowl. You'll thank me later."

She gave me a little shove, and I headed in the opposite direction of the punch bowl. My luck, Granny was talking about Michael, and I would be stuck there for the next hour talking about nuclear fusion. Cute, but so boring.

The sad part about living in a small town was when someone had a birthday or there was a special occasion, everyone in the town was invited. My face hurt from smiling, and I was tired of dodging Michael. I went outside to sit on the porch rail to get some fresh air. I needed to figure out if I was really marked as a key player. If I was, then I needed to know who to talk to about becoming un-marked. I mean, surely there was someone in charge.

One minute I was looking at the beautiful garden and plantation oaks then poof—it all just disappeared. I couldn't blame it on the punch bowl being spiked because thanks to my avoidance of Michael, I hadn't had any punch. It took me a second before I realized I was having a vision, which was confusing because I was nowhere near Jo.

The dark stranger pulled on his open collar and grimaced. "Okay, James, let's try to make this as quick as possible. I feel like I'm in hillbilly hell."

Jamison stopped walking up the steps of the building. Wait. I recognized that street and the building. It was the town hall. "I happen to like this small town, CG. What do you find so distasteful?"

He gritted his teeth. "You cannot possibly count this as a town when there is not one damn red light. The nearest airport is an hour away from here, and the worst part is I cannot understand a word anyone says. It's like they are completely incapable of putting G's and T's on the end of their words."

As CG opened up the town hall door, Jamison laughed and clasped his brother on the shoulder. "Quit being so pessimistic. I like to think they talk like this because it's more efficient. Quicker to the point without all those letters that aren't needed, and you have to admit their drawl does sound charming."

"Let's just find what we're looking for and make sure we don't leave here without it."

Both brothers stood out like a sore thumb. One light. One dark. Both were around six feet four inches tall and muscular; their suits fit them snugly. They scanned the crowd for someone when the busty brunette, Stacy, made a beeline for the brothers.

James smiled his disarming smile and murmured to his brother, "Please let this be her. I call dibs."

The pretty brunette grabbed both brothers' arms and purred, "Well, hello boys, I'm Stacy. I don't know what has brought you to this small town, but I find myself very thankful. Would either of you like a drink?" She batted her eyelashes. "What can I get y'all?"

Before James could say anything, CG said, "We're looking for someone. Sadie Grey?"

My heart sped up, but I couldn't shake myself out of the vision. Poor Stacy looked like she was about to spit fire. "Well, of course, you are." She made a big production of studying her nails. "I just saw the tramp dodging Michael as she slipped out to the back porch."

Both boys started moving towards the doors leading to the back porch.

James turned around and winked at Stacy. "Thanks, sweetheart."

Stacy stopped pouting for a second to return the smile. "Anytime, big guy." With that, she was on to her next pursuit. Freaking wall-crawler.

The dark one opened the doors and saw a profile of a girl straddling the porch with her focus on the garden in front of her. His nose flared. Emotions welled up inside of him and then like a faucet, he turned them off.

It was the blond one who broke me out of the vision.

Jamison said, "I sure as hell call dibs."

chapter seven

I blinked my eyes several times. Both boys were staring at me, and I realized that I didn't see the future. I was seeing the present. I unabashedly studied two of the hottest men I'd ever encountered in my life.

I hopped off the rail to go and search for Jo; she would know what to do, and this time I wouldn't let her weasel out of giving me answers.

The black haired boy stopped me from leaving. "Excuse me, are you Sadie Grey?"

I gave a nod. I needed to remain calm. They didn't know me. Or maybe they did? Maybe these were the bad guys my mom talked of. I couldn't let them know I was scared to death. I crossed my arms over my chest and tilted my chin up. "Last time I checked. And you are?"

"I am CG Bradford, and this is my brother, James," CG said. "We hate to interrupt your birthday celebration, but we need you to go with us."

"So much for subtlety," Jamison said.

I looked at both brothers like they had just lost their minds. "Um, yeah, not really that kind of girl."

The angelic one leaned a hip against the rail, as if he was enjoying his brother's discomfort.

Scowling, CG started again. "I apologize. What I should have said is, it is imperative that we go somewhere to talk. This is a very time sensitive matter, and unfortunately what we need to talk to you about cannot wait."

I studied CG. His aura was many different colors, so beautiful I wanted to touch it. The colors swirled to me and I inhaled deeply. Was that normal? What was normal anymore? That was a better question. I needed to leave immediately. I could feel panic bubbling up inside me as I started edging around CG to stop a few feet away from the door. My nostrils flared. "What is that sweet smell?"

The dark one cocked his head. "All I can smell is your fear."

Just great, I was siphoning off of them. I didn't even know how I was doing it, so I sure as heck couldn't stop. Whatever they were, they could smell my fear. So much for trying to put up a brave front. I tried to calm my heartbeat and build my walls.

I slowly headed towards the door leading back to the party, where there were people also known as eyewitnesses. "Well, guys, thanks for stopping by. Make sure to take a piece of Granny's famous strawberry cake with y'all when you go." I reached for the doorknob when the blond lightly grabbed my elbow. That was when the other one growled.

The angel dropped my elbow, sending a knowing smile to his brother. "I can only imagine what you are thinking right now, but you must know that just like us, the Degenerates have their own soothsayers and seers. They know what it is going to take to stop the Lux from getting their hands on the keys. Just as we know that you will play a part in winning this war, they do, too, and I can promise you that if they aren't here now, they will be soon."

CG nodded. "You will be safer with us."

"You know, that is a great offer, but I'm going to have to sleep on it. If you boys have maybe a card, you can leave it by the snack table, and I'll be sure to pick it up later."

With my hand on the knob, I was so dang close to being away from hotter and hottest when the, "I'm bad, and I know it," one shook his head at me. His black hair fell over his forehead, and my hand froze. In a menacing tone, he said, "You are making a mistake. The others that come for you will not be as kind as me."

I could think of a thousand words to describe that man, but kind wasn't one of them. Kind was something I associated with soft and nurturing. He was neither. I didn't run back to the party, but I definitely walked as fast as I could because if he was part of the good guys, I didn't want to see how fierce the bad guys looked. My mouth was suddenly dry, so I headed for the punch bowl. I looked over my shoulder to see hotter and hottest walk in the building and take a seat at one of the empty tables. Guess some people couldn't take no for an answer. Go with them? Yeah, probably not. Hadn't they ever seen *Forensic Files*? Or *Date Line*? Both were Granny's favorite shows. Come to think of it, Granny might have some serious issues, but I would worry about her mental health later. I currently had more pressing problems.

chapter eight

almost tripped when I saw what awaited me at the punch bowl. It sure as heck wasn't Michael. My whole life, I grew up around cute, all-American boys. Now all in one night, I saw three men that looked like they could be in any cologne ad in a high-end magazine. This man was not quite as tall as the brothers, but he was still every bit of six feet. He had perfectly mussed, rich brown hair and big brown eyes that were currently boring a hole right through me. I finally got my feet to start walking again properly. I picked up a glass off the table and avoided his eyes.

I poured some green punch, doing my best to not cave under the intense gaze of the model in front of me. "You are even more beautiful in person, Miss Grey."

"How do you know my name, Mr....?"

He smiled at me, and Lord help me, he had dimples. "Just call me Stephan. I hear that they are soon going to start dancing. Would you save me a dance? I promise to answer all of your questions."

This man oozed charm. I had no clue why I said, "Sure," but I did. He smiled at me like he wanted to devour me before he left me standing all alone at the punch bowl.

Jo came trotting over with a lopsided grin on her face. "It's like a smorgasbord of hotness in here. So, care to tell me who all your little friends are?"

I gave her an exasperated look. "Jo, I'm sure you know exactly who they all are, but I'll play your game. The hot, mysterious one over there by the snack table is Stephan."

Jo sighed. "Holy crap. He is the hottest thing I have ever seen this side of the Mississippi."

I laughed. "Just wait." I scanned the room until my eyes landed on a little checkered table. There I saw the angel sitting with my Granny of all people. "And the angel over there flirting with Granny is James, but I have dubbed him 'hotter' because he is about hotter than anything I have ever seen."

Jo's eyes darted from Stephan to James. All she came up with was, "Damn."

I searched for the other one and finally found him leaning up against a wall with one foot propped up and his hands in his pockets. That hoochie, Stacy, was all in his personal space, laughing and twirling her hair. I turned back to Jo and pointed behind me with my thumb. "And that one over there is hottest. Also known as CG something or another."

Jo looked behind me and said, "Oh, the one that is currently staring at the back of your head?"

It took everything I had not to turn around. Bonus points for me. Jo still stared at CG.

"I don't know if one is technically hotter than any of the others. I would have to see them head to toe naked before I made that kind of judgment call."

She might have a point.

"Remember, build your walls. You can do it." I was about to ask her about the crazy vision I had outside when she grabbed my cup from me. "Here, let me hold that for you."

My eyebrows drew together. "Why?"

"For the dance, silly."

A couple of seconds later, some music started up, and Stephan walked over to claim me. I thought of an indestructible wall. When his hand landed on the small of my back, I sighed with relief. Jo was right; I could do this. If I could keep up with my Granny's crazy lingo, I could build a stupid wall. I was concentrating so hard on my wall that it took me a second to realize I was dancing. I gazed into Stephan's eyes as he slow danced with me around the floor, and I had to break the awkward silence. "You're not from around here. Let me guess; you think that I can help win the war in some way, and you need me to help you."

Stephan pulled me in just a little closer. "Smart and gorgeous. I came here tonight to see which side you're going to be batting for."

I looked into his puppy dog eyes and asked, "Which team are you on, Stephan? The good guys or the bad guys?"

He leaned in and whispered in my ear, "Whichever one suits me best at the time. I'm a selfish bastard."

I glanced back at him and laughed. "Well, at least you're honest." I gazed around the room, seeing the angel still talking with my Granny, and he looked up at me and smiled. I immediately sought out his brother. I found him frowning at me from the same place I saw him last time, with the same ho draped all over him. Stacy. Ugh.

Stephan said, "Do not worry about him. He always has a murderous look on his face."

"What do you know about the brothers?"

Stephan pursed his lips, as if he was in deep thought. "I know that honor boringly binds them. They have an overzealous sense of justice. I can assure you without a doubt they are here to get your help to rescue a key. I'm intrigued to know who they will get the key from."

"They don't look like they need my help. Why me?"

"I wish I knew. I do know that you have been marked as one of the players and because of that, you will need protection."

I was so wrapped up in what Stephan was saying I barely noticed the band had started playing another song. "Whether you want to be involved in this war or not, you will be. I came here tonight to offer you protection," he said.

There seemed to be a lot of that going around, but who would protect me from the protectors? I pushed back from him a little bit. "I appreciate the offer, but I barely know you. If I must be involved in this war, the best thing for me to do is to get prepared. I can at least trust myself."

Stephan stopped dancing but kept his arms around me. "When you need me, call me, and I will be there."

He gave me a white card. The only thing on the card was a phone number written in small, black numbers. Then he leaned in like he was about to kiss me, and two things happened at once. I accidentally let my walls down, and his aura hit me like a freight train. It exploded from him, red as blood, which meant I siphoned off of him. I felt a huge power surge. As I closed my eyes, I could hear things I shouldn't be able to hear, and I wanted... blood? As I was trying to come to terms with Stephan being a vampire, the second thing happened, also known as hottest. He was in between us so fast I didn't see him coming.

CG said, "It's about time for you to leave, isn't it, neck biter?"

Stephan backed up two feet with his hands in the air. He looked over at me and winked. "You let your walls down. It was a rush, was it not?" Then his eyes roamed over my body. "You know where to find me." He turned around and walked out the front door.

"People are starting to stare, and we don't want that, do we?" CG pulled me into his arms. I immediately stiffened, and he whispered, "Relax, I don't bite. The last one did but I don't."

I glanced up into his beautiful face. "Not sure if that was supposed to be a joke or not. It is tough to tell with that serious look on your face."

CG smiled, and my heart skipped a beat. "It's been a hard night for me, too. I assumed that when I came here, you would understand that it's imperative you leave with me for the safety of you and your family. And if I hear the phrase, 'bless your heart' one more time, I might just throw up."

"What do you mean, the safety of my family and me? Are you threatening me?"

CG let out a frustrated sigh. "No, I'm not threatening you or your loved ones. But there will be those that come after you who see you as a means to an end. They don't care what they have to do to secure a blood oath from you, which binds you to fight on their side."

There was a lot that had happened to me in a short time. I should be completely out of my mind with fear but I wasn't. I was scared for sure, but not freaking out. It could be because even though Jo couldn't tell me my future, she wouldn't have let me dance with either boy if they were ax murderers. Not to mention the fact that I'd caught a couple of glimpses of her, and she was wearing a goofy grin while giving me a thumbs up.

I tried to get my thoughts in order while trying not to think about how muscular his arms were underneath my hands, but I was having a hard time focusing. This creature holding me ever so gently had my hormones in overdrive.

"Mr. Bradford, I need you to understand that before today, I had no powers. None. I had heard rumors of the war and had basic knowledge of the keys, but I am, by no means, a fountain of knowledge when it comes to the Lux or the Degenerates. I need time to think about my options."

"But—"

I shook my head. "Thank you for the dance."

As I tried to extract myself from him, his grip tightened. "Don't think too long, Miss. Grey."

I patted his shoulder and shook my head. "Bless your heart." I swear I heard him laugh as I walked away.

Three mysterious, handsome strangers in our small town. I knew tongues were wagging, and fingers were pointing, but I also knew the reason the three strangers were allowed to stay in our town was because of Jo. She must have foreseen something and ran it by my dad because he wasn't threatening to kill anyone. Plus, the three strangers made it past our magic barriers. Someone had to agree to let them in. Dad walked across the floor where I had left hottest and was in a deep conversation with CG, patting him on the shoulder and smiling. What in the world was going on? I felt like everyone was in on a dirty little secret I wasn't privy to. Jo had definitely told my father something. I was so tempted to corner them both, but I knew it would be a complete waste of time. I wasn't a diary writing kind of girl, but if I kept one, I would definitely title this day, "weirdest day ever."

chapter nine

As I lay awake in my twin bed, I couldn't help but think what a crazy day I'd had. The dud had finally received her powers, but not just any powers, the best power to obtain ever. And who did I find this out from? My dead mom. Seeing three hot guys in my podunk town, much less at a birthday party for yours truly, was ludicrous, to say the least. But the real nail in the coffin? I'd been marked as a player in a game I knew nothing about. Being part of a community that had mostly witch-like powers meant I had never been around other factions. To come into contact with a vampire, and whatever the brothers were, almost felt surreal. All three gentlemen, and I used that term loosely, wanted to use me to find one of the seven keys. I had apparently lived a very sheltered life, which was okay when you were a dud. And to top off my night, my best friend had just disappeared. I came home to an empty trailer and found a note on the fridge.

It said, *Scared you will ask too many questions, and I won't be able to fend you off. Happy Birthday. Love, Jo.*

What a coward. I mean, of course, I was going to ask her questions, but it wasn't like I was going to duct tape

her to the wall and torture her until she gave me some answers. At least I don't think I would have because I didn't have any duct tape on me, which was an outright sin in the South. It was in the top five things for a redneck to have when in survival mode.

I tossed and turned until I realized sleep was just not going to happen for me anytime soon. I threw the covers off of me and headed toward the kitchen in search of some pie. It wouldn't help me sleep, but at least I would enjoy being up. As I reached the kitchen table, I glanced out the window and realized my night was about to get worse. A black aura emerged from the ground and headed towards me from the forest. My head started swimming, and my knees almost gave out, as I reached for the back of the kitchen chair to steady myself. I could feel the excitement of hearing my heartbeat. But it wasn't my excitement. It was someone else's, and they were also using all of their senses to pinpoint where I was in the trailer, which could only mean I was freaking channeling someone. And they were coming this way. I grabbed a kitchen knife and ran as fast as I could. Diving to the back of my closet, I hid behind some long dresses and prayed they would cover all of me. I barely had time to sit when I heard the screen door suddenly squeak open.

I heard a laugh then a deep rumble. He was speaking in some sort of foreign language, but for whatever reason, I could understand him. "Hmm. I hear a fast heartbeat and smell fear. I guess someone knows that I'm here. Shall we make this easier by you coming to me?" I heard a couple of footsteps in the tiny living room before he stopped. "No? Fine. Stay where you are, and I'll find you. Or better yet, get up and run. I love a good chase."

I tried as hard as I could to calm my beating heart, but having something evil searching for your crappy hiding spot was not a calming thought. Before I could even come up with a plan, I was snatched out of my closet by my hair. My feet dangled three inches off the ground, and I cried out in pain and terror because the thing in front of me was a demon. I wish that I would have paid more attention to what Mr. Boring had said about demons! This one was almost as wide as he was tall, and he was pretty dang tall. With two black horns growing out of his head, he stared at me with onyx eyes that were utterly soulless.

"Found you." His head cocked to the side. "The boss man is going to love you in so many ways. Pretty."

The shock wore off and panic set in, and I started kicking and punching. I remembered the knife I still held in my hand and rammed it into his stomach. With his free hand, he pulled the knife out of him and tossed it to the floor. Well, that didn't work out too great.

My weak attempt must have amused him because he laughed. "I like that you're feisty." He threw me across the room like a ragdoll. My head cracked into the wall, and I briefly saw stars.

Slowly, he walked over to me. I was barely holding on to consciousness as he gripped my ankle and started dragging me through the trailer. I grabbed onto everything I could, but it didn't stop him—it didn't even slow him down. He walked right out the front door, hauling me down all three steps, my head hitting each one.

Just as I thought this was it for me, and I was going to die at the hands of some ugly, two-horned freak, I heard, "Let her go, and I promise I won't torture you before you die."

The demon released my foot, and I crawled backwards on the grass as far away from him as I could. A man stepped out of the shadows. One that I didn't think I would see again so soon. CG glanced my way, and his face hardened even more, if that was possible. "Never mind, demon. I will play with you before you die."

The demon laughed. "You are too late. She's mine." He turned his back on CG and attempted to grab me. Quicker than the eye could trace, CG appeared behind him, punching the demon in his kidney. The demon whirled around to attack, but he swung at nothing but air. CG tapped the demon on his shoulder, and the demon turned around once more to find a different version of the dark stranger. CG had morphed into something larger. I had never seen a werewolf up close before, but the pictures in the textbooks didn't do them justice. I should be terrified, but I found myself enamored instead. Every inch of him had elongated, and he was so much larger. CG grabbed the demon by his throat and slung him fifteen feet into the air. The demon made contact with an old oak tree and slid all the way down.

"Demon, you must not recognize me. I am the King of were-creatures." The demon's black eyes looked to the ground as he pushed himself up. "Ah, now you show fear. You wanted to play, so let's play."

The demon wiped at a trickle of blood dripping from his nose. "I have no qualm with you. I came for the girl, and I must leave with her, or my life is over."

CG clearly understood the foreign language as well. He took a couple of steps closer to the demon and smiled a terrifying smile. "So, demon, I guess you have to decide, would you rather be killed by your king or by me?"

The demon looked at me one more time before he ran into the woods. CG sighed and ran after him. My adrenaline was wearing off and I was hurting. I gave myself a couple of minutes of just sitting there on the cool grass until I finally found my way to my feet.

CG strolled out of the woods and was beside me as I climbed the first step to go back in the trailer. His eyes searched my face. "Are you okay?"

His once pristine, white shirt was bloody. "You... you gave him a choice of fighting you or someone else, and he chose to run. Did you still kill him?"

"Of course, I killed him." CG's handsome face scrunched up like he was stumped. "Don't sympathize with him. If I hadn't shown up, he would have had his way with you before he gave you over to the Demon King. If I let him escape, every demon in the world would know that you were with me, and I don't want anyone to know who has you yet. Not until you are stronger."

I had so many questions popping through my head it spun. Or maybe I felt like I was on a carousel because I had a concussion. "How did you get here so fast? How did you know I needed help? And what do you mean by you don't want anyone to know who has me?"

CG was scanning the woods as he half dragged me through the front door. "I have been patrolling the woods around your home because I feared others would know about you and something like this would happen. Word travels fast, does it not?"

I was still in shock as we went through the trailer. Somehow, he knew which bedroom was mine. As soon as we entered the small room, he made me sit on my bed while he walked into my closet and found my only suitcase. He threw it beside me.

"What are you doing?"

He quickly grabbed as many clothes as he could and tossed them into the open suitcase. "Packing. You're coming with me."

I stood up and put both hands on my hips. "Listen here, douche bag, I'm not going with you or any other creep for that matter."

CG took a giant step toward me. "Yes, you are because the others that come for you will try and use your loved ones as pawns. They are safer with you far away from them."

He opened up my panty drawer, and I said, "That is enough!"

He turned around so sharply it made my blood freeze in fear. "There are more in the woods. At least four. Leave everything and follow me."

He grabbed my hand, and I immediately felt an overwhelming amount of power flowing through my body. He looked over his shoulder at me, as he pulled me through the small trailer to the back door. "You have no clue how powerful you are, do you?"

I had a hard time finding my voice with all his power pumping through my system, so I just shook my head.

He squeezed my hand. "Don't take too much from me. We don't exactly know how much power you can handle at one time, or what the consequences are if you overload." My eyes widened as I realized how much power I had been siphoning off of him. My senses were so sharpened I could hear four supernaturals heading for us. As he opened up the trailer door, I noticed my night vision was off the charts as well. As soon as we stepped on the porch, it made a sound under our weight that was like an explosion to my new hearing. With my hand in his, we took off at a dead run through the woods, and thanks to his power, I was able to match his super speed.

"I parked my car a mile down the road. We're going to circle back around to it."

I glanced down at my bare feet and was amazed I wasn't complaining about all the thorns and stickers I could feel jabbing into my skin.

"You know someone is waiting at the end of the road for us?" From my peripheral vision, I could see him nod. "Yes, I'm aware of that, and it's good to see that you can sense her, too." I didn't want to point out that even though I could sense someone, I had no clue if they were male or female. CG stopped running so quickly he almost pulled my arm out of my socket. My nostrils flared at the sickening sweet smell rolling off of me, but there was nothing I could do about it. Fear was coming out of every pore in my body. The only thing keeping my knees from knocking together was the adrenaline pumping through my body.

"They have split up to attack on all sides. Stay behind me."

I heard the demon before I saw him. He ran full force towards us. My throat almost closed in panic when I saw that he was twice as large as the other demon. I had a feeling this was it for me and the werewolf. Both demon and wolf leaped into the air to meet one another. When they landed on the ground in a heap, CG was on top. Without hesitation, he punched the demon in the chest twice. The first time I heard ribs cracking, and the second hit was to find what was underneath the rib cage—the demon's heart. I felt my knees buckle as he threw the heart on the ground for some wild animal to find.

He grabbed my arm and shook me. "Pull it together right now. We don't have time for any hysteria."

I thought seeing someone rip a beating heart out of a demon was an excellent time for hysteria. Before I could voice my opinions, the remaining three that had been chasing us now stood in a triangle formation. Two demons and one human?

The biggest of the two demons said in perfect English, "Adorjan always did jump the gun."

The demon on the right side of him had tattoos all over his face. His lousy ink job scrunched together as he smirked. "I told him his lack of patience would be his undoing."

CG dragged me behind him. I turned around, so our backs were together and to keep an eye on the big-boned brunette headed my way. One look at her black eyes and I realized this demon must have found a body to take over.

She said, "Boys, please focus. We need the girl alive, but the wolf can die."

With her words, all hell broke loose. Both demons attacked CG at once, and the brunette lunged for me. Thanks to my borrowed power I was stronger than I'd ever been, and I used that strength against the Amazon. She grabbed me by my hair and I got pissed. Having my hair pulled twice in one night was the straw that broke the camel's back. I kicked her so hard her kneecap dislocated. She released me as she howled in pain. My dad had always told me, "don't ever kick somebody when they are down," but I figured this was the exception. It felt natural to open myself up and draw power off the surrounding creatures. When I felt dizzy with the amount of energy coursing through my veins, I charged the Amazon. Jumping in the air, I wrapped my thighs around her neck, clenching her throat as I twisted my upper body. I heard a snap an instant before both of our bodies crashed onto the ground. I jumped up and spun around to see how CG was faring. Both demons were splayed on the ground with gaping holes in their chest where their hearts should have been. He repeated the process with the Amazon. My stomach was rolling as CG leaned over and wiped his bloody hands as best as he could on the tall grass.

"Here I was worried about you, and it looks like you handled yourself exceptionally well." He finally looked up at me, taking two steps towards me. He went to grab me, but he stopped himself, glancing at the stains on his hands instead. His arms dropped down to his side and to be honest, I was thankful. "How bad are you hurt?"

"I'm not hurt. I'm just really dizzy, and my head is pounding."

"Sadie, some blood is dripping from your nose."

I swiped the back of my hand under my nose, and sure enough, it came away red.

"I'm not sure what happened. Maybe I took too much power from you, and this is a result?"

"It looked like you were taking power from the demons, too. That's pretty dangerous, considering you're new to all of this."

I shook my head in dismay. "I can't believe that I just snapped that girl's neck like it was nothing. I have never killed anything in my life. I might be a little bit in shock. No, no, I'm definitely in shock."

Bloody hands or not, I was in desperate need for some emotional support. I took a step forward and rested my forehead on his chest. His arms wrapped around me as I tried to steer myself away from a panic attack. This guy was a complete stranger. But let's face it, if he wanted me dead, I would be dead. He just disabled demons like he was swatting at flies. Right now more than anything, I needed comfort, so I just stood there while he gently rubbed my back.

"First of all, that was a demon, not a human. She lost her soul a long time ago, and second, it was self-defense, and technically, she wasn't dead until I removed the heart." I looked up into his reassuring turquoise eyes, and I felt mine tearing up a little as I nodded. "But the demon had inhabited a human, so tonight she died, but so did the human, right?"

"Sadie, once a demon takes over a human's body, there is very little that anyone can do to save that person. After the demon possesses them for so long, the human mind breaks from the things it has seen and been forced to do." After I had somehow managed to stop the tears, he said, "I won't force you to go with me, but more and more Degenerates will be coming your way. Will you leave with me?"

"My family and—"

"Your family has already come to terms with you leaving. Your friend, Jo, gave your dad and grandmother a heads up."

That's what Dad had been talking to him about at the party. That also explained why Jo was currently unreachable. "If what you're saying is true, then I would like to tell them goodbye."

He grabbed my hand and started walking through the woods. "We don't have time for you to track each of them down to say goodbye. Would a phone call suffice?"

"Yes." He handed me a black iPhone from his pocket. I tried to think of who would answer. My granny was always home, so I found myself dialing her number.

She answered on the first ring. "Hey, sugar britches. It's about time you called. Jo's sitting here with me having a cup of coffee, and she told me about how you kicked that demon's ass."

"Granny, remember that guy from the party? The—"

"Have you ever in your life seen such smoking men? Don't get me wrong. I loved your grandfather, but holy cow. Those boys were fly."

My granny was always trying to keep current with the new slang, so I didn't have it in my heart to tell her that "fly" was about twenty years too old. For whatever reason, the nineties phrases were what stuck with her the most.

"Yeah, Granny they were fly." I knew the wolf could hear every word my granny was saying because he was fighting a smile.

"I mean, Sadie, their bodies were bangin', and that wolf of yours, he is swoll."

The said wolf's shoulders now shook with laughter, as I trailed behind him in the woods. How freaking embarrassing. "Yeah, Granny, but he's not my wolf."

"But Jo said—" The phone hit the ground, and I heard some mumbling. Then Granny said, "Well, shit, Jo! Quit trippin'."

"Um, Granny?"

"Yeah, yeah, I'm here. Listen, we know that you're going with the wolf. Have fun and call us when you can."

"So, you're okay with me leaving with a complete stranger?"

"If Jo is okay with it, then so am I, and so is your father. I don't mean to cut this short, but me and Jo are going to play *God of War* on the PS4, so I've got to bounce. Oh, and Sadie, if you need the sex talk, remember—"

"Granny! I'm losing signal. I can't seem to hear you. Are you there?"

"Girl, don't lie. You do know I'm sitting right beside a psychic, right?"

"Then you should know I'm about to hang up. Love you. Bye."

I quickly ended the call before she could embarrass me anymore. I knew my cheeks were bright red as I handed the phone back to CG.

"I told you that your family was fine with you leaving with me. Your grandmother had a long talk with me. She said there wasn't a boy in this town who wasn't half in love with you. Then she went on to list every single one of your attributes. It was all kind of hard to follow, and I think I lost her somewhere around not buying a cow if you get the milk for free."

Mortified. That's what I was. I felt like I owed him an apology. "I don't know what came over my granny."

"Don't worry about it. I liked her, and I don't like too many people." CG jumped up a steep six-foot bank, reaching down for my hand to pull me up. "My car is right behind those trees." After dropping my hand, we walked around some giant shrubs towards the road. He whispered, "Listen, I don't want you sharing your abilities with Celia. Understand?"

"Um, no. Who's Celia?" Someone cleared their throat, and I don't know what first grabbed my attention, the pretty redhead with mile-long legs or the sleek, black Porsche she was currently leaning up against. She stopped filing her nails and narrowed her eyes at me. "So, this is her? Really? What a joke."

I didn't know what her problem was, but it wasn't mine. I stuck my hand out. "I'm afraid I don't know who you are. As you've guessed, I'm Sadie."

She looked at me, then at my extended hand, and rolled her eyes while she shoved off the car. I dropped my arm back down to my side. I had a feeling this girl was going to make Stacy look like chump change. She went around to the other side of the car and opened the passenger door.

CG said, "Climb into the back, Celia."

She jerked the passenger seat up so hard I thought it was going to come completely off its rails.

I looked at CG, trying to figure out a way to calm the waters. "I don't mind riding in

the—"The look he gave me was menacing. "Front seat it is."

As soon as the Porsche roared to life, I asked, "So, where are we headed?"

"To an airstrip. We're going to take a plane." CG kept looking into the rearview mirror every couple of minutes. "It will take us to my ancestral home. It's different from my other estates."

I needed to build my walls and turn off this whole siphoning thing. I could smell Celia's anger coming off her in waves. I didn't know why she was so mad, or what I had done to anger her, but I had a feeling this was going to be a long drive. I turned as much as I could in my seat, so I could see CG better. Trying to make light conversation in a hostile environment was near impossible. "How is this home different?"

He looked over at me briefly then focused back on the road. "It was the home I grew up in. It's located in the middle of three hundred acres. Considering that you live in the middle of nowhere, I think you will like the seclusion."

Celia snorted. "Of course, she will like it. Did you see the dump she lives in? Before she leaves your house, you might want to check the silverware drawer."

I refused to feel shame over where I lived. Money didn't define a person.

CG gripped the steering wheel so hard his knuckles turned white. "That will be enough, Celia. Not one more word. Don't make me regret flying you out here."

Why Celia hated me was beyond me, but it was clear she thought very little of me. The good news was that Celia was more scared of CG than she hated me because she shut up. The rest of the ride to the airstrip was turbulent but quiet.

chapter ten

s I boarded CG's private airplane, I knew I made the right decision to leave, especially with my family and Jo confirming it. If I had stayed home, there would always be someone trying to capture me or trying to use my loved ones as leverage. CG never threatened my family but gave me an option to leave with him after he saved my life. For right now, he was the answer. I wasn't sure of all of his motives regarding the war, but if I believed for one second that he would be willing to sacrifice my loved ones or me to defeat the Degenerates, I would find a way to escape him. But that was borrowing trouble. I just needed to focus on the here and now.

When we arrived at the airstrip, I had to keep putting one foot in front of the other. My first time away from my little town and I was traveling by plane with a wolf and whatever the heck Celia was. There was little doubt she disliked me, if the daggers she kept shooting in my direction were any indication. The three of us boarded the plane. I overheard CG telling Celia that his brother had an important business matter to deal with and flew out on another private flight an hour earlier. CG then spoke to the pilot and with my adrenaline gone, I felt dead on my feet.

I went to take a seat but Celia stopped me. She grabbed my arm and pushed me towards the back of the plane. "You'll be sitting in the back."

I held my tongue and started walking towards the back. I dropped in one of the seats closest to the bathroom. CG walked down the narrow aisle, and to Celia's and my surprise, he took the seat right next to mine. Maybe it was because he could still smell my lingering fear, and he thought sitting next to me would bring me comfort, or maybe it was because he would rather sit next to the newbie than the girl who had resting bitch face down pat. At this point, I couldn't care less about his reasoning. My body was exhausted, and the anger coming off of Celia was enough to make me want to crawl into a ball. Siphoning other powers had mentally overwhelmed me and I'd learned the hard way that building walls was almost impossible when you're exhausted. CG somehow sensed I was distressed. His head jerked up, his eyes roaming over my face before he looked over at Celia. He gave her a hard stare, and she finally dropped her gaze. Whatever her problem was, maybe she would get over it soon. I was too tired to be dealing with her childish drama. Today had taken a toll on me emotionally, so I laid my head back on the seat and closed my eyes.

CG's voice was warm and low. "Sadie, I know everything is happening quickly, but this was your best option. I will keep you safe."

I didn't reply, opening my eyes and unabashedly studying him. He was back to his normal size, but that was anything but ordinary. His black hair curled in the back and around his ears and was ruffled like he had been running his hands through it. Stubble grazed cheeks that looked like a master sculptor had carved them. Specs of blood were all over his shirt. The hottie sitting next to me was mouth-watering, even after all we had been through in the woods. I must still be in shock to have such thoughts after I'd witnessed him rip four demons' hearts out. I rubbed a hand over my chest. I just had to make sure he didn't get mine.

He must have read my mind because he said, "I'm not going to hurt you."

With every part of me, I believed his words. His body turned rigid and then he jumped up from his seat. A screeching sound assaulted my ears, and the entire plane trembled from whatever force had hit it.

CG yelled at me, "Stay here and don't move!"

I watched him exit the plane while Celia, looking none too worried, sat in her seat reading a magazine. I followed his directions for exactly thirty seconds before something smacked the side of the plane. I was up and running towards the exit. As I started down the ramp, I heard an evil laugh coming from above the plane. Stopping, I glanced up, and my mouth dropped open. The ugliest creatures I'd ever seen flew around in circles, cackling. Their long, stringy black hair covered their deformed faces, and their puke-green skin made them appear even more hideous, if that were possible. What was even more startling was they had no auras. I noticed two of the creatures on the ground, decapitated. The remaining creatures flew circles around CG, and I was shocked to see Stephan. He fought beside CG, so one could hope the vampire was on our side.

CG looked at me and shouted, "Get back on the plane. One cut from their claws and you will be poisoned."

I turned to go back in but I couldn't. Celia had shut the door. She put her face right up to the glass window and smirked at me. Well, shit. I turned around again, facing the flying creatures. Their rotten skin oozed off of them, making a hissing sound when it plopped on the runway.

One of the creatures said in a hoarse voice, "Quick, kill the girl."

Oh, great, we're back to "let's kidnap or kill Sadie" because that game was so much fun. One of the creatures soared straight towards me. Just as she was about to reach me, CG grabbed hold of the back of the broom-like object she was flying on and pulled it from underneath her. She crashed to the ground. He broke the wooden handle in two making it into a wooden weapon, throwing half of it, and piercing her neck. The others shrieked. I covered my ears as CG took the other half of the wooden apparatus, hurling it at the creature hovering closest to me. It pierced her heart, and she spiraled to the ground.

The remaining female tilted her head back and made a gut-wrenching sound, causing bumps to rise all over me. She came at me, and I knew CG would never make it in time. I was frozen with fear as Stephan jumped in front of me and intercepted her, knocking her to the ground. With blinding speed, the vampire stepped over her and broke her neck.

The skin on his hands was almost entirely gone from where he touched the creature. I tried to make words form,

but nothing came out of my mouth, so I just pointed at his burns.

"It's okay." Stephan held his hands up for my inspection. "Don't worry. I heal quickly." I watched in fascination as his hands began to repair the damage.

CG barked, "Are you all right?"

It took me a second to realize he was talking to me and not the vampire. I gave a small nod. The stench wafting from the creatures made my stomach roll. I put a hand over my mouth and nose and tried to calm my queasy stomach.

Stephan yelled, "There are hundreds more coming from the west. We need to get on the plane."

I glanced over in the direction he was pointing. It looked like a huge, dark cloud coming our way. Celia opened the door for us before going back to her seat.

CG grabbed my elbow as he steered me onto the plane. "Why the hell were you not on board?"

"I wanted to see what was going on, and then I couldn't get back on because Celia locked me out."

With her actions, she had literally tried to kill me. But why? What was in it for her? Even though I didn't know this girl, she had definitely let me know exactly how much she despised me. It was one thing to be hostile to me and another thing entirely to try and send me to my grave.

CG turned his wrath onto Celia. "Endanger her one more time, and you'll answer to me." Then he growled at Stephan, "And what the hell do you think you are doing, vampire?"

Stephan smiled, showing his dimples. "Well, it looks like I was saving all of your asses. Listen, you don't have to thank me now. You can wait."

CG ran a hand through his black hair. "I know your kind. You always have some ulterior motive. Give me one good reason I shouldn't kill you right where you stand."

Stephan laughed. "Well, first, you would ruin your upholstery. Blood stains are a bitch to get out. And second, I hate to let an instrumental part in winning the war out of my sight. Not that I don't trust you and your dog friends, but all the same, I would like to keep an eye on her."

It all happened so fast. CG grabbed Stephan by the throat and slammed him into the ground. He pulled a knife from his boot, and it looked like CG was about to make slow work of decapitating Stephan when the vampire procured a silver blade from somewhere and was about to stab CG through the heart.

I screamed, and they both stilled their weapons. My voice didn't even sound like mine. "CG, you will not hurt him. He just saved my life seconds ago." Stephan smirked, and I pointed a finger at him. "And you vampire… if you stab him, I'll stake you myself. If I'm such a hot commodity and everyone wants to acquire me, don't you think the more people protecting me, the better? Let go of one another!"

Celia sighed. "And things were just getting interesting." CG seemed to squeeze Stephan's neck tighter. "If at any point I think you don't have Sadie's best interests in mind, I will torture you before I kill you. Do you understand?"

Stephan gurgled, "Perfectly."

CG hopped off of him as fast as he took him down.

Stephan slowly stood up and brushed imaginary dust off his pants. "Well, it looks like I'm out of the dog house." Then he walked over to where I stood and pointed to the seat next to me. "Is this seat taken?"

CG looked like he was about to tackle him again, and I was so over this whole day. "You better take the one in front of me instead."

He chuckled. "Where is your sense of adventure, Sadie?"

I sat back down in my seat, pointing at the one in front of me. "I can't do any more fighting or drama today. Unless someone decides to throw Celia from the plane then I'm all for that. Otherwise, I am literally about to check out."

The plane took off, and although it was my very first plane ride, I couldn't feel any excitement over flying through the clouds or dread over possibly crashing. I was too tired. I glanced at CG. It was evident he was going to give Stephan the death stare for the next couple of hours, and the vampire was going to ignore him. I had nothing to say to either of them or Celia. She'd made an enemy out of me today. At least my anger replaced the sickening smell of fear. I was tired of a lot of things, and that smell was pretty high up on the list. I curled my feet under me and closed my eyes. I was going to rest for a minute. My only wish was that when we landed, I would get a break from people trying to steal or kill me.

chapter eleven

After arriving at the landing strip, we all hopped into a large, black SUV that cost more than Jo's and my trailer. After a short drive, we arrived at CG's family estate. I was amazed by what I would call a rustic mansion. The house had four levels made up of stones and hardy boards that were natural, earthy tones. Several chimneys jutted out of the roof that sported many gables. I could easily see a whole family of wolves being raised in a house like this.

CG came up behind me. "You look like you are about to fall on your feet. Let me get you up to your bedroom where you can sleep. We will start with your training bright and early in the morning."

His words reminded me of a previous conversation. I let out a crazy laugh. "Damn that Jo. She knew you would be training me, but could she give me a heads up? No. I said, 'my brother is coming in to train me,' and she said, 'oh and yeah, you'll be getting the best training,' which I thought had a little bit to do with her infatuation with my brother. But she knew!"

He gave me a nod, and that's all I got from him. It wasn't that CG lacked emotion; it was that he just seemed so matter of fact all the time. Good for him that he had his stuff together, but my ducks weren't in a row. Hell, somewhere along the way, I'd lost my ducks. I didn't have any ducks to give. I both laughed and sobbed at the thought.

"I know today has been crazy, Sadie. Let me help you to your bedroom." His words were kind, but there was no empathy in his voice.

I was homesick, overwhelmed, and the guy in charge of my safety acted like a robot. Just as I tried to maneuver around him, he swooped me up in his arms. He was probably scared I would endanger myself going up the steps. Posture stiff, he carried me down a long hallway and somehow managed to open the door with me still in his arms. After he gently sat me on the huge king-size bed, he shocked us both by brushing a stray hair away from my face.

"My room is beside yours. I'm close if you should need anything."

"Also, you'll be able to hear if anyone sneaks into the house in the middle of the night and tries to steal me. If I'm a key to saving this world, it would just suck for you to misplace your ace in the hole."

CG leaned down to my level. "What other reason would I have for guarding you? I have a job, and you're part of it."

What a jerk. "Got it. We're not going to be friends. You stay in your lane, and I'll stay in mine."

"I can't let you be anything else. I have enough friends." He stood and walked to another door. "We share a bathroom. If you need me at all through the night, you can come find me. I'll shut your door, but I will leave mine open."

"Thanks for the hospitality."

"Good night, Sadie."

I'd been through hell and back today, and this was just day one. I wasn't saying I wanted CG to tuck me in at night and tell me bedtime stories, but jeez. One would think if he needed something from me, he wouldn't be such a douche. Maybe I was overly sensitive, but in my humble opinion, a little Southern hospitality would have gone a long way.

I took off my dirty clothes and left them in a heap by the bed. Crawling between the sheets, I wiped a tear from my face. I was just tired. I was almost kidnapped… twice. Practically killed. Had to leave the only town I'd ever known. Didn't get to say a proper goodbye to my loved ones. I was entitled to feel the way I felt. I would have this night to feel sorry for myself but tomorrow… Well, tomorrow, I would come out swinging. I finally got my power, and I was going to learn how to use it.

chapter twelve

I woke up to the sound of silence. Jo wasn't swearing we were going to be late for school. My granny wasn't calling to make sure we weren't going to be late for said school. Obviously, Jo had let Mr. Boring in on where I would be the final week of school. That had to be the reason for his impromptu history lesson on the key players. Hopefully, he would talk to the headmaster and explain my situation, and I would still get my diploma.

For the first time, I noticed my surroundings. My room was huge and masculine. There was no pretty floral bedspread or chic curtains. Everything was either beige or green, and the furniture was big and bulky. For once in my life, I was surrounded by expensive, lavish things, and all I wanted was to feel my mustard-colored shag carpet from the trailer under my feet. If I made it out of this thing alive, I was going to use this whole crazy situation as a life lesson. One must be careful for what they wished for.

I got up, naked as a jaybird, wrapping the sheet around me. I glanced out of the huge window to get an idea of my surroundings. The land was no longer flat but had rolling hills. There wasn't the tell-tale sign of sand, but instead lush green grass was everywhere I looked. The trees weren't the kind I was used to. They were massive, and the branches were thick with leaves. The Carolina mountains were different than the coast. I was so tired last night when CG showed me to my room that I barely remember crawling into bed. I shuffled my way to a door that I prayed was the bathroom. I groaned, as I realized it was a walk-in closet. I went to the opposite end of the huge bedroom and opened another wooden door. Bingo! After peeking into it to make sure CG wasn't in there, I went to the opposite side of the humongous bathroom to shut his adjoining door, so I could take a shower. A clean body might not help the situation, but it wouldn't make me feel worse. As I grabbed his door handle, I heard a throat clear. My head swiveled to where CG sat shirtless in an armchair looking sexier than ever. Why did someone so rude have to be so freaking hot?

"Good morning, Sadie."

"Um, good morning. I need to take a quick shower, and then I'll be ready."

His gaze raked my body with… hunger? Then as if he realized what he was doing, he waved me off like I was a nuisance. "Take your time. I'll meet you downstairs in the kitchen."

Before I could shut the door, he said, "Oh, and Sadie, we wouldn't want you running around in a sheet. I put some clothes in your armoire while you were sleeping. I hope that you find them to your liking."

"Oh, okay, thanks."

Not sure how I felt about him coming into my bedroom while I slept, I quickly pulled the door closed and locked it before I felt comfortable hopping in the shower. Well, today was going to be interesting, but I hoped the theme of today wouldn't be awkward.

Totally miscalculated that one. The theme wasn't awkward; it was total crap. Everything I did turned to complete crap. In fact, so much so, that I was thinking of opening up my own fertilizer store.

"You are not focusing," CG snarled for the hundredth time. "You need to try harder. This is not a game. In case you have forgotten, it has been foretold that you will be instrumental in finding one of the lost keys. Therefore, there will be a lot of innocent people who will die if you are not capable of defeating the Degenerates."

Wow. No pressure or anything. I blew a long strand of hair out of my face and rolled to my feet on the training mat. There was a theory that once I siphoned off a supernatural I could call upon their powers at any time. My body was supposed to naturally store their auras into a storage bank. The problem was I hadn't figured out how to call auras to me, and my teacher wasn't a patient one. I put my hands on my hips and glared. "Believe it or not, sunshine, I am trying. I'm doing the best that I can."

He picked up the tail of his shirt to wipe his sweaty face. His chiseled abs glistened. "Well, if that's your best, we're all screwed."

"Maybe it's your teaching that sucks." I was at my breaking point an hour ago. "Hey, just saying." It was true; something wasn't clicking for me. It was as if I was purposely trying to sabotage myself. All the power I was around was getting to be too much, so I built a wall, and I wasn't entirely sure how to let the wall down while keeping my sanity.

CG started circling me. "You have to concentrate. Reach out with your mind and feel for the surrounding powers near you."

I shifted from one foot to the other. "Why can't I just touch you and siphon your power?"

CG sighed. "All right, try it."

I went to touch him, and before I knew it, he had his hand on my throat. I was pinned to the ground with him straddling me. He looked at me with that arrogant expression I was dying to wipe off. "Having to touch your enemy puts you too close to danger. I could have broken your neck before you hit the mat. You need to learn how to siphon from a distance, or you won't live to see your next birthday."

I knew how to do that. Every time I concentrated on a person, I saw their aura and felt their power, but I was tired, and my temper was getting the better of me. "Get off of me!"

He put his face closer to mine, appearing even more intimidating. "Did you hear anything I just said?"

I put both my hands on his thighs. His nose flared and his pupils dilated. My touch distracted him, so I was able to take enough energy without him knowing it. His body flew through the air. Too bad he landed on his feet. I was hoping for his head.

"Yeah, I heard you, but did you hear me?"

Clapping sounded from behind us, and both of our heads turned in the direction of the intrusion. Stephan stood propped up against the doorway to the gym. With one of his crazy vampire abilities, he flashed beside me on the training mat. He leaned down to grab my hands and helped me to my feet.

"Thanks, Stephan."

He raised one of my hands up to his mouth where he placed a kiss. "Anytime, love."

CG growled, "What the hell do you want?"

Stephan took his time looking at me before he finally focused his attention to CG. "I do have things to do and people to see. How long am I to be trapped here?"

CG crossed his muscular arms. "Ahh, so you found out about our little protection spell surrounding the property. The great thing about it is not only does it keep others out, it keeps all of us in until I remove it. Remember, you wanted to have Sadie in your sights. Why would you need to leave?"

Stephan smiled. "Hey, I don't need to leave. Just bored, my friend. The blood supply is a little low around here. I had to resort to chasing wild game in your woods last night. It would be nice to be able to hit up a bar where there is more appealing game. Maybe I should resume training with Sadie to help my boredom?"

CG smiled back. "And maybe I should just stake you."

"You could try," Stephan said. "Touchy and brooding fits your surly personality so well. But this sensitive? One has to wonder why, unless that someone is me and has already figured out why." Stephan turned to me. "Beautiful Sadie, should you require a less grouchy training partner, I would be more than happy to accommodate you. In the meantime, I'll be in the library killing time by laughing at all the numerous history mistakes."

After he left, I glanced at CG. "What's the deal with you two? And how old is he if he knows mistakes in history? Like are we talking about when the first cell phone was invented, or when Christopher Columbus set sail?"

"Some personalities don't mesh together. I think he's a conniving, selfish bastard, and I can only imagine what he thinks of me. I don't hate him enough to kill him. Yet. And I'm not sure of his exact age, but considering he's Prince of the Vampires, I'm assuming a couple of thousand years or so."

My mouth fell open. "Are you serious? Is he really that old?"

"He is that old and deadly as well. You should do your best to stay away from him."

"How old are you? Please tell me you're twenty-one." He gave me the first smile I'd seen from him since we'd arrived at his estate. "I'm a few hundred years younger than the vampire."

All these hot guys around me and they were all crypt keepers. "That is so gross."

CG shrugged his broad shoulders. "I guess maybe to you it is. What do you say we call it a day? We can pick up tomorrow?"

My muscles were starting to hurt. "Yeah, sounds good. Um, I saw a bathing suit in with all the clothes that you got me. Which, by the way, I appreciate. I don't know how you knew my size, but all the clothes fit perfectly." He just grunted, so I continued, "Anyways, when I saw the bathing suit, I was hoping there was a swimming hole somewhere."

CG had walked over to his gym bag and pulled out a clean T-shirt. He took off his sweaty one, revealing a shoulder tribal tattoo that looked amazing with its lines and swirls. I pulled my gaze away from his stunning form, just in case he was a mind reader as well.

He said, "I'm sorry, a what?"

What the hell was I talking about? "Um. A swimming hole. You know, a pond. Lake. River. Something. I'm not picky."

"Well, we have an indoor pool. I assume that will work as well as a swimming hole?"

I squealed. "Yes, even better!"

He turned around and almost smiled again before he caught himself. What was his deal? "I take it someone likes to swim?"

"Yes. My dad always said I was like a fish. Wherever there's water, there I was. My granny used to joke that maybe my superpower was a mermaid."

"Why don't you go put on your swimsuit? I'll come up and get you in a couple of minutes and show you where the pool is."

"I guess in a house like this I could get lost, huh? Okay, I'll see you in a minute."

Before he could change his mind, I ran out of the gym and through a series of hallways and stairs. Only having to backtrack once made me feel accomplished. As soon as I got to my bedroom, I took off my clothes and put on the little black bikini. He hadn't guessed my correct size on everything because my boobs looked like if I dove into the pool, they might pop right out. Feeling a little self-conscious, I wrapped a towel around me just as there was a knock on my bedroom door.

"Come in."

CG stood in the doorway in a pair of swimming trunks, T-shirt, and a towel thrown over his shoulder.

"Oh, that was quick. I just got ready. Are you going swimming, too?"

"Yeah. I try to swim every night. Maybe I was supposed to be a mermaid, too."

Was that a joke? I had a feeling this man was like an onion. There were so many layers, and I hadn't even scratched the surface.

chapter thIrteen

After a couple of minutes of walking through hallways and corridors, I realized I seriously would have gotten lost. On our way to the pool, we passed a magnificent room. The walls were painted gold and the floors were white sparkling marble. I had to go in to explore. If he was aggravated with my curiosity, he didn't show it. There were swords pinned along a wall and different weapons hanging on the opposite wall. At the very back of the room was a throne. The arms and legs of the chair represented a wolf's paw. In the middle of the intricate chair rested a crown. It was made of solid gold and small, pointy things appearing to be antlers wrapped around the whole crown. There was an identical smaller crown in a glass case right next to the throne.

"What is this room?" I asked.

"It is where our pack meets on business. It also holds our family heirlooms."

"Do you sit on the throne while you go over your business?"

"Yes."

"And do you wear the crown?"

He looked like he was ready to change the subject. "When I have to, yes."

He exited the room and didn't wait for me to follow. I should mind my business, but I was too curious. I caught up with him.

"Hey, what's up with that room? You look agitated."

His pace quickened. "That crown belonged to my father. That throne belonged to my father. That room belonged to my father."

Before I could ask any more questions, we went through some glass doors. The swimming pool was shaped like a tropical island. One side of the pool you could walk right into, and the other side was at least twelve feet deep.

CG placed his towel on a chair then made a motion for mine. After a moment of hesitation, I handed it over. His eyes bulged out of his head, and he made no move to grab the towel from me. Finally, he cleared his throat and snatched the fabric. He was clearly attracted to me, and it was as if the thought of that more than anything was what pissed him off. Perhaps in his thousands of years roaming this world, he'd found true love and lost her. Maybe he thought feeling attraction for anyone else was a disservice to her memory? And maybe I was reaching, trying to explain away his odd behavior. As he stormed past me, I decided to ask him what his deal was. I watched him gracefully dive into the deep end.

He swam over to where I stood. His voice was gruff. "I thought you said you could swim? Are you going to stand there all day or get in?"

I smiled. "I was just waiting for you to get a little closer."

"Excuse me?"

I did my best cannonball I could muster without landing on him. When I emerged from the water, CG was wiping water off of his face.

"What are you, four?"

"What? Is Mr. Grumpy Stripes afraid to break out of his stuffy box and have a little fun? Or is it that you're too old and don't remember what fun is anymore?"

His brow furrowed. "I'm not that old. Do you want to see fun? Let me tell you what I think that cannonball needs. A little height."

He grabbed me with one arm and turned me around in the water. My back momentarily met his chest before he pushed me an arm's distance away. There were definitely some issues there. His massive hands grabbed both sides of my waist and he launched me.

He threw me ten feet into the air, and I had plenty of time to roll my body into a tight little ball before I hit the water.

I came up laughing. "That was awesome." I made sure my teeny-weeny bathing suit was in place before I swam over to him. "Let's do it again."

He turned me around and said in a mocking voice, "I think the old man can do it one more time. You ready?"

He was so busy enjoying the moment and actually having fun that he didn't notice how my body pressed up against his. But I noticed. I bobbed my head up and down, not sure I could find my voice. After a couple of seconds, I went soaring again into the air, but this time I jackknifed my body and did a shallow dive into the pool. I swam back over to him once more and stopped right before I got to him, still treading water because it was over my head in this section.

"It must be nice to be over six feet tall, huh?"

He grabbed my waist. "Here, let me help the little mermaid."

Before I could tell him I was fully capable of swimming to the shallow end, he was placing me on my feet.

The water dripped slowly off his muscular chest. He leaned into me. His nostrils were flaring, and almost bitterly, he said, "You are so beautiful." The back of his hand trailed down my face, and I was both thrilled and scared he was going to kiss me. That couldn't happen. Not when I needed answers. I had a feeling the moment his lips touched mine I would lose touch with reality. He wouldn't settle for anything less.

"Why do you hate me?"

He abruptly dropped his hand and stepped back. At the same time, the glass doors to the pool opened up and Celia walked in. She shook her long, flaming red hair behind her and put one hand on her hip. "Well, what do we have here? Hope I wasn't interrupting something. After all, I would hate to call the wedding off."

I could feel the color draining from my face. I looked over at CG, waiting for him to laugh, or tell her that she was a crazy lunatic. When neither of those things happened, I felt majorly disappointed. I had a bad habit of romanticizing things. I thought he was an ass because of some misplaced feelings for a lover that had gotten away. Not once did it cross my mind that he was engaged, much less engaged to a nasty, trifling ho.

Celia tilted her head back and snickered at my confusion. "Oh, I can see he must have forgotten to tell you that he has a fiancée. Well, hopefully, you didn't fall too head over heels for him and if you did, it will be all right; most women do, so don't beat yourself up about it."

"Celia…" There was a warning in CG's tone, one his fiancée clearly ignored as she continued glaring at me.

Well, hell. When it came down to it, I was Southern, and most of us Southerners had many admirable qualities. One of them was our pride. I'd be danged if I let either of these two get the best of me.

I smiled cheerfully at Celia like I was about to let her in on a dirty, little secret. "Oh, I'm sure mentioning you just slipped his mind, and you don't have to worry about me. I'm not most women. I only give my heart to those who deserve it. Now, if you will excuse me, I think I'm going to go soak in the hot tub."

As I climbed up the ladder of the side of the pool, Celia said, "Well, I just thought I would set the record straight that he is, what do you country bumpkins call it? Getting hitched? So, you should probably not get your hopes up."

"Nope. We're good. Nothing for you to worry about. He never once said anything about wanting to upgrade."

In my anger, I must have let my walls down and unintentionally siphoned off of her because as I walked away, I could feel her coming for me before CG yelled, "Celia, no!"

I instinctively stepped to the side right before she reached me, letting her rush past me, which made her even angrier. I could see her aura as bright as the light of day—reddish orange. Somehow, I knew she was a witch. She was back in front of me snarling. She raised a hand to slap me, and I quickly caught it. I wanted to take the brute power from the wolf behind me to send Celia flying into the pool, but he asked me to not show her my powers. Which was another question I could add to my growing list of "What the hell CG?" Instead of giving into my desires, I gave her hand a hard squeeze before I let her go.

CG quietly called out my name, but I ignored him as I made my way around the curved rock wall to where he had said the hot tub was. I should have just gone back to my room, but I was trying to act like what just happened wasn't a big deal. You know, that whole pride thing. I walked down the steps of the hot tub, grateful it was secluded with tropical plants growing around it for privacy. I didn't have to see CG and Celia, and they couldn't see me. After a couple of minutes of hearing hushed voices, I heard the glass doors open, and I prayed that both of them were leaving together. I laid my head back on the side of the hot tub and closed my eyes. Day two sucked. But on the bright side, even with its drama, it was still better than yesterday.

"*Ca c'est bon*. That's good. Real good stuff. But now don't cha worry, *Cher*. They done gone off together."

I jumped up, searching for whomever was spying on me.

"Whoo-hoo! Right *Cher*, darlin'."

I looked over my left shoulder, and there was this huge bug… No, a tiny person the size of my palm flew over the hot tub. My mouth dropped open.

"What? *Cher*, haven't you seen a fairy before?" I shook my head. At least she didn't look like she wanted me dead like the demons. Her Louisiana accent was heavy and left little doubt where she was from. "Well, now I ain't gonna hurt cha. I ain't never hurt nobody before that didn't deserve it. And I can promise you no matter what my ex Lynard says, he deserved what he got. Yes, he did, and it's not like he ain't never gonna be able to fly again. I think." She gave me a sweet smile. "Here, I'm a gonna come closer, and you can have a good look see. Just don't go gettin' my wings wet."

I leaned my head down close to hers, so I could get a better look at her. She was beautiful with skin the color of light caramel and black hair falling down in ringlets to the top of her shoulders. I said the first thing that came to my mind.

"Wow. You're gorgeous."

"*Cher*, you earned you some brownie points. Yes, you did." She pushed her hair up with her palm twice and winked at me. "Comin' from you, that's a huge compliment, and the way you handled yourself bag dare with that slut puppy." Then she saluted me. "I'm Lilly-Ana, but you can call me Lil, because I have a feelin' we're gonna to be great friends."

Now that I knew she wasn't going to hold my head underwater until bubbles came up, I went back to the bench and sat.

"Well, thanks, Lil. I could use a friend. And as far as those two go, well, they deserve each other."

She flitted over to the handrail running into the hot tub and perched on top of it. "Well, now, *Cher*, don't cha go a judgin' poor Camden. He's just doin' what he feels is best for his pack."

"Who's Camden? You mean, CG?"

She rearranged her little skirt. "Yep, that be one and the same. His initials stand for Camden Grant."

I pulled my feet up to rest them on the bench, so I could put my head on my knees. My severe go-to thinking pose.

"Why would them being together help his pack?"

"There's not just the one war you got to win, *Cher*.

"There are gonna be many battles before the huge war. All of us supernaturals who want to live in somewhat peace and co-exist with one another, well, we're a part of the Lux. Sweet Camden is different than most of us supernaturals. He is one of the most powerful out dere, and yet he got a conscience."

I rolled my eyes because, really, I had nothing to say about "sweet Camden."

"Whatcha don't know is that Celia, well, that girl's father ain't never picked a side between the Lux and the Degenerates. Probably because he likes the comforts of livin' here on this plane, but then he has no qualm about using the Degenerates' methods when he wants somethin' bad enough. The man is a yellow-belly coward. A snake in the grass."

I lifted a shoulder. "It must run in the family."

"Ain't that the truth. It's rumored that Celia's father, Merek, has somethin' that Camden needs. It's also rumored that Merek killed his brother for that somethin' I'm speakin' of."

Mr. Boring's words came back to me. He had mentioned that a brother had killed his sibling for something highly coveted. "He has the key!"

She gave a little shrug. "I ain't sayin' nothin' about no key. But I can tell you that there are only a few kings in our supernatural world. Merek wants his daughter married to one of them because of the power and the prestige that comes with the title. All the kings, fae and demon alike, want what Merek has in his possession. All are willin' to court Celia to obtain it, but Merek let his daughter choose which king she wanted to marry. And guess who she had to go and chose? Camden of course. I was all for Camden usin' some brute force on Celia's father and just takin' whatever it was that he needed, but he was scared the old fart would take it to his grave instead of spillin' the beans about where the desired object is."

I was trying to process everything Lil was telling me, but I was having a hard time.

"What in the world—besides the key—would be so important to Camden for him to marry someone like Celia just to get whatever her father has?"

"I didn't say that it wasn't the key." Lil fluttered over to the side of the hot tub, her hazel eyes sparkling with mischief. "I just said that's a question for him to answer and not me."

Her wings beat faster, and I could tell she was ready to change the subject, so I let her.

She flew closer to me and said, "It's been forever since I had a girl's night, considerin' Celia is the only other girl here. And I can promise you I don't need the company that bad. What do you say? You in for some hell-raisin'?"

"Sure, I could use some girl time, but how much hell raisin' can we do if we can't even leave this place?"

Climbing out of the hot tub, I wrapped my towel around me. She put both her hands on her tiny hips. "Oh girly, you just wait and see. Before the end of the night, we will have everyone in this place wantin' to hang with us. We will bring the fun bus. *Laissez les bons temps rouler.* Let the good times roll!"

My spirits were slightly lifted as we parted ways. She headed towards the kitchen; I went to my bedroom to change out of my bathing suit into a tank top and a pair of sweatpants. I put my wet hair into a ponytail, threw on some flip-flops, and down the stairs I went to meet my little friend. I was ready for whatever, as long as it didn't involve demons, witches, or wolves with blue-green eyes.

chapter fourteen

By the time I got to the kitchen, Lil had jazz music cranked up and was blending a pitcher of mixed drinks. She placed a steaming plate of food in front of me.

"Here girl, eat some of Lilly-Ana's famous Cajun stir fry and put some meat on those bones."

My belly started talking to me. When was the last time I had food? "Lil, how in the world did you have time to fix this so fast?"

"I'm a fairy, child, we don't do nothin' slow."

"I know that you are a fairy, but what are your powers exactly? I look at your aura, and it's so bright like the color of the sun."

"Well, *Cher*, that's not surprising because I'm like a ray of sunshine." She got a couple of glasses down from the cabinet, and I was amazed to see that she could fly with the weight of both of them. "Obviously, I can fly, but I also can put people to sleep with a little fairy dust, but if I give them too much, they don't ever wake up. I also can make little potions here and dere. Make people itch or make them hallucinate. You know, the average fairy stuff."

That was cool. I thought of all the people I would like to dust with an itching potion as I attacked my plate like a starving woman. Lil gave me a look, as if she expected me to swallow the fork. Silly fairy. I wouldn't do that, but I might lick the plate when she wasn't looking. "Oh, my gosh, this is pure heaven."

Lil had put her mixed drink along with mine on the counter right in front of us. She put a straw in her glass and was guzzling hers like a fish.

"Pure heaven, huh? *Cher*, we got to get chu a life."

"I've got to warn you. I've never drank before."

Lil was still slurping her drink like a champ. "Is that right? Well, this oughta be interestin'."

I started sipping on the mixed drink. "Well, I am underage, but considering that my longevity is looking slimmer and slimmer with every demon or ghoul attack, I say what the heck? I should live in the moment."

Before I knew it, I was at the bottom of the glass. "All right, sister, pour me another one."

"Yes! That's what I'm talkin' about." She fist pumped the air and I giggled. I realized that if I was already giggling after one drink, I should probably slow it down, but then again, I always did what I was supposed to and look where that had gotten me. I was far away from my loved ones, training for a war that I really shouldn't be a part of with a hot guy with personality issues, which was understandable considering he was engaged to a psychotic biatch.

At some point, the jazz music switched to hip-hop. My eyes blurred, but I could still make out Lil's form on the counter. She had her hands on her knees, and her small booty was going every which way. "Um, Lil? Are you convulsing?"

"What kind of small ass town are you from? Girl, this is called twerkin'." Her butt started vibrating faster, and her wings were flapping with the rhythm. She looked over her shoulder. "Sometimes, you got to look back at it."

What the hell was she talking about?

"Come on, *Cher*. Let me see your dance moves."

Dance moves? We did line-dancing back home. Not twerking. But when in Rome, twerk like the Romans. I stood up from the barstool and tried to mimic her by placing my hands on my knees, but instead of my butt moving, my ribs gyrated.

I stopped when Lil fell over with laughter. "You look like a dog that is tryin' to throw up a bone. Oh, child, just stop. I don't want to witness that no more. Lawd help me."

She was laughing so hard I was scared she was going to damage a wing. I somehow managed to find my way back to the barstool. The glass before me was half-empty. No, it was half-full. I decided to be optimistic about life, at least for tonight. Switch it up and try something different. I slurped down my drink as Lil said, "Aww nah, here comes the vampire. Whatever you do, don't cut yourself on anything."

I looked up and saw Stephan strolling into the kitchen; he grabbed his heart and pretended to stumble. "I feel hurt that there is a party going on and I wasn't invited."

"Buddy," I slurred, "Pull up a chair, and we'll pour you a drink."

"Are you offering up a vein?"

I wrinkled my nose in disgust. "Not in this lifetime."

"Well, a man can dream." He sat down beside me. "Unfortunately, alcohol doesn't do much for me, considering my high metabolism, but I can live vicariously through you."

I gave him a wink as other people strolled in. Where the hell were they coming from? I might have voiced that out loud. Oops.

Lil explained that the six supernaturals now studying me were part of the security detail, and they lived in CG's guest house. The rest of the werewolf pack, numbering close to three hundred—whoa, someone was breeding like rabbits—lived in cabins on the adjoining property. Thanks to the tequila, it didn't take long to break the ice, and before I knew it, I had some new friends. We were sitting around making jokes until Lil suggested we turn this into a karaoke party. For a second, I thought I should disclose that when I sang, it sounded like a dying cat in heat, but then it was all par for the course.

Celia came into the kitchen during one of the werewolves' renditions of Hank Williams's "Howling at the Moon."

She made her way over to where I was sitting beside Stephan and Lil. "Let me guess. You're going to do a country song about how you're trailer trash and proud of it."

Stephan tsked and said, "Oh, come on, Celia, why don't you sheath your claws for a night?"

She shot Stephan a sly look right before she pounced on me. She grabbed me by the back of my neck and slammed my head down onto the countertop. Her hand was still squeezing when Stephan flashed behind her. He wrapped his arm around her, and clenched her to his body.

His voice was low and deadly. "Release her now, or I will rip out your heart and feed it to you."

Lil flew over and landed on Stephan's shoulder. Her wings were beating too fast to track. "Don't do it, vampire. She ain't worth it."

Lil reached into her little skirt. Then she held a fist up to her mouth and blew. Fairy dust sprinkled all over Celia. Before she hit the ground, Stephan picked her up into his arms and carried her over to the pantry where he shoved her body into the small space and closed the door.

I sat up and rubbed my neck, glancing around to see if anyone had noticed the confrontation. All of the drunk werewolves were still swaying to the music. I was ninety percent sure they had heard and witnessed everything, but since it was a conflict of interest, they had let the vampire handle it.

"Are you all right?" Stephan asked.

I rubbed my sore forehead. "She really hates me."

"She's territorial over CG. What would help the situation is the next time she comes across your path, grab me and start making out with me like your life depended on it. I'm sure then she would not feel so threatened about you taking her man. Especially if she thought you already had one."

I rolled my eyes at him. "Well, thank you for being willing to take one for the team."

"I'll do what I can to keep the peace."

Lil burst out laughing. "He's a persistent thang, ain't he? Now, come on, y'all, let's not let Celia ruin our night."

I just wanted to go to bed, but Lil was right. If I went scurrying off now, it would look like Celia had won. Besides, I accidentally pulled a little power off of the vampire and my head no longer hurt. When she'd attacked me, I must have let down my walls.

Four songs and six mixed drinks later, I realized I couldn't care less if the world ended tomorrow.

Somewhere after my epiphany, I noticed the kitchen started to tilt. The massive granite counter top I was currently standing on—wait, why was I standing on it? Whatever the reason, it resembled a balance beam. I sat down on the counter and scooted off to get some air when I felt two strong hands grab me around my waist. I looked up and rolled my eyes. Of course, it had to be CG who came to my aid.

My words were slurred. "When did you get here? I thought this was an invite-only party?"

I pushed his hands away from me and started to go around him, but I couldn't figure out which way to go, considering the whole kitchen was rotating. I glanced around the room, trying to figure out which person was magically making that illusion happen, when CG swooped me up into his arms.

"First of all, it's my kitchen. I don't need to be invited. And secondly, I think we should probably get you in bed before you hurt yourself."

I rested my spinning head on his muscular chest. "The last thing I want is you anywhere near my bed. You're such a douche bag. And I can't leave just yet; I was going to ask Stephan if he wanted to do a duet with me. That vamp has layers, too. Not as many as you, but they are there."

His arms tightened around me as we climbed the steps. "Yeah, well, that's not going to happen, and I think you've had enough fun for one night. The way you were on my counter, grinding your hips, you—"

"Wait! What? I learned to twerk. Yes. I feel like I should give a thank you speech to Lil." And how long exactly had he been watching? I squinted up at him. Maybe he did have stalker potential. But I couldn't focus on that; I needed to go back to the party. I slapped his chest. "Halt, you massive beast. I command you to take me back down the steps at once. I need to express my gratitude to Lil." When he ignored me, I looked at both of him. "And why would you care about my hips and grinding? Did I say that backwards? What is it to you if I'm having a little fun?"

"Even inebriated, you ask multiple questions at once." As we rounded the last corner before my bedroom door, he asked, "How many marriage proposals did you receive tonight?"

I was so sleepy I was having a hard time thinking. "I don't have any clue."

The door magically opened, or maybe he opened it, and I just missed it.

"Five," he grumbled.

I shook my head. I was having a hard time concentrating. I turned my nose into his T-shirt, so I could smell his scent better. I grew up in a small coastal town, and the ocean was a part of me, but I had never been to a Caribbean island. I imagined the sand would be whiter, the water clearer, and the smell purer. His scent was what I imagined an island would smell like. Exotic.

"Five what?"

He placed me in the center of my bed.

"Five proposals you received tonight from men who are known to be some of the fiercest warriors out there, and you are making them into lovesick puppies. We could be going into battle any day now, and I'm scared that they will all be concentrating on your pretty behind instead of the task they are supposed to be focused on."

Maybe it was because I was drunk but I had nothing. No witty comeback. No questions. All I could think about was how good he smelled. "I want your T-shirt. Do you think I could have it?" Oh, wait, did I say that out loud, too? That was my last thought before I passed out.

woke up around ten the next morning. The drapes were closed, and CG was sitting in an armchair, staring at me. My mouth was so dry I squeaked, "Am I dead?"

CG rubbed his hand over his face. "No, but I'm betting right now that you wished you were."

I grunted. "Have you been there all night?"

He ignored my question as he stood and moved to my side of the bed. I was about to warn him to stay back, because I was pretty sure I was going to throw up everywhere, when he said, "I probably should just let you suffer to teach you a lesson, but we need to train today."

He sat down on the edge of my bed. As soon as he placed his hands on my body, I immediately felt less nauseated. "What... what are you doing to me?"

"I'm making you feel better."

After a minute, I felt better than incredible. "How did you do that?"

He searched my face and then gave a satisfied nod. "You do look better. And as far as my healing powers, well, it's a long story; one that I don't wish to bore you with."

He started to stand up, and I grabbed his wrist. "What if I beat your butt on the mat today? Will you tell me then?"

He smiled and started for the door. "If, and that's a big if, you can outfight me today, then yes, I'll bore you to death with my stories. I'll meet you in twenty at the gym."

I jumped up and headed to the shower, more motivated than ever to kick his hind end.

I had just gotten out of the shower and donned a new hot pink sports bra and black yoga pants. I hated to admit it, but my new wardrobe was more beautiful than anything I had back home in my closet. I was tying my shoes when a knock came on my door.

"Come in."

The door swung open, and there stood a woman, her age undefinable. If I had to take a guess, I would say a hundred plus some. She had kinky gray hair that was a hot mess all around her shoulders. But it was her eyes that were the most disturbing. They were milky white, and she had no irises. I wasn't entirely sure she could see me.

I waited for a second, and when I realized that she had no intention of speaking, I asked, "Can I help you, ma'am?"

She pointed one crooked finger at me and in a gravelly voice said, "No, but I can help you."

Well, this was weird. "Who are you?"

She tilted her head like I'd seen Jo do so many times before. "Yes, I'm like your Jo, but much more powerful. Your young friend has not learned how to control her power yet. She lets her power control her, and if she's not careful, it will eventually make her crazy. I see all things, but I choose what I want to haunt me. The things that don't interest me I shut off. But that's not what you asked, is it? My name is Ariana."

This little old woman was making me very nervous. "How can you help me?"

"The walls that you build are necessary. Like a buffer between you and others' powers. Somewhere in between a fortress and a blank canvas is where you have to be. A battle is on the horizon, train and train well, so the mistakes you make will not be in front of your enemy."

That made absolutely no sense to me. None. She started to turn away, but I stopped her by lightly touching her arm. Her head tilted back and she sighed. I jerked my hand back, hoping I didn't just commit some sort of faux pas. "I apologize. I did not mean to startle you. But please, don't go just yet. Is there anything else you can tell me?" Preferably something that would actually make sense.

This time she looked at me a little differently. Maybe she had picked up on something when I'd touched her.

"Yes, child. Know this. Camden is equally as powerful as you but in different ways. Do not worry about him in the battle. What you see is not so."

"Um, maybe that'll make sense at some point. I have another question for you, if you don't mind. I just touched you, which was completely foolish on my part, but the good news is I didn't get anything from you. In fact right now, I'm trying to see your aura and I can't. Why is that?"

Her face wrinkled more when she gave me a gummy smile. "Everyone has an aura, but some are off limits to you. Whether it be because the power would be too much for you to consume or if it's nature's way of limiting what you are capable of doing or becoming." She gave a shrug. "Who knows?"

"But you know, don't you?"

"Of course, I do. You want to know, so I'll tell you. It's both. My power personally would kill you... slowly. You would eventually go out of your mind. Count your blessings when you can't see someone's aura. You shouldn't be able to see Camden's and yet you do. Interesting, isn't it?"

Before I could ask any more questions, she glided back out of the bedroom, leaving me with more questions now than before she'd showed up.

chapter sixteen

I got to the gym and noticed Lil, Stephan, and a couple of werewolves whose names I had already forgotten from our little karaoke party last night, sitting on some bleachers facing the mats. I waved to the group and walked over to them.

"Hey, guys. What are y'all doing?"

Lil flew over to me. "We've decided to come out and be your moral support today."

Did I need moral support? This would officially be the second day of training. What was so special about today? CG strolled into the gym. His white T-shirt was snug over his muscles, and he looked like a well-oiled fighting machine.

Lil swatted me on the ear. "Are you eyeing up the boss?"

"Eww. What? No." Well, maybe. Crap. I had to keep that in check.

"I think you were," Lil said. Stephan laughed, until I gave him a murderous look.

"No, I wasn't." I definitely was. "Guess I should go stretch. Thanks for the support."

I kept my eyes down as I headed over to the mat. Lusting after an engaged man. What was wrong with me? Even if he was single, I shouldn't be lusting after him. He was stuffy and just not my type.

Out of the corner of my eye, I saw him stretching. His shirt raised up an inch to show his tan belly. I turned to face the wall while I stretched. It was safer. Yeah, definitely not my type.

"Sadie, are you ready to start?"

"Yes, Camden, I am ready."

At the sound of his first name, he tilted his head sideways. His eyes trailed my body head to toe and back up, a corner of his mouth tilting. He seemed to be thrilled that I called him by his real name. Note to self, he shall be Camden from here on out. I had to stop noticing the golden flecks in his blue-green eyes and start focusing on training, so I didn't die in some battle.

Closing my eyes, I found my center, slowing everything down in my mind. Once I was focused, I began looking around the room at all the different auras. I was getting better and better at calling their auras to me. Lil's was the familiar bright yellow, Stephan's was red, and the werewolves were different shades of orange. When my eyes landed back on Camden, I studied his aura that resembled a rainbow. Very strange. So far there had been only one color for each supernatural, but he had so many different vibrant colors. I wondered if his brother's were as colorful. After I was done kicking his butt, I was going to have to ask him about his strange aura that looked like skittles.

I started slowly circling him, but before I could come up with a plan, he charged at me. I pulled power from Lil, and the next thing I knew I was in the air, hovering over Camden. My arms flapped beside me. "Oh, my gosh. Oh, my gosh. Oh, my gosh. I'm freaking flying!"

I heard Lil say to Stephan, "Please tell me I don't look like that when I'm flyin'. That girl looks like a one-winged duck flyin' in circles."

Camden attempted to hide a smile. "Yes. Yes, you are. Now, come back down here and fight me."

The werewolves on the bleachers were cheering and clapping. They were all so excited for me that I didn't have the heart to tell them that I didn't know how to get back down. I closed my eyes and focused on lowering my body to the ground. As soon as my feet touched the floor, I let out a sigh. That took a hot minute.

Camden chuckled. "I could have gotten you down if you needed help, but I knew you would figure it out."

"At least she did something interestin'," Lil said. "Round one goes to my girl."

Camden was like a streak of lightning. He came at me so fast I didn't see him until it was too late. He took the wind right out of me as he knocked me flat on my back.

Lil groaned. "Ugh, and round two goes to the stud muffin."

He crouched beside me, partially blocking our audience's view of me. "Are you all right?"

I nodded because that whole pride thing reared its ugly head up again. "Yeah, I'll let you have that one. Since you're so old and everything. I didn't want the newbie to school you in front of your friends."

He smiled that sexy smile of his. "Don't worry about my feelings. School away."

Instead of just focusing on one aura, I concentrated on all of my new friends' auras. Since I hadn't figured out how to collect auras from the 'storage bank' that I supposedly had built inside of me, I was lucky I had so many different supernaturals in the room with me. Letting my walls down, I reached out my hand like I was trying to gather them all together. I watched the different colors wrapping around one another. With my other hand, I reached out to stroke all of Camden's different colors, pulling them towards me as well. Then, with both hands, I shoved all the different energy I had collected towards Camden.

He went flying across the room until a wall stopped him. He jumped up with a smile on his face. The things that made him smile. So weird. "That a girl, Sadie! Sadie?"

Why was I so dizzy? Lil was asking me something I couldn't decipher. I knelt on the floor while she cooed Cajun words to me. What was that dripping sound? I glanced down at the floor where a constant drip of blood hit the mat between my knees. Well, that wasn't good.

Camden knelt in front of me as he took off his shirt and pressed it to my nose to stop the bleeding. "Sadie, what happened?"

My head pounded. Ariana's words played back to me. My reaction had to do with letting my walls completely collapse and taking in Camden's aura, but I didn't know that for sure. "I think I might have just overdone it. I took everyone's aura and swung them at you like I would a bat. Then I got sick to my stomach."

His eyes scanned my body with such worry. He had one hand on the back of my head holding me still, and the other hand was stanching the blood flow with his T-shirt.

I grabbed hold of his wrist and in my most convincing tone said, "Camden, I'm fine. I'm learning all of this as I go, and I can't learn if I don't make mistakes."

Stephan came up beside me. "The blood has stopped; that's a good sign, but maybe you should take a break."

I started to stand up. "No. We're not taking a break. I met Ariana this morning."

Camden rested his hands on his thighs while he studied me. "She does not like meeting new people, but she wanted to meet you?"

I knew I couldn't keep the conversation I had with Ariana a secret, and it wasn't like she asked me to. Her being the great psychic and all, she probably knew I would spill the beans, anyways.

"Ariana told me that our first battle is imminent, and I need to be prepared. So that means that I need this. I need to train."

Camden seemed to understand what I was not saying. He stood and nodded at me. "All right, if you are sure, then we will continue."

Unfortunately for me, he decided not to put his now bloody T-shirt back on, and he chucked it to the side. Great. Just great. I was trying to learn how to control my powers, and now I was going to have to fight while being distracted by his beautiful body. No, I wasn't distracted. It would take more than a six pack to break my concentration.

I glanced over at Lil who was sitting with the wolves. "Where did Stephan go?"

"Once he saw that you were okay, that vampire bailed. It was the blood. He gone just like that. Good thang, too. You ain't no buffet, girl."

"Does it matter where the vampire went?" Camden asked. Well, didn't he sound jelly? When I didn't answer, he growled. Yep, definitely jelly. "If you are sure that you are ready, then we can begin."

"I'm ready."

"I'm not sure what happened earlier, but when something feels wrong, back off. Whatever you feel like you can control right now is what we will work with. All the rest will come with time."

He danced around me, coming towards me, only to back away again. It was like he was afraid to attack me. Frustration bubbled up inside of me.

"If you're too afraid to train me, just say so, but I'm not going to stand here all day while you decide if you think I'm too fragile."

Something came into his eyes, almost like he was… proud of me? Then he charged at half of his usual speed, but that was a start. I pulled just enough energy off him that when he grabbed me, I flipped us, so he landed on the mat first with me on top.

He threw me off of him and just as I was about to crash on the floor, I channeled Lil and floated to the ground. He was right beside me, with his hand behind my head, trying to protect me as I fell. Except I didn't.

He smiled down at me. "Good girl. You are learning so quickly."

I returned his smile after I rolled to my feet. "Yes, but you can't train me by trying to fight me, then trying to protect me at the same time. The enemy won't be as gallant."

Camden took a couple of steps towards me. He reached out and brushed my hair behind my shoulders. That gentle touch had me stiffening. "Now that I know what you are capable of, I won't worry about you anymore."

I heard Lil from the bleachers snort. "Liar. That boy is whooped."

"Did she just say I'm whipped?"

With him this close, I could smell his exotic scent, and it took everything I had not to stare at his glistening chest. He looked like a Spartan warrior standing in front of me. One that I shouldn't be noticing. Camden cleared his throat. Oh great, I had been caught staring.

"Yeah, but it's kind of hard to be whooped when you're engaged to another, isn't it?"

A shield fell over his eyes. Good. He nodded as he took a step away from me. I told myself that I didn't regret my comment or the lack of his closeness. We went a couple more rounds with him tackling me and me countering by throwing him against a wall. I knew he was holding back from me, and honestly, I appreciated it. I already had bruises popping up from this current training session. I could only imagine what I would look like if he socked it to me.

"Sadie, it's not that I mind being thrown into every wall in here, but what would happen if you tried something other than swinging auras at me like a bat?"

Well, that was a good question. I pulled from Lil and centered all my energy on Camden, trying to make him float. I put too much oomph in it because he hit the ceiling right before he crashed to the ground. He moaned and rolled over onto his back.

"Wow. I guess I should have been content with the walls. Do you know how tall the ceilings are in here? Twenty-four feet."

I knelt beside him. "I am so sorry. I think I know what I did wrong; try it again?"

"I've created a monster," he groaned. "All right, let's do this until we get it right."

We both stood to face each other, and once more I pulled off of Lil and sent Camden flying again, but this time I stopped him right before he hit the ceiling. Control was the key. I slowly lowered him back to the ground. He came over to me and gave me a side hug.

Color me twenty shades of what the hell was going on. He was stoic and stuffy one second, telling me we couldn't even be friends, then the next minute he was jealous over Stephan. The saga continued with gentle touches, his need to protect me, and a partial hug. Either they were putting crack in my frosted flakes in the morning, or Camden had layers all right. Layers of crazy. The deeper I went, the more insane it got. "What was the hug for?"

"That was for not shoving the ceiling down my throat again."

"You need to work on your trust issues," I joked, because why not? If you can't beat them, join them.

"Well, considering you've hit me into every wall in this place a thousand times, not to mention that I received a dislocated shoulder and three broken ribs for my efforts, there might be some trust issues there."

I looked at his magnificent body and shrieked, "I did what?"

He put his hands up to try and calm me. "It's nothing to worry about. My body has already begun healing itself. Another thirty minutes and I'll be good as new. But I am starving. What do you say we call it a night?"

I nodded. "Oh. Okay, sure."

He went and grabbed his bloody shirt. "So, what do you say we give ourselves an hour? That'll give us enough time to get cleaned up and the chef time to prepare a meal."

"What?"

He winked and said, "Dinner. Remember? I owe you a story."

Layers and layers. Hot. Cold. Gruff one minute, winking the next. He was a cornucopia of emotions, and it was starting to mess with my head. "I technically didn't win. You didn't even go hard on me you just… You just—"

"Was your human punching bag? You had to train with your powers, and since I heal quickly, I was your best option. So, dinner?"

I could only nod. Maybe I needed speech training, too.

As soon as he walked out of the gym with the remaining werewolves, Lil flew over to me.

"Whew, that man is so hot he makes my wings skip a beat. Too bad they don't make that version in a tiny size. Well, what the heck you standin' there for with your mouth open? You gotta hot date to go prepare for."

"It's not a date! And I refuse to drool all over him while he's engaged."

Lil squinted her eyes at me. "Yeah, well, good luck wit dat."

I had a feeling I was going to need a lot of luck, and some hardcore determination on my part, if I planned on not letting that man get under my skin.

chapter seventeen

After I took a quick shower, I styled my hair while I debated what to wear. Ugh. It wasn't a date, so what did it matter? I wasn't trying to impress him. To prove that it didn't matter, I closed my eyes as I picked an outfit from the armoire. I pulled out an orange sundress. Nope. That's wasn't going to work. Orange was not my color. I returned the dress, and this time I peeked a little. I was so screwed.

I slid into a black dress and was putting on a pair of sandals when I heard a knock. Camden was on the other side of the door wearing a fitted polo shirt and a pair of faded jeans. No matter what he wore, whether it was an Armani suit, gym attire, or a pair of jeans, the man always looked like he was model-ready for a photo shoot. It was almost annoying. Almost.

He had a bag in one of his hands. "Hey, I brought you something."

"You brought me something? What?"

He handed me the bag, and there had to be at least four folded T-shirts in solid black smelling of a faraway ocean.

"Um, are these your T-shirts?"

He leaned into the door jam and crossed his arms. One side of his mouth lifted up into a smile. "Yes, they sure are. Last night you asked for one of my—"

"T-shirts," I finished for him. "Well, I was pretty toasted."

Maybe it was my lack of gratitude that made him give me a curt nod. "Shall we? I think I owe you dinner and a story."

"All right, let's go." He walked me down a couple of halls and pulled open the door to show a hidden elevator. We stepped in, and he hit the fourth floor.

"We are going to the top floor? I haven't been there yet."

The doors opened, and I stepped out with him. "That's because it's my floor, and I don't usually let anyone up here."

I didn't know what to say to that, so I didn't respond. Dinner that wasn't a date in a private place. No biggie. His private quarters though, wow. It was amazing. After we exited the foyer, we entered a huge open living room that had a rock fireplace. The living room flowed into a warm kitchen.

I was hoping he was going to give me a tour, so I could see the rest of his private space, but instead he led me to yet another door in between the living room and the kitchen. It opened to a set of stairs.

"We're going to the roof." He waved me through. "Ladies first."

The narrow stairs led to a lush garden with beautiful flowers everywhere. Who would have thought that the ornery werewolf had a private terrace on top of a roof of all places? Layers. Lots and lots of layers. My fingers gently touched a rose petal.

Camden smiled as he came up beside me. "I take it that you like it?"

The more important question was, did it matter what my opinion was? But that would be too snarky even for me, so instead, I said, "Are you serious? I love it. It has to be the most beautiful thing in the world."

He still hadn't taken his eyes from me. "Almost."

"Why do you do that?"

"Do what?"

"You are all over the place. Nice one minute, standoffish the next. Then you say things that I consider flirting. The problem I have with that is you're engaged, so I guess I'm asking, why?"

My whole life had been turned upside down, and I believed I was doing my best to adjust to the new circumstances. I didn't know what was going to happen tomorrow, but I was pretty sure what I didn't need was to hook up with a hot guy currently engaged to another woman.

He started to say something, and I held up a hand. "You look like a man who commands respect. I can't give that to you if you lie to me. So, if you want my respect, give me the truth."

He nodded. "After dinner, I will answer your question." He didn't wait for me to reply as he grabbed my hand, leading me around some beautiful statues and down a lighted path. There, in the middle of the roof, was a table set for two with a white tablecloth and two candles.

I stopped walking, and since he still held my hand, he stopped walking, too.

"What's wrong?"

I pointed at the table. "That kind of looks romantic. I guess I had it in my head that we would be eating something messy like ribs in the downstairs kitchen with other people coming in and out, not a candlelight dinner for just two."

He dropped my hand and cursed under his breath. "You're right. I don't know what I was thinking." He turned around to walk back the way we just came from.

As much as I knew that I should keep my distance, I didn't want to. One thing was certain: I liked spending time with him. I was still a little shocked when I heard myself say, "Wait. It's fine. Let's eat and I can ask my questions."

After sitting in one of the chairs, I looked around nervously. Camden studied my face before asking, "You're not afraid of being alone with me, are you?"

"No, I'm not afraid. I'm from the South. We fear nothing except God, bad tea, and outdoor weddings that take place in August. I mean, seriously, that is just torture." He shook his head and did that sexy smile thing he had down pat. Awkward moment over. That was me, Sadie the icebreaker.

"All right, then let's eat."

A chef appeared from who knows where and set one plate in between us. He poured two glasses of what looked like red wine for us both. I took a tentative sip out of my glass, as I still remembered what the tequila had done to me. Never again.

He pointed at the plate in between us. "Care for some sushi?"

I shifted in my seat a little. How to tell him I wasn't cultured enough for sushi? "Um, about that. Where I come from, we use sushi as bait. I'm not sure if I could stomach eating it."

He laughed, and it warmed my insides. No. No, it did not. That was the wine. That one teensy sip of wine. He moved the sushi, so it wasn't in front of me. "No worries. Some real food will be here soon."

The chef appeared again in a couple of minutes and put two plates of salmon and rice in front of us. My belly growled in appreciation.

I took my first bite and moaned. "Wow, this is great, Camden."

His Adam's apple bobbed, and his blue-green eyes stared at me with such intensity I grew self-conscious. "You know, I think I could get used to that."

"What?"

He cleared his throat. "Nothing." Cleary, it was something, but I let it go.

"Why don't you tell me that story you promised while we're eating?" I forked another bite of salmon into my mouth and made a hand motion for him to begin.

"I'll start at the beginning to give you a better understanding. My parents had several miscarriages before I was born. My dad sought out Ariana because she was the most powerful witch and soothsayer to have ever been born. He thought she could help my mom carry to term. Ariana told my parents she could help them, but only because the fates allowed her to do so. She said the future told her my mom would conceive two boys instrumental in winning the war."

He took a couple of bites of food before taking a sip of wine, and I had to curb my impatient nature from screaming, "Then what?" He winked at me, so he must have guessed what I was thinking.

"She explained to my mom she was going to give each of her sons extraordinary gifts of power. Jamison and I are both werewolves; however, unlike others in our pack and other packs in the world, we don't have to change into werewolf form during a full moon. We prefer it, of course, but we can fight it. She also enhanced our given powers, so we are faster and stronger than other werewolves, with speed like a vampire, and intuition comparable to a witch. She blessed us both with the ability to heal ourselves and others. Healing others is a power were-creatures and shapeshifters do not have, so in that we are different. The only thing that can kill us is a silver bullet through the heart or decapitation."

That didn't sound that special. "But wouldn't that kill all werewolves?"

"Any silver will kill a werewolf. A knife to the heart or silver injected into the bloodstream. But to kill my brother and I, the silver has to be left in there. If someone stabs one of my pack members in the heart with a silver knife, they are dead. But if someone stabs me with a knife, it has to be left penetrating the heart because if I remove it, I'm back in business."

"So, how many of your enemies know how to kill you?"

"Only Jamison, Ariana, and I know."

I sat back in my seat. He could have left out that last part. Why was he telling me?

"Because of that and our added powers Ariana bestowed upon us, we are the most powerful werewolves ever to exist."

"That is why you are King of the Werewolves, because everyone knows they can't challenge you?"

"Oh, they did at first, but not here lately."

"Does Ariana live here?"

"Sometimes. She likes to watch over my brother and me."

I nodded. "Ahh, I see. She wanted to keep tabs on you both to make sure your powers were used for good. Kind of like the whole Spider-Man thing."

"The what?"

"You know, the whole 'with great powers comes great responsibility' and yadda, yadda, yadda."

He smiled. "Yes, like that. And to be honest, Ariana has become like our grandmother. I don't know what I would do without her. She keeps us in line."

I had finished my plate and was leaning back in my chair, trying to imagine how stinking cute he must have been as a kid when I had a thought.

"You said she gave you the ability to heal quickly. Is that how you were able to heal me?"

Camden had finished his plate as well. He stood up and extended a hand. "Do you want to go for a walk?" I took his hand and nodded. He never released me as I walked beside him, until he led us to a bench underneath the stars. "Technically, you could have siphoned off me and healed yourself. And no, I don't have the power to heal others without consequences. What I did was take your pain."

I was shocked. "You mean that you took my pain and what? Then you had to deal with it?"

"It's not like that, Sadie."

"So, you didn't just take my pain for me?"

"Well, maybe it is like that." I glared at him. "Fine, I did take your pain, but first of all, it was from a hangover, not a gunshot wound, and I heal incredibly quick. Remember? In the scheme of things, it's not that big of a deal."

Understatement of the year. Everything with him seemed to be a big deal. "Camden, I appreciate you telling me about your powers. I promise I will never tell a soul about what you confided in me."

He gave a little laugh. "Well, that's good because if my enemies knew, I'm sure they would try to bury me somewhere deep with the bullet still in me."

"With not even an X marks the spot, huh?"

"That's exactly right."

"Why are you telling me instead of your fiancé?" The million-dollar question. "I would like the truth, please."

"I'll be blunt, then. All supernaturals have a mate, and it's said that once they cement the bond between them, one cannot live without the other. Sometimes, it takes thousands of years to find your mate, but it only took my dad fifty years. He loved my mom with everything he had, and when a rogue werewolf killed her, my dad followed her to the grave. I lost both parents within days of each other. Life became very hard for my brother and me. If it wouldn't have been for Ariana, I don't know what we would have done. I will never put my children through that kind of misery and because of that, I haven't looked for my mate."

I was sure confusion was all over my face. "Okay?" I didn't mean for that to come out as a question.

"Even though I wasn't looking for her, I still found her. Or better yet, Ariana made me find her. Sadie, you're my mate, but I can't accept you because I won't be like my parents."

Anger replaced my confusion. Who the hell did he think he was? "Whoa! Hold on a second. I never wanted you to accept me as anything. I'm sure there has been some kind of big misunderstanding. But thanks for explaining your bipolar emotions when you're around me. It sounds like you're the one struggling, buddy, not me. You have all kinds of issues, but I can promise you, I am not one of them."

I started to get up, but he placed a hand on my thigh, cementing me in place. "Sadie, please let me explain. My father knew other wolves in different packs had heard about the power my brother and I would grow into. He also knew they would try to eliminate us, so they could be king. Yet, he chose not to stay around and protect us. In the end, his love for my mother made him choose death instead of us. Do you know how old I was when I had to make my first kill?" My stomach knotted with dread. "Twelve. A werewolf from a nearby clan snuck into my room and tried to behead me. He tried to kill a child, so his child could grow up to be king. I had no one to protect me."

Some of my anger died. "I'm sorry, Camden. I'm sorry that you didn't have an easy childhood, and there was no one there to protect you. I'm sorry that their love for one another left no room for their children, but Camden, you're not your father."

"I can't fall in love with you."

"That's understandable. But do you know what would help? You not flirting with me or inviting me to romantic dinners. We are both here for a reason. To find a key. We have to work together but…" I made a motion with my hand, as I looked around the rooftop. "This isn't necessary. From here on out, no mixed signals. We need to install boundaries, and there is no reason for us to cross those invisible lines." I was confused, pissed, and underneath it all, my feelings were hurt.

His elbows were on his knees, as he rested his head in his hands. "I'm trying. I'm trying, but every part of my soul recognizes you as mine."

"And what does your soul think of Celia?"

"Celia is a means to end. Nothing more, nothing less. I have no feelings for her, but her family has something I need, and I aim to play the game the way it should be played in order to get it. I just didn't factor you in. You make everything so—hard."

"Then I'll make this easy for you. I don't belong to you." I stood up from the bench. "Thank you for explaining some things and for dinner. Please give my compliments to the chef."

"Sadie, wait—"

"For what?" I snapped. I was angry, and I wasn't entirely sure why. Well, maybe I had an idea. An attractive man who I felt a magnetic pull toward wanted me but couldn't have me because of his past, and I had no say in any of it.

He held both hands up. "I just need a minute to get some more clothes for the room I'm sleeping in downstairs, and then I'll escort you back down."

"You have this huge living area; why don't you just stay up here? If our enemy comes, I'm sure you will know in advance; besides, I'm only a few levels below you. I'll be safe. There is no reason you have to stay in a room right next to mine."

"I'm sleeping downstairs." His voice left no room for argument, so I just rolled my eyes. Neither one of us spoke as he gathered his things or while he escorted me back to my room. The silence was awkward, but I didn't know what to say. "Hey, but we can still be friends," or "Does your fiancée know that she's not your mate" all sounded like I cared way too much, and at this point, I couldn't afford to care.

At my door, he wished me a polite goodbye, and I mumbled something about seeing him tomorrow. I wished I could talk to Jo right now or maybe slap her. She must have foreseen this. I held up my middle finger and spun around slowly in my bedroom. Maybe I would get lucky, and she would see this, too.

I shed my dress and slipped on one of the T-shirts he gave me—only because it was handy, not because I loved his scent. The smell of the ocean wrapped around me, comforting me in ways I couldn't explain. I repeated the word boundaries over and over again until I fell asleep.

chapter eighteen

A tiresome week went by of more training. Camden was extremely polite if distant, which was fine, considering what he had shared with me. I had come to terms with me possibly being his mate, but if that were true, did it mean the one person I was supposed to be with didn't want me? Also, if he were my mate, wouldn't I know it? I mean, I did feel a spark of energy every time he touched me, but that could've been because he was freakishly hot. No matter how hard I tried not to notice, my eyes always seemed to track him. Considering that the vampire was freakishly hot, too, and I didn't even to notice him when Camden was in the room spoke volumes.

Speaking of the vamp, he was restless. One day at training, he was watching—or maybe studying was a better word—Camden and I spar, mostly out of pure boredom. He noticed how Camden always made sure not to touch me if it wasn't absolutely necessary, yet he wouldn't allow any of the other wolves to spar with me. Stephan made a comment under his breath and Ariana, who came out of hiding to just torture him I thought, said, "Oh, your mate will give you twice as much trouble when you find her...

and that will be soon." The word "soon" made him look like he was about to go into epileptic shock. Since then, he had been acting weird. Maybe all of the hot guys had commitment issues.

I was getting ready for our morning training session when Camden strolled into my room.

"Um, have you heard of this thing called knocking?"

He apologized, even though he didn't look the least bit sorry. "I wanted to alert you to some news. A portal has just been opened."

"What?"

"Since the keys have gone missing, I've had scouts around the closest portal to us. I just learned that the man who has one of the keys, Merek, has recently opened the portal. My scouts reported at least twenty coming over before the portal was closed. Out of the twenty were three powerful supernaturals. One being a mind controller. The good news is that his power is extremely limited. From what I've heard, his power is good for about fifteen minutes, and then he is drained for at least a day. I'm not sure why Merek opened the portal, but we need to be prepared for anything."

"What exactly does this mean?"

"It means we train harder today than we did yesterday. You'll need to be able to use your powers with precision and intent. Intent to harm whoever tries to hurt you. Being able to siphon powers is a big deal. It'll be an even bigger deal when you learn to harvest powers from someone and use it when they are not around. In a battle, you will have to assess which powers can help you the most. Remember, it's also important we tell no one about your ability, so only show what you can do if your life is at stake."

I nodded as he ticked off the list of things he had for me to do today, as I simultaneously gave myself a familiar pep talk. I would slay today. Totally crush it while not thinking of the hunky werewolf. Because I could do both. Maybe. Ugh. If I was being honest with myself, today was going to be hard to concentrate. This was the first time since our rooftop dinner that we'd had a lengthy conversation. Even if it was work related. He claimed I was his unwanted mate, and I had a hard time not staring at him. Why did he have to smell so good? That should be a sin in itself. I hated to admit it, but I'd missed him. Really missed him. How could I possibly be so attracted to someone after such a short amount of time? Boundaries! Must maintain boundaries.

Chapter Nineteen

After a long day, I had come back to my room and crashed. One minute I was asleep, dreaming about a hot werewolf that I had no business dreaming about, and the next minute, I couldn't breathe. It took me a second to realize I wasn't dreaming. There was a heavy weight on my chest. I tried to push it off me, but it wouldn't budge. I started to panic, realizing I was going to die. Hell, no! I wasn't going to die. I was a powerful manipulator. I stopped struggling and placed my hands on whatever was on top of me. I was pretty sure it was a boob. Well, that went from scary to awkward as hell real quick. I drew power from her, and whoever she was went flying across the room.

I jumped up, crouching on top of my bed at the same time Camden came rushing in. He flipped on the light switch, and there was Celia, standing with a bloody nose. Faster than I could track, she pulled a gun from her waistband.

She took aim, the barrel pointing at my heart. "Can you dodge bullets, bitch?"

Before she could pull the trigger, Camden attacked her with such force I heard one of her bones break. He wrangled the gun from her, pressing her face down into the carpet of my floor within seconds.

I knew she was crazy when she started laughing. "I want her dead. Or I will tell my father. I wonder what he will have to say about this? The deal was you make his little girl a queen by marrying her, and in return, he would tell you where the key to the portal is hidden."

Camden growled. "Screw the key."

"And have a part in ruining the world? I don't think so. You couldn't stomach it. Let me up, and I'll make quick work of killing her. Then I'll take you to my father's estate where we can get married tonight, and you can have the key in your hand the minute after we wed. Think about it, CG; don't you need that key to protect all of your pack and loved ones? If you don't have it, you might as well sign their death certificate yourself."

This time it was Camden's turn to laugh. "Celia, I thought I could go through with marrying you. Entering into a loveless act in order to protect the ones I love? I didn't think twice about it. But it is you that has ruined your chances of becoming queen."

"No, that's a lie! It was her." Her face was buried in the carpet, but I didn't have to see her eyes to know she was talking about me. "You have always been indifferent to me, but with time, I could have won you over. Until she came, that is. You've done nothing but watch her every move. With her out of the way, you can concentrate on me and your true desire—obtaining the key."

"Yeah, maybe your plan of marrying me and becoming queen could have worked out. You've ruined that plan. My plan is still the same, however. Get the key. But now, I'll have to do it the hard way because you made me choose, and just so we're clear, I would never choose you over her."

There was so much venom in his voice. "Are you going to kill her?" I asked, voice shaky.

"Would it overly upset you?"

Yes! No. Maybe? Oh, hell, I didn't know. "Maybe you shouldn't."

He had a knee in her back, pinning her to the ground, and a hand over her mouth. She was shouting into his hand but I ignored her. "I can't just let her go since she wishes you dead." He grabbed her by her arms, yanking her up. "I'll have to put her in the dungeon. No one's been in there in a couple of years. It's a little dusty. Hopefully, she won't mind."

On his way out the door, he looked over his shoulder at me. "Sadie, you know you can come down now, right? Or you can stay up there until I get back." Then he winked at me.

What? I was currently floating above the bed. Well, that was relatively embarrassing. How did I not know I was floating? I slowly let myself fall, so I landed on the bed, where I immediately got up to pace until Camden returned. What just happened? Celia tried to kill me… again. Camden admitted to us both that she was nothing more than a business transaction, telling her he would always choose me. That crazy wolf wanted me just as much as I wanted him, and neither one of us knew what to do with this… thing between us. I wanted to succumb to it, and he wanted to fight it. But I couldn't focus on that right now because I had a plan. He was going to be so excited when I told him he didn't need to have Celia's father tell him where the key was hidden because he had his own key: me.

Forty-five minutes later, I was still pacing when Camden walked back into my room. "Are you all right?"

I went over and sat on the edge of my bed. "Yes. I'm great. Did you see me floating?"

He came to me and placed one hand on my forehead.

I swatted it away.

"I'm not in shock. I'm fine. Really. Do you see Lil here? No, she's not here, but I was floating. Do you know what this means? It means that I found that storage bank of power you were talking about. We now know I can call back up someone's power for a certain time frame." Maybe forever. Who knew? This was uncharted territory.

"I knew you would be able to do it. I just didn't think it would take a jealous, gun-wielding witch to get you to tap into your stored energy. Now, tell me why you think your powers are on a time frame?"

"Okay, so my friend Jo is psychic, right? And when I was coming into my powers, I touched her briefly and had some glimpses of the future. I can't see anything now." I laid a hand on his arm to show him what I was talking about. "I'm picking up nothing from you. No

visions of the future. Even when I first came here, I had no more visions. I think it's because I touched her and didn't channel her aura, so her power only lasted with me for so long. But don't quote me on that. The point is, Lil is nowhere close, and the last time I pulled from her was days ago, and yet I can still fly."

"Your powers are extraordinary."

I turned my face, gazing into his eyes. "Oh, you don't know the half of it. Mind readers are almost completely extinct, aren't they?"

Camden nodded. "Yes, because that is one power everyone is terrified of. No one wants someone to be able to know their plans and course of action, especially in war times. And because that is usually the supernatural's only power, they are easy to dispose of."

I winced a little at that remark. "Well, there is one that is not extinct. My dad is a mind reader."

"Impossible. If there were a power like that available, I would assume both sides would already know about it. Both sides would want to persuade that individual to join their cause."

"Our town is made up of witches. If they didn't want someone to find out about the town and what the residents' powers are, then they could make sure no one ever knew. That's part of the reason I was so confused when you and your brother showed up. Someone had to have known you were coming, and they would have to have allowed you both in. Then I realized Jo wanted you both to come because it was part of my fate. She allowed the demon to terrorize me in our home because she knew it would spur me into action. She wanted me to go with you."

"Powerful witch community or not, Ariana could have found your dad if she wanted to. Or maybe she already knows about him, but then again she's the most powerful soothsayer that there is."

"You know that night that I first came into my powers, I accidentally siphoned off of him. Not only that, but I sought out his aura, and it wrapped around me like it was hugging me. What if I can tap into it?"

His muscular arms crossed in front of his chest. "Try."

Concentrating on the man in front of me, I called to my father's aura. It was warm and kind.

This won't work, but if she wants to try, there is no harm in that. Her snow-white hair is braided back from her face, showing all of her angles. She's the most beautiful creature I've ever laid eyes on, and it's been hard to be around her without touching her. These last few weeks have been torture. Even now, I can walk through the house and smell her everywhere. The smell of sunshine makes me long for her. But I just... I just—

My eyes opened, and I gave him a sad smile. "You just can't. I've understood since you told me about your past."

His mouth dropped open in shock. "Sadie, I—"

Shaking my head, I held up a hand. "If you can get me close to Celia's father, I think I can tap into him, and I can probably locate the key."

Anger radiated off of him. "You are crazy if you think I would let you anywhere close to him. No. We will get the key, but we will figure out another way."

I pointed a finger into his chest. "The whole reason you brought me here is to use me. Remember? Ariana told you I was instrumental to winning this war. How can that possibly be if you make me stay on the sidelines?"

He grabbed my hips. Pulling me into him, he said, "I care for you, damn it." He didn't sound too pleased about it. "I don't want anything to happen to you."

I put my hands on his shoulders, and then he was kissing me. His mouth parted my lips, and before I knew it, I was kissing him back with just as much enthusiasm. There was nothing gentle or shy about the kiss. As my tongue touched his, I heard him groan softly. His arms tightened around me, and I was engulfed in his warmth. When the kiss ended, we clung to each other without saying anything for several seconds. I knew no matter how great the kiss was, it didn't change anything for him and to be honest, I didn't want to be anyone's mate. I was a teenager, and mate-hood sounded like a forever kind of thing that one shouldn't take too lightly.

"Sadie—"

I didn't want to know what he was about to say. If it was regret, it would destroy me, so I cut him off. "I will meet Celia's father tomorrow, but try not to stress because you will be there, and you're, like, indestructible. With you by my side, what do I have to worry about? You'll protect me."

His grip on my hips tightened. "Sadie, you're mine to protect. If we do this, we do it my way. You will listen to my every command, or when I meet with Celia's father, Merek, you will not be there. Understood?"

I didn't know what he meant by the "mine to protect," but I assumed he meant while I was under his roof, because any other conclusion I could draw would mean we were crossing boundaries. I stepped back from him, so he could see how serious I was. "If I was going to be in danger, don't you think Ariana would let you know?"

"Yes." He gave me a stern look. "But I mean it, Sadie. I *need* to protect you."

"Protect me. But don't box me out. I'm here to do a job. I can't do that if you keep me on the sidelines."

"Go to bed and get some rest. I'm going to wait here with you until you get to sleep."

I was still a little shaken up by Celia the maniac, so I wasn't going to argue. Having him in the same room made me feel safe and something else... It made my stomach flutter and my heart race, which made me blush. I knew the werewolf sitting eight feet away from me could tell how much I liked him. The attraction I felt for him was so intense I felt like I could burst into flames at any moment. He cleared his throat and shuffled his feet. Yep, he knew I was attracted to him. Ugh. I immediately started thinking about the time I had to wash out Granny's pantyhose for her. That extinguished the fire real quick. Yep. I would just focus on Granny until I went to bed. Whatever it took to douse this need I had for him. I climbed in the bed as Camden was turning out the lights. I could make out his shadow as he headed over to the chair beside my bed.

I asked in the darkness, "Can I ask you a question?" His voice was smooth.

"Yes, but I might not answer."

"If the keys are so important, why doesn't Merek keep it? I get that he wants his daughter to be queen, but wouldn't he be more powerful by holding onto the key?"

"He's not a strong enough warlock to control whatever comes across the portal, at least not without help. Even with the portals containing the weakest beings, he would still be no match for them. But I am. He thinks that his daughter can enthrall me enough to do her bidding, which will really be his bidding. He assumes if I make his daughter queen, then they both can use me to open the portal and let over some Degenerates to join my pack."

"Why does he care about your pack?"

"He doesn't. When the Lux were dragging off the worse Degenerates—the ones who had committed crimes—into the portals, his son was one of the first to go. Merek's brother, Devon, had the key in his possession, and he was said to be a powerful warlock, but he knew you couldn't just pick and choose who comes through the portal. To retrieve Cecil, he would have to allow thousands of Degenerates over, and there was a chance that Cecil, Merek's son, might not even be alive. When Devon refused to help rescue his nephew, Merek began to plan. A week later, he killed his brother in his sleep and has been holding onto the key ever since then."

"So, it has never really been about getting his daughter a crown; it has been about finding a king or someone with enough power who can open the portals to find his missing son."

"Before you start sympathizing with Merek, let me tell you that Cecil is about as evil as they come. Those demons that tried to take you on the first day are nothing compared to Cecil."

"Wait! I remember my history teacher saying something about Cecil. Didn't he kill a psychic? And doesn't he have his own key? How did he get stuck in a portal?"

Camden chuckled. "I love how you always ask multiple questions at once. The girl he killed wasn't a strong psychic because she hadn't come fully into her powers. Yes, he did kill her for the key, but when he was arrested by the Lux, he didn't have time to grab the key. The Lux searched for it everywhere but came up empty handed. Wherever he hid the key, he didn't disclose its whereabouts to anyone. When Merek couldn't locate the key either, he pleaded with his brother, but I've told you how that worked out. Merek, unfortunately, wasn't dragged off to a portal with his son because the Lux didn't have enough evidence against him to do so. Everyone knows that Merek killed his brother but there's no proof."

"Obviously, you need the key, but why didn't you just take it by brute force?"

"Ariana said that if I followed that path, it would lead to loneliness and destruction. If I would have taken the key from Merek when I first learned he had it, I would've—"

"You would've what?"

"I would have never met you." He cleared his throat, and I started thinking about Granny again, so he couldn't smell how much I liked his words. "If he would have offered the marriage of his daughter for a key to another king or someone with enough power, then who knows what would have happened? Think how many Degenerates

154

would have been let into this world. I couldn't let that happen."

We couldn't let that happen. "If I can't read Merek's thoughts and this doesn't work tomorrow, what will happen if we don't find the key?"

"Then we have let down mankind."

He could have saved the world by marrying Celia, but we'd botched that plan, and I couldn't help but feel like it was my fault. In a hectic moment, Camden had chosen me over Celia and the key. I had to help him find the key tomorrow. I couldn't let me be his downfall, especially when it came to him saving the world. He might not forgive me, and I couldn't live with that.

chapter twenty

I woke up madder than a wet hen. I had no clue where the heck I was, but I knew one thing for sure: I wasn't in my assigned bedroom. I jumped up out of bed, still in the cute little pajamas I went to sleep in, but everything else was different. I opened the bedroom door and started walking down a hallway that looked vaguely familiar.

I'd be damned. There was Camden in his kitchen. He was bare-chested, showing off his beautiful tattoo and wearing a pair of loose sweats hanging low on his hips. It should be a sin to look that good in the morning. He was cracking eggs into a bowl while he whistled. He must have heard me before he saw me because his lips lifted into a smile.

"Good morning, sunshine."

"Um? Hello!" I shouted.

"Whoa. Did someone wake up on the wrong side of the bed?"

I marched over to him. "How about waking up in the wrong bed period. How the heck did I get here?"

He flashed a lopsided grin. "I knew you would not agree to move up here, so I waited until you were completely asleep before I moved you. You're definitely not a light sleeper. All your stuff has been moved, too."

I started sputtering, and he held up both hands in mock surrender.

"Before you get too mad, please listen to reason. This is exactly like our downstairs arrangement, except your room is bigger, and you are safer here. No one can get to this level without an elevator key, and the only other person who has one besides me is Ariana. Plus, I don't have to keep lugging clothes downstairs."

I guess he had a point, but I was fully committed to being mad, and once I was committed, there was no giving in easily. My dad didn't raise no quitter. "Whatever. But in the future, I would like for you to ask me before you assume that I won't have a problem with something." I turned on my heel to go take a shower, calling over my shoulder, "I like my eggs scrambled." That was not me giving in easily. That was making sure my belly was satisfied.

After a steaming hot shower, I felt a little less grouchy. I shook my head as I opened up a large walk-in closet and saw all my clothes had been moved, too. Camden was confident, arrogant, and presumptuous, and yet here I was, hurrying to get ready so that what? So, I could spend some time with him? No! It was because I was hungry. Yeah, that was it. Those eggs smelled delicious, and everyone knew eggs weren't good cold. Boundaries, Sadie. Boundaries. I put on a bright blue sports bra, yoga pants, and my tennis shoes and headed towards the kitchen.

By the time I scarfed down breakfast, Camden had come out of his bedroom with his hair wet, dressed in his gym attire of a black muscle shirt and black gym shorts.

"You ready to head down to train?"

I nodded, and we both made the long journey to the gym. When we got there, we did some stretching and a couple of warmup drills.

"There is no going easy on you today," Camden said apologetically. "We're down to the wire, and we need to see what you're made of. You ready for this?"

"For you to stop holding back? Definitely."

He gave me a nod and came to stand before me. "Don't pull off me today. Or the vampire. I think it's too much power for you, and I don't want you to have a bloody nose or something worse. Not when we're meeting with Merek tonight."

Without using his power, I would be no match for him, but I nodded. The next two hours were pure torture. I called upon the auras I had previously tapped into, including some of his werewolves and Lil, but with his strength and speed, it was almost impossible to stay one step ahead of him. I was constantly tapping into all of the previous supernaturals that I had, at one time or another, siphoned off of, but I made sure not to tap into him or Stephan. None of the supernaturals I had ever pulled from were nearly as strong as Camden or Stephan, so most of the time I felt like I was on defense. In the end, I almost gave half as good as I got. I was tempted a time or two to siphon from him to wipe that smug look off his face, but I decided a nosebleed and a headache wasn't worth it.

As we were cooling down on the mats, Camden said, "We leave tonight to go to Merek's estate. It's not that far away by plane, but since Lil won't fly—"

"Whoa! Wait a second. Lil won't fly? Isn't that irony at its finest."

His laughter warmed my insides. "Since she won't take a plane, and I really would like her to be there, we will take a car, so we won't arrive until eight in the morning tomorrow." At my nod, he continued, "I need to give you a rundown on what to expect. Merek has some employees who are very powerful individuals. Remember, we talked about the infamous mind controller named Zander? He is strong but his powers are limited. After about fifteen minutes he is left weak as a babe. But it's those first minutes that I'm worried about. If things go wrong, we will need to take him out first. His other top dog is Zander's twin, Chron. He's telekinetic. Merek also has several rogue vampires working under him. All and all, there are about a hundred there at his estate."

"Hmm. How many are we taking with us?"

His blue-green eyes met mine. "Here's where it gets interesting. I could call in my pack, but we can't take an army in with us because we will lose our advantage. It'll look like we're preparing to fight instead of just paying a visit to my future father-in-law. I thought you could go in there like a Trojan horse. Tap into Zander's and Chron's powers, so you can use them again in the future. Or for as long as your powers allow you to. The more supernaturals you tap into, the more powerful you will be."

I smiled at him. "Heck, yeah. I'll be a floating, flying, speedy, mind controlling, mind reading, object-moving beast. Mama likes. Now, seriously, how many are we taking with us?"

"Six, including us."

"What if he knows why we are there? Or worse, what if he knows that you have his daughter in a freaking cell?" He was crazy. "Suicide. That's what this is. I'm not the greatest when it comes to math, but I can tell you right now those odds suck."

Camden grimaced. "You are right. This is a bad idea. Maybe you should stay here."

I rolled my neck to stretch out the sore muscles. "Of course, it's a bad idea. And no, I'm not staying here. I just wanted to bitch a little. Considering that you're taking me on a suicide mission, I think you listening to me is the least you can do. Have you talked to Ariana to make sure that us going in there is not like lambs going to the slaughter?"

"I've never been considered a lamb. I don't think I like it, and yes, I did ask Ariana. She said something discombobulated, but the gist was that we both had to go to be put on the right path."

"Let's just hope the path doesn't lead us to death."

He helped me to stand up, and his lips met mine in a brief kiss. My heart raced, and I felt tingly everywhere. This attraction wasn't fading; it was getting stronger, and it was going to be the death of me. Not demons, ghouls, or warlocks, but my attraction to this man.

"You've got to stop doing that. Remember, we have boundaries?"

His teeth slowly raked his bottom lip, and it took everything I had to quit looking at his lips. "I'm trying."

"Try harder." I gave him a shove. "We need to go get ready. Move it!"

We had a couple of hours to kill before we began the drive to Merek's estate, so we sat on opposite ends of the couch from one another and watched a movie. Camden thought it would relax me and calm my nerves. A popcorn bowl sat in the middle of us, and we were both trying to pretend that the distance between us wasn't awkward. I couldn't help but think what it would be like if we were just two regular people, watching a movie together, and had no battles lurking in the future. His doorbell rang, jarring me from my thoughts. My whole body tensed with worry.

His nostrils flared slightly. "Relax, it's Ariana."

We stood up together and walked to the door. Sure enough, it was the strange old lady. She glided in and placed one hand affectionately on Camden's cheek. "My boy. I've come to wish you luck. You come back to me in one piece."

Camden leaned into her hand as he kissed her palm. "Of course."

She cleared her throat. "I'm thirsty."

"Can I get you something to drink?"

She smiled up at him. How she saw him through those milky white eyes, I hadn't a clue. "Just a sip of water, please."

He ran off to do her bidding. As soon as he was in the kitchen and we were left alone, she turned towards me and crooked a finger in my direction. "Come here, child." I reluctantly shuffled my feet closer towards her. This lady scared the crap out of me. When I was standing right in front of her, she whispered, "Yes, you will do well tomorrow. So much strength and you haven't even really tapped into all of it yet. Tomorrow is not the end for you. As long as my boy is around, he will not let anything happen to you, for it would break him if his mate died and he knows this."

We weren't on the same page. "Oh, but we've unofficially agreed to ignore that I'm his mate. We're not bonded or anything."

I raised my eyebrows at her chuckling. I was about to ask her what was so funny when Camden interrupted us. He handed her a glass of water. She took one sip then nodded at me. "Make sure you take Stephan with you tomorrow."

Camden looked like he was about to argue, but Ariana cut him off with a wave of her hand. "I've come here to do what needed to be done, now I shall go."

We both watched her as she left. "I'm not sure if I fully understand the point of her visit," he said.

"It was strange." I turned around to face him. "She knew that I'm your... um, your mate."

"Of course, she knows. She knows everything. Ariana told me the day you were born but other than that, she has never given me any information about who you are or your whereabouts. When I stepped into your town hall, I thought I could sense you, but I was hoping that I was mistaken. But when I saw you, I knew. I also knew the real reason behind her wanting me specifically to go after you."

"She wanted you to find your mate? Even though she knew how against it you were?"

"Ariana is a master at planning everyone's life." His fist clenched beside his body before he inhaled deeply. The anger that colored his face was gone as quickly as it came. "Let's go finish the movie."

We went back to the couch to resume our movie, but I couldn't help but think of the crazy soothsayer. Camden almost seemed bitter that Ariana was behind the scenes planning his life, but he still trusted her so wholeheartedly, and yet I was on the fence. When the key rested in Camden's hands and we were both still standing, then maybe, just maybe, I would start to trust her.

chapter twenty one

That night everyone moved in silence as we got ready to go to Merek's estate. The six of us met outside, pretending to be prepared for whatever came our way. Celia was still locked in Camden's dungeon. If I never laid eyes on Celia again, it would be too soon.

We all started loading up into the Hummer. The charming vamp, two werewolves named Garren and Evan, and Lil climbed into the backseat. I sat in the passenger seat, just as Camden was jumping into the driver's seat. He started the Hummer, and we began the drive to Merek's estate.

To kill off some nervous energy, I turned around, facing the backseat to ask Stephan a couple of questions I had been dying to know. "Stephan, how is it that you're able to walk around in the daylight? Is it just a myth that vampires will burn in the sunlight?"

Stephan kept looking out the window instead of making eye contact. "No, it's a rarity. I am the Prince of the Vampires, and that in itself allows me to be a daytime walker."

There was a heck of a lot more to that story, but I knew that no matter how many drunken karaoke parties we had together, that's all I was going to get out of him. Hello, steel trap. I veered away from any conversation having to do with his past and asked, "So, if it's an uncommon thing, we probably don't have to worry about too many rogue vampires strolling around Merek's property?"

Camden answered me. "Right. That's exactly why we are going to meet with Merek and his clan during the day." Then he addressed the group. "I have told Merek that I wanted a meeting, but I failed to mention over what. He probably assumes it's about his daughter or the wedding. Lil, I want you to hide somewhere on Sadie."

Lil flew over to the console between the driver and passenger's seats. She crossed her little arms over her chest. "First, you insist that I come along because I might need to fairy dust some people, but then you tell me I need to hide my beautiful self. You better be glad I like you."

Camden did his best to stroke her ego. "Think of it like this… you're our secret weapon."

"What's the plan?" I asked. "And what is our reason we didn't take Celia?"

"You should pretend that you're the weddin' planner," Lil said. "When he asks about his crazy daughter, tell him that she's off with her life coach. I mean, seriously, has anyone else noticed how messed up in the head that girl is? I can understand being biased when it comes to your own children, but the fact that he thinks CG would fall head over heels for a basket case is a little funny, no?"

Stephan and Camden laughed. Finally, they were bonding. I didn't point out the bromance because I didn't want to ruin the moment. "So basically, we have no plan; we're just going because Ariana told us to."

"Nailed it," Lil said.

Stephan weighed in. "Can someone please explain to me why we don't just take the key from him?"

"We don't know where it's hidden," Camden said.

"So, we torture him." The vamp shrugged like torturing someone was no big deal. "I bet I could make him squeal like a pig within an hour."

Camden sighed. "I've already thought of that. Ariana said that if we go that route, I'll lose the key for good."

I trusted Jo with my life, but I wasn't sold on Ariana. I didn't know why she didn't just tell us straight up where the stupid key was. Why all of this running around? It was like she was playing chess, and we were the pieces she moved around on the board. Yeah, the jury was still out on that one.

Lil floated over to my knee. "Sadie, are you sure you can read Merek's mind?"

"I'm positive. Camden asked me earlier to read his mind."

I almost sighed with part frustration and maybe a smidge of lust when I thought of where his mind had been and the kiss afterward. Perhaps a lot of lust and maybe I had denial issues.

Lil sat on my leg and narrowed her eyes at me. "All right then. Tell me what I'm a thinkin'. Pretend that we're at the circus. Dance monkey, dance."

"Um, that is not insulting at all." I still did what she asked. "Yes. Theo James does look a little like Stephan, and Camden could pass for Jason Momoa, and no, I'm not following you. Who is Markie Mark? But popcorn with extra butter always sounds good."

Lil stood up and started twerking. On. My. Freaking. Leg. Just as I was about to move her, she flew over to the console.

"Who the hell is Theo James? And there is no way that he comes anywhere near my stunning good looks."

"Whatever, vamp." Lil said to everyone, "I was thinkin' that if we make it out of this alive today, it would be fun to have a Mark Wahlberg marathon with some popcorn."

The next three hours were of me guessing Lil's thoughts. I swear, I was never going to be right in the head again. The fairy was as perverted as they came.

Thanks to Lil, I was happy to pull up to the gate outside of Merek's subdivision. The fairy jumped onto my shoulder and draped my hair around her to make a curtain. She whispered in my ear, "This is demeaning. But let's say hell freezes over and we do this again, remind me to buy you a pair of hoops, so I can at least have a place to sit."

I said, "It's a deal."

Then everything got quiet as the security guard at the main gate stepped up to the Hummer. "Can I help you?"

Camden said, "We have a meeting with Mr. Merek Davis this morning."

The guard talked into his walkie-talkie for confirmation. "All right, you can pass."

Camden put the Hummer in gear, and we started up a curvy drive. We finally pulled up to a normal looking Tudor home, appearing as if it could have belonged in a subdivision housing a soccer mom or a business executive. The house was humongous but completely normal on a nice sized lot. There were no nearby houses, which was great. No innocent bystanders. As a group, we marched up the six stairs and the butler let us inside Merek's house where we were intercepted in the foyer by two beefy guards. A robust man with ruddy cheeks and a full head of gray hair came clopping down the stairs. He wore suspenders over a pristine, pinstriped, collared shirt. The only thing that would have made him look more like a 1920s gangster was a cigar.

He came over and slapped Camden on the back. "My future son-in-law, have you come to visit with me, or is this meeting of a business nature? And why is my princess not here with you?"

Camden said, "She is currently planning the wedding. We've taken your advice to heart and moved up the wedding date to next month as you suggested."

Lil whispered in my ear, "So much for my 'she's trying to better her life' speech."

Hmm. Note to self, never play poker with Camden. I could have sworn he was telling the truth by just looking at him.

Merek grumbled, "I'll have to tell her later that I am disappointed with her for not coming. Please, let's go into the study to talk about your business, and perhaps you can explain to me why the Prince of Vampires is with you."

Camden nodded at Garren and Evan, who took a stance outside the door to the study right off the foyer. I was uncertain of what I should do when Camden motioned for me to follow him. Stephan didn't wait for an invitation but followed us both into the study. Merek walked around an antique desk, gesturing for us to sit. I took a seat in one of the leather chairs, and both Camden and Stephan remained standing on either side of me. Merek pulled open one of his desk drawers and pulled out a Cuban cigar, and I had to stifle a laugh. I so called it. Gangsta. He snipped the tip of the cigar then walked back around his desk and sat on the corner. Two men entered his office, and my nerves began to triple. One man was beefy and bald. He headed towards the bookcase looking bored. The other man was maybe five feet tall if he wore heels. He went to the right of Merek's desk and sat on the windowsill.

We waited impatiently for Merek to get his cigar lit. I started to channel him. His aura was a bluish-black color, and my body didn't want it anywhere close to me, but I fought through the disgust. Concentrating on pulling my father's powers forward, I applied it to Merek. Bits and pieces started coming together, and I felt physically sick. We had been played.

I started to stand. "My head is pounding and—"

With steel in his voice, Merek commanded, "Sit."

The bald man standing by a bookcase was obviously a teleporter like my brother because in a flash, he was in front of me, and the next second I was in his arms. Before I could blink, we were now behind the desk facing Camden and Stephan. Did I show my cards? Before I could make the decision, the short man strolled towards me and grabbed my arm. Now, I was in between both men while Merek clapped.

Camden and Stephan took a step forward, but Merek stopped them both with his next words. "She will be dead before you reach her. As you can see, I've acquired new employees." He pointed to the tall, lanky bald guy who had snatched me. "Carl, here, is a teleporter, and Ricky is pretty handy to have around also. Can you guess what he is?"

I glared at the short man holding my arm. "He can nullify powers." With the way he was clenching my arm, his power must only work if he was touching someone.

Camden made eye contact with me, and I could tell he knew how dire of a situation we were in. "What are you doing, Merek?"

"Let's cut the bullshit, shall we? Your infamous soothsayer, what's her name? Ariana? She called this morning before your arrival and said there was a chance I would never get my son back if I didn't get a blood oath from you at this moment." He took a long drag from his cigar. "She also mentioned that the wedding was off. So, here is the deal. I want a blood oath that you will go through portal fourteen tonight and not only find my son, but bring him back to me alive. I also want a blood oath that my daughter will be returned to me alive as well and no later than tomorrow morning, or the girl dies."

Why? Why would Ariana betray Camden like this? This made no sense. This was a trap, and we walked right into it.

"What if your son is dead?" Camden asked.

"He's not. Your soothsayer said that not only was he alive, but she could see his path. Soon, he will be engaged to the Zombie Queen." He chuckled. "It's just like Cecil to come back and make up for lost time."

Camden and Stephan exchanged a look, and I knew Camden was about to agree to the terms. Then what? The game would be over before it could even begin.

"Don't do it," I said.

Merek smiled at me. "Oh, but I think he will."

Camden stepped forward. "I vow that if your men release Sadie, I will immediately take a vow to find your son and bring him back to you and vow to return your daughter alive."

Merek chuckled. "Smart man."

"I'm assuming you will be giving me your key, so I can cross through the portals?" Camden asked.

"You assumed wrong." Merek smirked. "Since we couldn't work things out between us and we must part ways after you deliver my children, I insist on keeping my key. I think I should let you know that the key is not here, so looking for it would be futile, and you'd be wasting precious time. Rumor has it that the Vampire Queen has a key in her possession. Go retrieve that one."

Stephan snarled, "Not likely."

Merek shrugged. "There is also another rumor that the Undertaker has one or is about to retrieve one. Go get his."

"Death?" Camden scoffed. "You want us to stroll up to Death and take his key?"

I assumed Death was a major badass the way both Camden and Stephan were shaking their heads. Camden sent me another look. "We will figure something out, just release her."

As soon as both men let me go, I took in their auras and teleported across the room just in the nick of time. The man who had suppressed my power had a knife in his hand and was jabbing at thin air.

Merek clapped. "It appears my daughter might have been wrong. Interesting. Do you know what a power manipulator is worth? I want her. In fact, I'd trade the key to you right now. What do you say, King of Wolves?"

"I think I'm going to have to decline your offer."

"If I can't have her, I don't want you to have her either." He turned to the guy who'd short-circuited my powers. "Next time be faster, Ricky. I'm disappointed in you."

Camden let out a string of curses. Merek shrugged. "You said 'release,' not let her escape unharmed. You've really backed yourself into a corner. Now, your other vows, please."

While Camden recited his vows, I cleared my mind and focused on all of the auras in the room. I wanted to visually see them in case I needed to use my powers, or rather their powers, quickly.

Merek hit a button on his intercom. "Please send Zander and Chron in."

My palms started to sweat. As soon as the two men stepped into the room, I could sense the power radiating off them. Both were identical twins, and with a few choppy words directed to Merek, I realized they were of Russian descent. They had matching cropped blond hair and pale blue eyes and were more than six feet of pure muscle. They didn't need the guns in their holsters for them to look menacing. I started searching for their aura, gently tugging both dark blue auras into my body. Aww. They had matching auras. Cute. Merek stood up and started for the door.

He nodded at Zander and Chron, as they went around us to stand behind the desk. Carl, Ricky, and Merek headed for the door. "Our meeting is over. Find a key and bring me my children." Right before the door closed, he said, "Oh, and I was serious about not letting you keep the power manipulator." The door shut and a quietness filled the air. Great. Just great. When we left here, I was going to kill Ariana.

One of the twins sat down at the desk and opened up the bottom drawer, grabbing a large wooden box. He laid the box on top of the desk and opened it, revealing several different sized knives.

Lil, who had been deathly quiet until this point, whispered into my ear, "If that large white dude starts going into serial killer mode, I'm gonna be gone, like yesterday."

"Zander," the other twin said, as he stood off to the side. "Make the vampire kill the manipulator."

Stephan started to tremble. His voice sounded like he had swallowed gravel. "CG… get her away from me." He raised his arms like Frankenstein and took a giant step towards me before he started laughing. "Yep, hate to break it to you, you oversized salt shaker, but mind control doesn't work on me."

Zander's gaze swung to Camden, who wore a bored expression on his face. "I'm not as good as the vampire when it comes to theatrics, so I'll just go ahead and tell you that you're wasting your time."

The twins stood together holding hands, looking like overgrown *Children of the Corn*. It was not a good look but it was intimidating. I'd give them that.

Stephan's brow furrowed. "Um. That's interesting."

Camden was pulling on his legs. "What the hell? I can't move my feet." He glanced over to Stephan, who nodded in return.

"What's going on guys?"

"I'm assuming," Stephan said, "that twinkle dee and twinkle dumb are combining forces somehow."

Lil flew off of me. "Hold on, y'all. I got this."

Zander threw his hand out towards Lil, focusing his energy on the fairy, giving Stephan a bit of reprieve. The tiny fairy flew by Stephan and hit the wall. She flew backwards just to repeat the action. Without moving his legs, Stephan reached out a hand and snatched her before she could do more harm. Zander was trying to make her kill herself.

Camden was equally frozen like he was rooted in concrete. But both guys were strong enough that they fought Zander's power. Every second that passed, they were able to pry one foot off the ground, putting them a step closer to Zander and causing the man's eyes to widen in fear. He was having a hard time just controlling one of them, much less both. The other twin, Chron, made a motion with his hand, and all of the knives left the case. Hovering in the air, they pointed towards me. Their objective.

Stephan still held Lil gently in his hand. She was hurt but alive. Her voice was light. "Tell me you have a plan, fanger."

Camden laughed. "We have a plan." His head tilted towards me, and I gave him a wink. That was my cue. Let's hope I didn't disappoint.

I concentrated on Chron, using his power against him. I made the seven blades rotate, and now they were pointing at his chest. Let the games begin! Shocked, he lost focus, and I sent the blades flying. All seven embedded in his torso, pinning him to the wall. The twins' connection was weakened, and Camden and Stephan were able to move once again.

Lil's voice was tired. "Checkmate, Bitch."

"He's bleeding out," Camden said. "Find out where the key is and I'll handle Zander."

Camden had Zander by the shirt collar. "I feel you poking at my head, but you're not strong enough. It's over. Tell us where Merek hid the key." I cringed as Camden reared back a fist. I knew what was coming and by the looks of it, so did Zander.

Stephan handed me Lil, and I gently cradled her to my chest. I watched as the vampire walked over to the pinned Chron. "Do you know where the key is?"

Chron grunted in pain. "No."

Stephan smiled at me. "He is lying."

I felt an eyebrow reach my hairline. "Vampire trait?"

Stephan gave me a wink. That vampire was as charismatic as he was hot. Too bad my damn body didn't want him like it yearned for Camden.

Camden shook Zander. "I have a feeling they are both thinking of the keys, so now would be the time to extract your information, Sadie."

I concentrated on reading Zander's mind because Chron looked like he was about to pass out. Stephan removed one of the blades from Chron's arm. He tossed it to Camden who caught it in midair. With an air of boredom, he held it against Zander's throat.

"Whoops," Stephan said, "Chron is officially dead."

"Good thing we didn't need him," Stephan said. "Sadie, work your magic on blondie over here."

I was trying. If they would both just hush for a second, it would make my job a helluva lot easier. I made sure not to look at Chron, who was still pinned to the wall, with his pale blue eyes open. I tried not to shudder. I did not like death. Even if the dead person was someone who just tried to kill me. I stood in front of the other twin who had murder in his eyes, even with the King of Werewolves pressing a blade hard enough into his throat to draw blood.

He was thinking of murdering us all right at the moment, and that just wouldn't do. We needed him back on task. "The key, where is it?"

"Go to hell," he spat.

He didn't have to tell me because I now knew where it was. He was thinking about it.

I gave Zander a wink. "Thanks."

Camden asked, "Are we good?"

Considering that I knew neither man wanted to go hunting the Undertaker, I said, "Good news. It looks like there will be no reason to visit the Vampire Queen… yet.

We have a key we can use for the portal. There is just one small problem."

Stephan groaned. "Please tell me the key is located in the middle of a harem of beautiful women, and you want me to go in single-handedly to retrieve it. In fact, I insist on not listening to any other problems that might come from your lips."

I rolled my eyes. "Yeah, sorry to disappoint, unless you alter your illusion a little bit. For example, substitute beautiful women for ugly ogres in a cave just down the road."

"Repeat that one more time," Camden said.

"There is a cave a mile away from here. When Merek used the key to open up the portal, there were three ogres that came over before he closed it. Zander here was able to control the ogres long enough to reinforce them magically with collared chains. They are currently surrounding the key in the cave."

"Merek is a weakling. How is he managing to keep—" He gave Zander a disgusted look. "To keep mediocre supernaturals in check?"

Zander spat at his feet. "Go screw yourself."

The vampire looked offended. "Why the hell would I do that? I'm not desperate for feminine attention."

"It's because Merek has everyone fooled into thinking he's as powerful as his brother. You know, the one he offed."

Camden grunted as he removed the blade from Zander's neck. "Do you want to live or die?" Zander lunged at the Werewolf King. I thought I heard Camden sigh before he reached out and grabbed Zander by the neck, twisting it at an awkward angle. "Guess that answers that."

I should have been used to all of this death but nope. My stomach rolled at another life lost.

Lil was lying still in my hand, having passed out from the pain long ago. Camden came over and gently touched her broken body. I knew he was healing her but not enough that it would raise questions. From where Stephan stood, it looked like Camden was just affectionately touching her. I was smiling at him when a phone on Merek's desk rang. We all looked at one another before Camden finally answered it. With all the power I'd siphoned, hearing the conversation was easy.

"Hello."

"CG, you will find Cecil, but he needs to remain alive."

"May I ask why?"

Ariana sighed. "Without him, several others will fall off their course. We need him to right their paths."

"If you're sure, Ariana."

"I am."

After he hung up, I was fuming. "You're seriously not thinking of listening to her, are you? She alerted Merek and suggested you take those vows. I could have been killed!"

"But you weren't." I glared at him, and he held up both hands. "It's the truth. If she thought you would've died here, she wouldn't have let you come. Some people are supposed to play a role in this war—"

"You mean her game," I interrupted.

"I mean that she cares for the key players. They are her chosen ones. The ones she trusts more than anyone to guard the seven keys, and she wants all of them to be on the right path. If she thinks keeping Cecil alive will help the key players to win this war, so be it."

Stephan sighed like he was dying his second death. "Please don't tell me that she cares for the key players, because that woman has done everything but bake me a cake in the last week. I'm just waiting for an invite to watch reruns on the Hallmark channel with her. Next thing you know, she'll be planning my wedding."

I was pissed. Whatever her reasons were, I didn't like her. "Let's just go."

We opened the study door to a completely confused and disoriented Garren and Evan. Apparently, Zander had given them a command as he passed by them. The poor werewolves were ordered not to move. They couldn't even blink until Zander died, then they were free from his command. Their ego was bruised but they were fine. After we gathered our crew and left the house, Stephan put a hand around my bicep to stop me. "None of my business, but I do think Ariana is trying to help all of us."

"You're right. It's none of your business," I said, as I sidestepped him to the car.

Stephan turned to Lil, who was awake now and looking like she felt much better. "Is it just me, or is she getting sassy?"

"That child has always had potential to be a smartass. Just wait and see," she said.

I was exhausted, but we were far from being in the clear, and I was sick of death. Despite the blood trickling from my nose, I convinced Camden and Stephan to let me use Zander's power. Every one of Merek's goons let us pass, thanks to my newly acquired ability. They were like confused zombies as we passed by. I wasn't sure how long it would last, so we hurried outside. We all loaded back into the Hummer to head to the cave. I knew one thing: Camden might have promised that soothsayer he wouldn't harm anyone, but I hadn't made any promises. As soon as I was seated, I glanced at Camden's profile and thought of what I would personally do to Ariana if she killed someone I lov—um... liked. Liked strongly.

chapter twenty two

inding the cave wasn't the hard part. The hard part was convincing Lil to stay in the car. She wasn't healed completely and looked exhausted. We would all be worrying over her, and we didn't need the added distraction.

"Three werewolves, a handsome vampire, and a manipulator walk into the woods—"

"Stephan, please," I grumbled, as I tripped over a branch.

"Too early for jokes?" Stephan asked.

Camden held up a hand, stopping us at the entrance of the cave. "Let's be quick about retrieving the key. In and out. Sadie, stay back a safe distance to use your powers."

I wasn't sure what I expected when we entered the cave, but what was before us made me speechless. Three ugly beasts made a triangle around a black object on the ground in the middle. All three ogres were giants. There were collars around their necks connecting to metal chains bolted into the cave walls. I looked around for the beanstalk. Two of the ogres were viciously trying to reach us. I assumed to grind our bones for their bread. The third ogre sat with his back against the wall, his knees drawn up to his chest, and head in his hands. He looked pitiful. Camden targeted the largest of the ogres, and Stephan charged the other. The two werewolves, Garren and Evan, went for the one sitting down.

I stopped them with one word. "No." This one was different than the other two. He wasn't salivating from the mouth or pounding his chest ready to fight. He looked... broken.

They both looked at each other before they nervously allowed me to approach the ogre sitting down. Using my father's abilities, I searched his mind. I was shocked at his thoughts. Hurt and anger over the loss of his family. The injustice of his whole family being sent to a portal just because his uncle had done something horrible. Memory after memory popped into my head of his loving mother and his fierce brothers. The joyful memories were mixed with the painful ones. The Lux had dragged his baby brother away from his mother, and she was crying and pleading. That was what he had been doing so close to the open portal. Searching for his baby brother. Now, he felt he had failed them all. His pain was almost too much to bear. Tears trailed my face as I sat crossed legged in front of the giant.

"I'll help you find them." His sad brown eyes lifted to mine and I whispered, "Friend."

His voice was hoarse. "Friend?"

"Yes, and I'll help you. You have my promise."

Confusion marred his wide face, and I winced to see that Camden and Stephan had fought and won their battle with the other two ogres. "Were they part of your family?"

The ogre shook his head. "Bad."

"They were bad ogres?"

He nodded as Camden and Stephan strode towards me.

Camden shouted, "What are you doing? Get away from him!"

I stood up to protect him, even though sitting down the ogre was still taller than me. I fanned my arms out. "Do *not* touch him."

"Now is not the time for you to take on a pet," Camden said.

Stephan straightened his cuffs. "And if you insist on a pet, you should adopt a kitten or something equally cuddly, not something that could smash your head like a grape."

Now, the ogre decided to pipe up. "Grape?"

Camden gave me a knowing look as he crossed his muscular arms over his chest. "Why don't you step away from the ogre, and we can talk about this."

"You are not hurting him, so there is nothing to talk about, Camden."

"Camden," rolled off the ogre's tongue, like he was trying it out.

"To you, I'm CG," Camden said with a death stare.

I faced the ogre again. Using Chron's skills, I forced the steel collar around the ogre's neck to open. He sighed when he was finally freed from the chains.

Stephan sputtered, "Did she just?"

"Yep, yep she did," Camden replied.

I was glad to see the boys bonding, even at my expense. The ogre held out a hand for me, and I placed my small one in his huge catcher's mitt.

He stood. "Friend?"

"Yes." I smiled up at him. "Friend."

Camden pinched his forehead. "Twenty bucks says I have to kill him in the first twenty-four hours."

Stephan nodded. "I say the first twelve."

Garren and Evan were backing up from the ogre with a look of horror on their faces. Changing the subject of the ogre's life expectancy, I asked, "So, you have the key?" Camden pulled out a small, black ball from his pocket.

It was about the size of a baseball.

"That's what the key looks like?" I asked. Back in school, there were no pictures of the infamous keys that opened the portals.

He turned the key, and it split into two halves. He placed each half in his pocket. It wasn't the most secure spot, but I guess it was the best he had. "Yes, and now we need to go. Who knows how long your control over Merek's guards will last?"

Stephan asked, "What's the plan?"

"You're free to go," Camden said.

Stephan laughed. "I've always been free to go, magic spell or not. However, Ariana told me to stay, and there is something about her that is extremely creepy but reassuring at the same time. I'm feeling conflicted."

Camden pinched the bridge of his nose again. He looked like a man on the edge. "I need to find Cecil and return him and Celia to their father."

"You never vowed not to kill Merek," I said.

"No, I did not." Camden headed towards the mouth of the cave. "After all of this is said and done, everyone except Cecil is fair game. I only vowed to return Cecil and Celia to him alive. Once she is returned, anything can happen."

I had to bite my tongue. I didn't agree with Ariana on Cecil's lifespan, but my opinions weren't needed right now.

"I only have a few hours to enter portal fourteen. Stephan, you drive Garren, Evan, and Lil back to the estate. Sadie can teleport me to the location and then teleport herself back to all of you."

Stephan nodded as he headed towards the car. I rested a hand on Camden. "Wait a second. I'm going with you through the portal, and we're not leaving the ogre behind."

"No, you're not, and I don't know what to do about him."

"Um, yes, I am." Keeping my voice calm, I said, "Ariana told me that as long as we stayed together, I would be safe." Truth. "She also said I was to go with you after our meeting with Merek." Lie.

He studied me for a second. "She said this?" I nodded. "Well, then, there must be a reason she needs us to stick together. And she said that you would live?"

What was one more lie? "Yes, she swore it."

The vampire stood directly behind Camden, and my eyes met his. He knew I was lying. I wondered if that was a skill all vampires had or just the prince. As impressive as that was, what was more interesting was that he didn't rat me out.

Stephan did point at the ogre who was now eating leaves off of a tree. "That is not riding back with me, even if he could fit in the car."

I scoffed. "Of course not. He will stay with me."

Camden sighed. "Sadie—"

"Don't Sadie me. I've witnessed first hand the horrors that he went through. He is not like the other ogres but because he is one, he has been lumped in with the Degenerates. Do you know where portal forty-two leads?"

"Yes," Camden said. "The portals are labeled one through forty-two. The lower ranked a supernatural is in power means they got sent to a lower numbered portal. If a Degenerate is sent to a higher portal number, then they are perceived to be the strongest and most evil of the supernatural world." He pointed at the ogre who had taken a limb off of the tree, so he could eat the leaves better. "That ogre might be strong, but no one would have sent him into the realm of suffering."

Stephan put his hands in his pockets and rocked back on his heels. "I agree. I might be a forty-nine, but that ogre is a solid ten."

I huffed. "Well, then someone screwed up because that is where he was. Portal forty-two."

Both boys studied the ogre for several minutes before Camden said, "If he threatens you in any way, I will kill him."

"He won't." I was almost a hundred percent positive. "So, I'll agree."

Camden's brow raised. "I wasn't asking."

We all hiked through the woods together until we reached the Hummer. After quick goodbyes, we watched

our friends pull back onto the road. They had a long drive ahead of them, but soon they would be back at Camden's estate safe and sound.

The ogre waved goodbye, and that gesture had me smiling and Camden scowling.

To break the tension, I asked Camden, "So, where is this portal fourteen?"

"Have you ever been to Key West, Florida?" I shook my head. "Usually, one can only teleport to where they have been, and we need to go to a hole-in-the-wall bar in Key West."

"I've seen pictures of a sandy beach in Key West. Does that count?"

"It'll have to work. Try to teleport me first. And then after we complete our mission, we will come back for the ogre."

I squinted at him. "No way. He's coming with us." I grabbed the ogre's hand. "I'll teleport him first then come back for you."

Camden shouted, "Don't you even think about going by yourself—"

For a second, I thought my organs were going to explode as I teleported us to a beach. I took a moment to breathe in the saltwater and listen to the seagulls before I started to hide the ogre.

"Look mommy! That statue looks real," a small boy with freckles said as he and his parents headed to the beach.

The dad laughed. "Yeah, real ugly. I swear, artists today can make total crap and call it a masterpiece."

The mom swatted the husband's arm. "Don't say crap in front of Sean."

"Um, but you just did," the dad said.

We waited for them to get farther away before I turned to the ogre. "Don't move okay? They will think you're just a statue." A bird came and landed on his shoulder, and his eyes swiveled in fright to look at the creature. "It's okay. It's just a pelican; it won't hurt you. I'll be right back. Don't move!"

I went back for Camden, who was pacing when I returned. When he saw me, he grabbed me and hugged me. "Don't ever do that again."

He was squeezing the life out of me. "Easy, big guy. I'm fine, but Key West might not be if we don't get back to the ogre."

Stepping back from me, his eyes traveled my body to make sure I really was okay. "Let's go, then."

I teleported him right next to the ogre, who still hadn't moved.

A slightly wasted couple walked up to us while we recovered from the teleporting. "Excuse me, Miss. Can you take a picture?" They motioned to the ogre, and I understood they thought he was an attraction.

"Sure." I took their camera and snapped away. Of course, I had my finger halfway over the lens, so the picture would be mostly of my finger. I didn't feel right mind controlling humans, so a blurry picture was the best I could do.

As soon as they left, Camden said, "You didn't get us next to the portal."

"Well, excuse me. I'm kind of new to this, you know."

Camden searched on his phone. "It's only a half a mile from here, so we will walk."

"The ogre is coming with us." Before he could argue, I said, "They will just think he is in costume."

"This is a horrible idea. He's eleven feet tall and looks like he fell out of a scary movie."

"Look around you, Camden. This place is full of attractions and drag queens. Lots and lots of drag queens. Look at Marilyn Monroe over there. She's wearing a boa in this heat while walking in the sand in stilettos. Anyone who sees us will think it's part of a show. They will assume he's walking on stilts. We can be at the bar in less than five minutes."

Camden sighed, but we all started towards the portal. Several times, people stopped to get a picture. Some complimented the ogre on his stage make-up, and some asked him how he could walk on stilts without falling off. He just waved and smiled. Camden was barely keeping it together before we reached our destination. The bar was colorful. The owner was probably trying to hide the fact that the whole building looked like it was about to collapse. Drunken customers were weaving in and out of the establishment. Camden steered us to the back of the bar. The portal that could only be seen by supernaturals was a thin piece of shimmering air beside a dumpster.

"Most portals strip supernaturals of their powers. Off the top of my head, I can't remember if this portal is like that or not. Just remember that you're different. I'm not positive that you will be able to use your powers, but if Ariana sent you with me, there is a good chance that you can."

Oh crap. Now would be a good time to tell him the truth, but I couldn't get my mouth to work. He took out the key, put it together, and placed it within the shimmery atmosphere.

"Humans will see nothing, but we need to hurry."

Camden went in first, then the ogre, and I went in last. I honestly couldn't believe I'd complained about my ordinary life. How foolish I was to crave adventure. If someone were to ask me now what I thought about adventure, I would say it was highly overrated. I just prayed that whatever was on the other side of that portal didn't try to kill me.

chapter twenty three

I turned fifty shades of red at what I saw, Camden cleared his throat, and the ogre shuffled his feet. Naked men and women ran around the streets, and people who I assumed were drunk were passed out in every lane. We were in some kind of market where people were trying to barter and trade goods ranging from animal skins to alcohol. They looked like humans, and they spoke like humans, but when I saw a woman lean over to kiss a man and her fourteen-inch tongue stroked his neck, I knew they were anything but human. As soon as I was spotted, catcalls sounded out, and Camden shoved me behind him.

He released a heavy sigh. "I wish I would have known that portal fourteen was where most incubi and succubi were sent. This is not going to go well."

"What should we do?" I asked.

"Put a paper bag over your face."

"What?" Just then a man tried to snatch me from behind Camden.

I squealed, as Camden grabbed the man's wrist and rotated it until his whole arm was at an abnormal angle.

His shoulder popped, and the incubus fell to his knees, where Camden drove the palm of his hand into the man's nose.

"Don't touch. Mine!" Camden roared loud enough to be heard by all the people in the market. His hand laced with mine as we walked down the cobblestone path. Most people got out of his way, but the braver ones leered at us openly, which he ignored, so I followed his lead. However, the moment they showed any sign of aggression, his hand would snake out and punch them so hard I feared their head would pop off. The ogre growled at a group of incubi, and they scattered like ants. It was hard to believe that everyone wasn't scattering to the wind after one glance from my companions. Either they were all very stupid, immortal, or were dying of boredom from being stuck on this plane. I took a couple of deep breaths. With Camden and the ogre guarding me, I was safe. I kept my eyes to the ground hoping to draw less attention to myself, but it didn't help block out the nasty sounds some of the incubi and succubi were making behind closed tents. This place was hella gross.

A curvy brunette in a sheer dress that left nothing to the imagination sidled up to Camden, blocking the path. "I would love an hour of your time."

Oh, I just bet she would. Tramp. I waited for him to punch her like he'd done to at least twenty others since we'd started walking through the market but nothing happened. I tapped my foot, as she ran her hands up his chest. Not letting go of my hand, he removed both of hers with one of his.

"Please step to the side," he said.

Oh, so now we were asking nicely just because of a couple of curves. Her whole body started to lean in towards him, as if she was a cat in need of affection. That was it. I'd had it. Jealousy reared its ugly head. I stepped beside Camden, almost falling off the narrow path and into one of the tents in doing so, and throat punched her. She grabbed her neck, making a gurgling sound.

Camden was trying hard not to laugh. I glared at him. "Are you going to lead the way or not?"

He pulled my hand to his lips and kissed it. "That took you longer than I would've liked."

Oh, the arrogant pig. I tried to pull my hand away, but he just held it tighter. Ugh. "Do you have a plan for finding Cecil? Or are we just going to walk the streets until we stumble upon him?"

"If he were anywhere close to the portal opening, Merek would've already opened it a long time ago and let him out, but instead he sends me to retrieve him. This tells me that Cecil is someone's slave here. We just have to find where they are keeping him."

Cecil had become someone's biatch. Things were getting interesting. The three of us continued on the path leading us out of the market and to what I assumed was where the majority of the inhabitants in this portal resided. There were lean-tos and pop-up tents on either side of the narrow cobblestone path. If only I had some red shoes and the trail was paved yellow because we sure as heck weren't in Kansas anymore, Toto.

"Hungry," the ogre said.

I patted his arm. "I know, big guy. As soon as we can find you something to eat that won't try to eat you back, we will feed you." I swear he stuck out his bottom lip. He was pouting. A freaking ogre was pouting. I squeezed his hand. "I can't keep calling you ogre. Do you have a name?" He just looked at me and blinked. "Okay, cool. How about Dan?" He shook his head, and for the next thirty minutes, I threw names at him and he refused every one.

Camden laughed. "If there weren't leering naked supernaturals poking their heads out from behind their tents to plot our death, this would be highly entertaining."

"Herold?" I suggested. The ogre just shrugged.

"In the film industry," Camden said to the ogre, "there was a massive beast that was highly misunderstood. He also protected a female with his life. He was feared by many, and everyone in Hollywood knows his name."

The ogre had stopped walking, giving Camden his full attention. His deep voice boomed. "Name?"

"King Kong," Camden said.

The ogre nodded his head once then twice. "Kong. Me Kong."

Seriously? I had just spent more than thirty minutes of my life trying to urbanize the ogre with American names like Steven and Kyle, but Camden came in with a fake gorilla name, and the ogre was all about that. Whatever.

Camden pulled me to a stop. His head tilted to the side, making his hair fall on his brow. "There is a mining cave. My guess is Cecil is somewhere in there working."

"Of course, he is," I grumbled. "Because lord forbid him to be in an air-conditioned bar."

I was sandwiched in the middle of Camden and the ogre—um, Kong—as we went into the open-mouthed tunnel. Two beefy looking men stopped us upon our entry. "Who are you, and what are you doing down here?" the one with no shirt asked.

Camden whispered, "Sadie, convince them that we have just been sentenced to this plane. Find a reason we need to be a slave, and make sure you ask them to escort us to their leader."

"Boys, you just found us. We were disturbing the peace. You witnessed us beating up a whole bunch of naked people. Now, you need to take us to your leader."

Both guards' eyes were glazed over as they gave each other a look before they nodded. Without saying a word, they started down the tunnel. Poor Kong had to nearly bend over as he trailed behind us. I was trying to keep track of the tunnels we had taken but after the fifth switchback, I gave up. The last tunnel we went through opened up to a vast underground cave. There were torches lit in all corners. The floor of the cave had stains everywhere bleeding through the dirt. I tried to avoid those spots as I followed Camden. A boy with no aura, about my age, sat on an old chair, and there were bones scattered in piles all around his feet. His rusty-colored hair fell to his chin, and he had faded blue eyes. This was who was in charge of portal fourteen? A kid? He made eye contact with me, and everything went incredibly still.

Was his hair rusty or was it the most beautiful burnt gold I'd ever seen? His eyes weren't just blue—that was too normal of a description. They were an aquamarine like the ocean, pulling me. I couldn't believe I didn't notice his chair was actually a throne fit for a king. Fit for someone like him. Someone magnificent. What happened to the bones and where did all the gold come from? So many beautiful jewels littered his feet. I glided across the marble floor towards him. He was a beacon of light in this dreary, dirty place, and I had to get closer. Someone was talking to me but I ignored them. The boy smiled at me and I almost tripped. He was so beautiful. I needed to touch him to see if he was real. That same annoying person dared to lay a hand on me to stop me from my goal, so I slapped at their hands. Then they blocked me.

I was beyond frustrated. I stared at the chest in front of me until fingertips forced my chin up. "What?" I snapped.

Camden wouldn't let my chin go when I desperately wanted to look around him to see the boy. "This isn't real. Whatever you think you're seeing isn't real. I need you to find your way back to me."

Back to him? I was trying to get around him, and he was stopping me. I think I hated him. "Let me go."

Camden never took his eyes off of me as he said, "If you do not let her out of this illusion, I will kill you."

The boy laughed. "But she wants me, and you're in my world now."

"This is my mate you are messing with; I won't ask you again to release her."

My eyes narrowed. Oh, now he was declaring me as his mate. Like he was proud of me, instead of denying our bond. Yeah, that wasn't going to work for me. If I recalled correctly, he didn't want anything to do with me. I was just about to crack that handsome face of his when the room became darker. A fog lifted from me and everything shifted. The floors were dirt again, there was no gold, and if I was guessing… I peered around Camden to the boy. Yep, he was no longer stunning.

"Cute trick," I snarled. The lively twinkle in the boy's eye only infuriated me more.

Kong patted me on the head. His meaty hand tried to be gentle, but instead he almost walloped me. I felt a headache coming on. "Not friend."

"Thanks, Kong, I got that," I sighed.

Camden was boiling with anger, and it was all focused on the boy who couldn't quit smiling at us. The tension was increasing by the second.

"So," the boy said, "welcome to my portal. I've ruled it for the last ten years, and since then I have renamed this plane to 'Rapture,' and my name is Monad."

Ten years and he couldn't come up with a better name? For his colony or himself?

He studied Camden briefly. "I can tell we are going to have a problem with you, so unfortunately I'll have to kill you, but first tell me, how did you get here? I do love a good story," Monad said.

"The Lux are still dragging degenerates through portals," Camden said. His voice never faltered.

"Rumor has it that the keys were misplaced. This is not true?"

"Apparently not," Camden said.

"You just came before the king of this place and threatened him, and you let some Degenerates throw you and your mate through a portal?" Something about the boy's tone said he wasn't falling for it.

Camden crossed his arms. "Things happen."

The boy stroked his hairless chin. "Interesting. And what did you do to land yourselves here?"

"Your guards there," I said, nodding to the two who were almost hidden in the shadows, "brought us here. Apparently, we were being too disruptive."

I realized the boy needed to believe the words coming from my mouth or none of us would be leaving this portal. I gently probed his mind. He didn't believe us, and we were in trouble.

Camden read my face. "See if your storage bank can help us."

That was code for make him believe us or we're screwed. I gave Monad a smile. "Listen, we need to go through those tunnels, so that's what we're going to do, and you're going to let us."

The boy's gaze raked over me. There was a brief moment of shock, or maybe I imagined that, and then he bowed his head. "Yes, of course. The guards will show you the way."

Something in his tone made me believe my powers didn't work on him. But then again, he was letting us go as I requested.

Before we moved in the direction of the tunnels, the boy stopped us. His gaze never left mine as he said, "When you get back here, I would like to proposition you. I would love nothing more than for you to become my lover."

Camden's voice was hard as steel. "No. That is not going to happen."

"You dare take that tone with me? Do not presume that you can come into my kingdom and tell me what to do. Make that mistake again and your bones will be lying at my feet as well."

What was happening? Was my power not strong enough? This boy's eyes weren't glazed over like the guards were, but he acted like he was under my control. After all, he'd granted my wishes about the tunnels. But he didn't have an aura. Was he acting?

Camden was an alpha, and he was struggling with backing down. Intervening, I tried again more forcibly this time. "Monad, we need in those tunnels."

"Of course, you do." Monad tilted his head and studied me. As I met his eyes again, I could feel him trying to cast another illusion. My eyes darted to the left of him and he laughed.

The boy got up from his chair and did a slow circle around us, stopping right in front of us both. "I can sense you are a wolf. Am I correct?"

"Not a very powerful one, but yes," Camden said with his eyes downcast, like he was embarrassed by the admission.

Monad looked pleased by his disclosure. "Regardless, your powers here will be totally useless. I'm the only one who can wield any powers. It helps keep everyone in check, you see." Facing me, he put his hands behind his back while he studied me. "But this beauty… what are you?"

"I'm a complete dud. Every once and a while when my concentration is at its peak, I can crawl walls. I know that's not useful, but we don't get to pick our powers." Thanks Stacy! I never thought that conniving heifer would be useful.

"Hmm. Interesting. Well, unfortunately, you won't be able to crawl any walls here. Like I said, powers are suppressed on this plane."

"We completely understand," Camden said.

"Good." Monad resumed his seat on his makeshift throne. "This will be our first time having an ogre here with us on this plane, so we will need to make sure you all are chained. Just as a precaution."

I was about to argue with him about the chains but I was starting to feel a little dizzy. Trying to convince him to do my bidding was like hitting a brick wall repeatedly. My voice was strained as I said, "We need to go now. Please send us on our way, and don't think of us for the rest of the day."

Monad nodded and waved us away with his hand. I had lots of questions, like why did I feel like my powers didn't work on him even though he was doing my bidding? We were escorted down a shaft where the guards put chains on all three of us, including a magical collar on Kong. My heart squeezed when I saw the panic in his eyes. I had just rescued him from chains to have him shackled again. Some friend I was.

I was about to apologize when Camden clapped him on the shoulder. "This is very temporary. Just hang in there, all right?"

When the ogre nodded at him, my heart swelled. Camden had lots of layers, but I was learning to appreciate every single one of them. He noticed me staring at him. I reached up on my toes and placed a kiss on each of his cheeks.

"What was that for?" he asked.

"For being nice."

"Remind me to be nice more often."

I started to laugh, but I felt something warm trickle down my nose. I was exhausted, and I hadn't had a moment to rest since Merek's. I tried to wipe the blood away before anyone could see it, but it was too late. Camden studied me with a look of concern.

He pulled my body into his, as we followed the guards. "You've done too much. Your body is giving you warnings. Listen to it."

I whispered, "This is a bad place to heed warnings. Especially since I might be the one that can get us out of this place."

"You're mortal. This could kill you. From here on out, bare minimum, understand? The powers that drain you the most, stay away from."

"That would mean no more mind control."

He winced. *Yeah, I'm right there with you buddy.* Whatever he was about to say was interrupted by the guards who handed us all axes. "Try not to kill each other or the other miners," the shirtless one said. He must be the talker for the both of them because the other one just glared. We all had our talents.

As soon as they left, we dragged our chains behind us to a partial tunnel jutting to the right of the central tunnel everyone was working in. As soon as we were all semi-hidden, I worked on removing our chains. Once that was accomplished, we went deeper and deeper in the shaft, stopping at every miner we approached, so Camden could see if they were Cecil. There was a guard about every hundred yards. Since we were supposed to be working on the wall in front of us and not traveling down the mineshaft, it was going to be tricky getting by them.

Camden asked me, "You didn't happen to swipe up the illusion talent for later, did you?"

"Afraid not, your boy back there had no aura. Go figure."

"Hmm. Maybe you can't manipulate some people."

"I know. Total shame." I studied the upcoming guard. "I could make him float?"

We weren't going to make it out of here alive if I didn't contribute in a big way. The guards would notice us talking to the miners if I didn't force them to look the other way. At every station, I convinced the guard he had an urge to go to the bathroom, or he had a headache and needed to lie down, or should go and inspect a miner's work. I was a busy beaver. A bloodied, busy beaver.

By the third guard, Camden was on to me, and Kong was becoming visibly upset, probably from the amount of blood spurting from my nose.

"Don't waste my efforts, Camden. Hurry. Find Cecil and let's get the hell out of here, so I can pass out without worrying about all of these rapey people."

He leaned in, whispering against my ear and sending shivers through my body. "I can't heal you. Please, don't do anymore."

I gave him a wink, hoping it would ease the tension, but I failed miserably. His jaw was clenched, but he did move at a quicker pace. Maybe we would find Cecil soon. After a few minutes, I said, "It is so easy to convince these guards to look the other way. I mean, if you don't factor in the blood loss, and yet I almost believe Monad didn't buy what I was selling."

Camden checked another miner, but he didn't fit the profile. "He didn't."

"Come again?"

"Your mind control did not work on him. Monad allowed us to come down here. He wanted to see why we're really here."

Kong grunted. Really? Even the ogre knew Monad was above my mind controlling skills.

"At what point were you planning on telling me that the psycho illusionist didn't believe the lies I wove and is probably planning his attack on us now."

Camden shrugged. "Been a little busy."

That was fair. I couldn't be mad anyways; my schedule was completely filled up with trying to avoid a panic attack. We were going deeper into the mountain. The funny thing was I never noticed I was claustrophobic. It was dark, the tunnels were narrow, and there wasn't a ton of oxygen. Camden sensed my fear. He grabbed my hand and without saying a word, his thumb gently stroked my wrist.

"When were you going to tell me that you lied to me about Ariana wanting you to accompany me?"

"That's a good question. I would honestly say probably never. I mean, no harm no foul, right?" Kong, the traitor, shook his giant-sized head. Oh, all of a sudden, he wanted to be judgmental. Whatever. "Let's look at it this way. Ariana is the best soothsayer there is, correct? I mean, those were your words. So technically, she knew I'd be here in this dark, claustrophobic place with you, and she

didn't try to stop me or alert you. So, in a roundabout way, she did give me the go ahead."

"A mate that lies to me."

"And now we're just going to accept this thing, whatever it is between us, all of a sudden?"

"Sometimes, you can't fight the inevitable."

What did that mean? I looked over to Kong and he just shrugged. Even the ogre was stumped. Good. I didn't want to be on Confusion Island all by myself. Somewhere along the way, I started to think less of the cramped space and more about what our future looked like. Not mine and Camden's, but our immediate future considering that Cecil wasn't in the tunnels. Everything we'd done so far was going to be a lost cause, and what about Camden's vow? What happened when you broke one of those?

I voiced my question out loud, and Camden said, "Vows are taken seriously. There would be heavy consequences."

"Death," I asked.

"Possibly."

My stomach clenched. He'd made those vows to protect me. I had peeled back another layer.

As we reached the end of the tunnel, Camden asked, "What do we have here?" He grabbed a short man up by his arm. His feet barely touched the ground, as Camden held him up for closer inspection. "Let me guess. You're Cecil?"

The man sneered. His red hair hung in dirty clumps around his slightly pudgy face. Freckles covered his face. Where Celia had long legs that went on forever, this poor soul looked like an oompa loompa. "Who wants to know?"

"We are going to get you out of this tunnel and back to your father, but you will do exactly as I say. Do you understand?"

The man blinked his eyes several times. "My father? I knew that crazy old man would eventually find me." Cecil studied Camden for a few moments. "Lead the way, wolf."

I grabbed a hold of the wall as a wave of dizziness hit me. I might have persuaded him to not ask any more questions. But honestly, who had time to sit and chat in a claustrophobic place while bleeding out. Not me. We all followed Camden, who was the only person who could smell fresh air, which also equaled the way out. To keep from passing out, I made a to-do list in my head. We would take care of the vows Camden made. He would have his key, and I would be free to lead a normal life. I looked up at Camden, who was now dragging Cecil by his chains. I felt a sharp pain in my chest at the thought of leaving him. But it wasn't like we had a future together. Just because he was admitting I was his mate didn't mean he wanted to claim me as his mate, and his strong feelings for me didn't mean he could ever love me. No matter how attracted we were to one another, or how fate had claimed us to be together, there could never be anything between us because of Camden's past. Those were his feelings. I didn't have to agree with them or like them, but I did have to respect them. Because when you loved someone, that was what you did and I loved him. With all my heart. A tear leaked out of my eye. Great. Now, I was losing all kinds of bodily functions. The pain in my heart was almost unbearable, but it wasn't necessarily a bad thing because it helped me stay on my feet. None of my feelings mattered; soon, I would be going home. Unless the siren blaring was any indication that Monad would now like a second meeting, in which case, I might be a permanent miner.

chapter twenty four

The four of us hiked back through the tunnel. Kong was still bent over, almost crawling. There was no way I could manipulate all of the guards at once, not without injuring or killing myself. They would know we were escaping, and there was nothing I could do about it.

Camden put a hand under my arm. "We need to hurry."

I didn't bother telling him we were already going as fast as we could go. We passed several miners that shot us fearful looks. Fear of us, or fear of what they thought was about to happen to us, I couldn't say. I couldn't pass any judgement because I was pretty afraid, too.

"Any minute now, someone is going to re-shackle us." Every step Cecil complained. "I should have just stayed where I was. We're all going to get caught, and you're just going to make my life harder now."

"If you don't stop your whining, I'm going to end your life now," Camden growled.

I should try to be the mediator, but the truth was I was tired of hearing Cecil's mouth, and I was about to encourage Camden to kill the little jerk until I thought of the vow he would break. Unfortunately, I didn't have any energy to waste on convincing Cecil to shut up, so I just ignored his blabbering.

We ducked into a partial tunnel as a group of soldiers stormed past us. As soon as we were in the clear, Cecil started up again. "I don't know what you were thinking. You have no plan. How are we to escape this? Maybe if I call the guards over now, they will be lenient on me. I've seen them torture people. I will not be subjected to that." From the look on Camden's face, I realized he no longer cared about breaking his vow. He turned around to face Cecil when Kong intervened. Hunched over, he put one beefy hand around Cecil's neck and bounced him on the ground a couple of times, and then he dragged Cecil behind him like a ragdoll.

Camden cuffed Kong on the shoulder. "Thanks. I don't know if I could have restrained myself from killing him."

Cecil dug his heels in the ground, but the ogre didn't notice. "Not friend. Bad man. Mouth stop."

I nodded. "Yes, you stopped his mouth, and I will be forever grateful. Drag him faster if you can."

Camden grabbed my arm. "There are many guards blocking the exit. I can hear them."

"I'll teleport Cecil to the market then come back for both of you."

"No," Camden said. "You are already bleeding. Can you imagine what teleportation will do to you? No, we will fight our way out."

"Fight!" Kong said, as he dropped Cecil behind him.

This was our only option. What if we couldn't fight our way out? What if Kong became a prisoner yet again?

No, I couldn't let that happen. Quickly, I grabbed Cecil's leg. I didn't want to even touch the weasel, but in a flash, I had Cecil in the market where some succubi stared at us, wide-eyed. I left him throwing up in the dirt as I returned for Camden and Kong. It took a second for my eyes to readjust to the darkness. They had moved to another tunnel veering off to the side.

Camden was pissed, but he'd get over it. "What were you thinking? Do you want to die?"

Ignoring him, and the way my legs shook, I grabbed Kong next. As soon as he was outdoors, he smiled. I didn't have the heart to tell him we were far from being out of danger.

Cecil turned around, his face a blotchy red. He pointed one of his fingers at me. "Why you—"

Kong took a meaty fist and bopped him on the head. As I was teleporting for Camden, I heard Kong say, "Again. Mouth shut." I was starting to love my ogre.

By the time I returned to Camden, guards surrounded him and I was in pretty poor shape. My body felt like it was about to shut down. Camden fought the guards in the tightly confined space with ease, his motions fast and accurate. He didn't hit to cause bodily harm; he hit to disable. Most of the guards were unconscious or holding their windpipes.

Trying to sound bored, I asked, "Do you want to stay and finish, or do you think we can blow this joint?"

"Waiting on you, beautiful," he said, dodging a fist to the face. "You are about to drop on your feet. I'll carry you back to where you left Cecil and Kong."

"Yep, sure. Or we could just—" I grabbed his arm and teleported him to where I'd left the other two. Camden looked like he wanted to throttle me, but after taking in our surroundings, he held me tighter to him. What awaited us was more than just unfortunate, it was flat out disheartening.

Monad stood there with a whole legion of soldiers. He was doing a slow clap. "Fantastic! Truly, that was something to see. So tell me, blondie, how is it that no one can use their magic in this portal but you and me?" He pointed to naked incubi standing fairly close to Kong. "I mean, they all still have the basics, even the wolf, but they are like fine cars stripped down to the bare minimum."

Camden was fighting like that, and that was the bare minimum? "Um, I don't know. This is your portal, you tell me."

The boy looked even dingier out in the light. "If I wanted you before, I definitely want you now."

"You won't be getting her," Camden said. I loved his confidence because right now, I had none.

Monad cocked his head to the side and smirked. I could hear a growl coming from Camden. We were too outnumbered to act hastily. I placed a hand on his bicep and squeezed. Not that I could hold him in place if he decided he wanted to fight our way out of this, but to calm him down.

"I felt you trying to control me. You are so very strong. But this—this was a surprise. So, you can teleport? But can you teleport out of this portal?"

Um. Good question. Before I could tell him I didn't have a clue, he whispered something to the guard next to him. The guard pointed a gun at Camden. "Those are silver bullets, love. I want you to try and teleport out of this plane. If you are successful but don't come back within thirty seconds, the wolf dies."

The crowd immediately started going crazy. They were hopeful I was their ticket out of this dirty place. Camden gave a bark of laughter. "She will do no such thing." The crowd became riled at his words.

Monad nodded, and a guard aimed at Camden. That was all the motivation I needed. I closed my eyes and pictured Camden's estate. Maybe I could bring the vampire back with me. We would need back up. My body began to travel, but then I was slammed into something that felt like a brick wall. My head began to pound, and my bones felt as if they were breaking in my body. I came hurtling back to where I had been just standing moments before. Camden caught me before I hit the ground. My nose was gushing blood, and I was seeing double.

Camden cradled me to his chest. "Why would you even try?"

"Because they had a gun pointed at you? Or maybe the loss of blood is affecting me. Does it matter? I tried. It hurt. End of story."

He gave me a look like I was slow on the uptake. "You don't have faith in me, do you?" Still holding onto me, he said to Monad, "Tell me when you're dead, who will rule this shit hole?"

A crazy looking incubus shifted from foot to foot so fast he looked like he was trying not to use the bathroom. "Me!" He waved one arm above his head, as if he was trying to flag someone down.

Seriously? Out of all the people here, they couldn't have picked someone that looked a little more stable? It must've not been a majority rules kind of thing.

Monad tilted his head back and laughed. "Like someone could dethrone me. I could cast an illusion so fast that—"

With Camden's 'basic' skills, he ran towards Monad, knocking two of the closest guards out of the way. His leg swept out, hooking both of Monad's feet, and making the boy fall to the ground. The boy cast a grand illusion turning everything pitch black. It was so dark I couldn't see my own hand. Over the cries of the crowd, I heard a scuffle, and then as fast as it went dark, the light returned. That's when chaos was created. All of Monad's guards rushed us. If I hadn't been scared for my life, it would have been comical seeing a bunch of naked people turn on each other. I saw things flopping in every direction.

Some things were never meant to be seen. This was one of those things.

Kong let out a roar and knocked guards over like pins in a bowling alley. Camden swung wildly at all who dared get close to him… or me. Naked people scattered, and I'd never been so thankful of anything in my life. I was on my knees, panting with exhaustion, as I watched Camden and Kong fight with abandonment. Neither one of them let anyone get close to me. Camden was choking one guard from behind as he kicked another guard in the face. I could hear the bone crunching from here. At least I wasn't the only one with a nose bleed. They were outnumbered, but they didn't need me, and I was perfectly fine with that. I would sit here and gather my strength.

Blinking, I found Kong standing next to me with a knocked-out Cecil over one of his massive shoulders. "We go now?"

Huh? I looked around at all of the fallen guards. There were some who had decided that this wasn't their fight, and they were leaving the area. The illusionist's body was crumpled on the ground. His eyes were unblinking, staring at nothing as blood trickled down from his mouth. Definitely dead. Camden stepped over him towards the crazy incubus.

"We are heading towards the front of the market, so I suggest you have a party celebrating your new leadership role. Anyone that follows us will die."

Kong nodded. "Crush."

The four of us traveled the football field's length it took us to get to where we had first entered the plane. Everyone stared after us, but wisely no one followed.

Camden pulled the key out of his pocket. "We have to be quick in crossing. We can't chance them jumping through the portal."

I pictured the curvy brunette that had propositioned Camden. He was right; we couldn't let a whole bunch of incubi and succubi take over Key West. Talk about *Girls Gone Wild*. After the portal was opened, we jumped through and were able to close it before any curvy skanks or creepy perverted men came through. Point for us.

Even with Camden healing me, I was beyond exhausted, but I didn't hesitate to take Kong, followed by Cecil and Camden, to Camden's estate. I'd never been so happy to see a place before in my life. It was daylight when we were walking up his drive.

"How many hours has it been?" I asked.

"Time operates differently on the planes. Most of them operate like Groundhog's Day. They are on constant repeat."

I wanted a bath, pajamas, and a bed. If I didn't get those things soon, there was a good chance that someone would pay. Only moments after being in his house, I knew that I wouldn't get any of those things anytime soon, and I was livid.

chapter twenty five

L il fluttered around, acting all mama bear on everyone, including Kong. She had taken an immediate liking to the ogre. Kong had free range of the downstairs thanks to the vaulted ceilings, and the ogre made good use of his time. He was like a toddler at the doctor's office, opening up every cabinet or drawer there was. Stephan tried to keep a respectful distance. In his defense, Kong leaned in close to Stephan and took a deep whiff of his neck, and that was enough to make the vampire nervous.

"If the ogre tries to eat me," Stephan said, "I'm out."

I shrugged. "We all have to draw the line somewhere." Cecil had woken up and did the unfortunate thing of opening his mouth, and now he was asleep again. Thanks to Kong, he was going to have so many knots on his head when he finally woke up, but I had no sympathy for him. One would think he would have learned by now that he did not have a friend amongst us.

Lil landed on Camden's shoulder. "What's the plan boss? Time is a-tickin'."

"We leave now to take Cecil and his sister to Merek's." My heart dropped. I wanted a bath. "We need to take the plane, so this time you'll have to stay behind, Lil."

Her hands wrung together. "I feel like I'm lettin' everybody down. Maybe I could just fairy dust myself for a bit and then—"

"Don't worry about it, Bumblebee. They will have me," Stephan said. "Who else could they possibly need?"

Surprisingly, Lil had grown attached to the vampire. Instead of reprimanding him, she winked at him like he just gave her the biggest compliment. I had gone through a portal, and they had bonding time. Didn't seem fair.

Camden went off to his study to call in his twelve guards to meet us outside by his private airstrip. Stephan went off to do whatever Stephan needed to do to prepare. Lil made the ogre several sandwiches, taking him out to the patio where he could eat, and she could question him in private. I think she could sense what I saw in him, and she wanted to know how deep his wounds went. Too tired to get off of the couch, I stared off into space, thinking about how much I missed Jo.

A phone on an antique table beside the wet bar rang. After the thirtieth ring, when I realized that no one was going to answer it and the caller was tenacious to say the least, I clamored to my feet.

I grumbled the whole way. "Hello."

"Dude. Did I not time that right? Why did it take you so long to answer the freaking phone?"

"Jo! You have no clue how much I have missed you."

The line was quiet for a second. "Why would I not know? I'm psychic. You know this. I know you're blonde but dang, girl."

"Oh, shut it," I laughed. "So, any more visions that I should know about?"

"Maybe. Last night I saw a wheel of crowns. They were going around and around like a merry-go-round. Where they stop no one knows. Crowns, keys. Keys, crowns. All connected. A hamster wheel and flustercluck of claiming thrones."

"Yeah, um. What am I supposed to do with that info?" She sighed into the phone. "Never mind. So, you've only got a minute before 'hottest' comes to get you. So, I need to ask you the important questions."

"Oh, I'm fine. I mean, you know the—"

"Dude, I know you're okay. When I said important, I meant like that kiss between you and Camden. I am so jelly. Now, on a scale of one to ten, what would you rate that? Ten being the highest. It seemed like a ten from my point of view. It was smoldering, intense, and looked like you would combust. I mean, smoking!"

I laughed like I always did whenever Jo was around. "You are medicine to my soul."

"Aww, friend," she said. "You so mushy today. Dial that Hallmark back a bit and tell me the number."

"Eleven." I thought about the kiss and sighed. "For sure."

"And with his awesome hearing, he just heard that. Considering he is at the doorway but don't worry. He doesn't know what we were talking about. But now he's intrigued because I'm still talking about the thing he doesn't know about, and I can promise you he will ask questions. If he doesn't, I'll quit my day job and start reading tarot cards."

I palmed my forehead. With friends like this, who needed enemies? "You are totally insufferable."

"Oh, stop," she sighed. "You'll thank me later. Again, it's a promise."

I hung the phone up, and of course, I found Camden exactly where she said he would be. He stood there, leaning on the doorjamb with tan arms crossed over his chest. His black hair hung over his brow, stubble was on his face, and he flashed a sexy smile. Whew, that man was so hot, he could make anyone combust.

"What's eleven?" he asked.

"My dad's shoe size."

His smile grew as he moved towards me. He stopped when he was right in front of me. Placing a hand under my chin, he said, "Maybe, but that is not what you girls were talking about. Try again."

"Don't we have a horrible man to go fight, and aren't we on a strict time frame in which to deliver the evil, red-headed siblings?"

He brushed my hair away from my face. "I think I have time, considering it's going to take my men half an hour just to fuel the plane. Tell me and we will go."

It was like ripping off a Band-Aid. The problem was I was the slowest ripper-offer in the world. "Okay. Fine. She asked me about our kiss. I rated it on a scale of one to ten."

He smiled as his eyes dropped to my lips. "And you rated it an eleven?" At my nod, he leaned in so close that I held my breath. "Let's see if we can get it higher."

"But... but we have boundaries."

Right before his lips met mine, he said, "I'm extending the boundary lines."

My hands traveled up his chest and through his hair where I gripped two fistfuls, bringing him closer to me. It was too much, and yet I couldn't get enough. Never enough. I felt every inch of him pressed up against me. The scent of something exotic wrapped around me like a cocoon. His stubble rubbed against my skin and it felt terrific. His hands were everywhere, and all I could think about was my need for more. The greedy need was what had me pushing away from him.

A look of hurt replaced the confusion on his face. I rubbed my swollen lips. "I just—we just can't. If you refuse to see where this thing between us could go, then I can't let myself fall for you."

What I didn't say was that it was too late. He was like an addiction. The more I was around him, the more I wanted him.

He shook his head like he was in a fog. "You're right, of course, and I already know where this will lead. To heartache. Lots of heartache."

My chin lifted. "Maybe. But being too scared to try for happiness, if only momentarily, is just plain cowardly in my opinion."

I took a wide berth around him and breathed deeply the whole way to the airstrip. I was trying my hardest to get his scent out of my mind and heart. The beautiful pine trees stood proud and strong, and that was how I would stand when my mission here was done. He had the key. He would keep his vow by returning the siblings, and my part in this game would be done. I'd be free to go home and do normal teenager things. One lone tear trailed down my face, and I angrily swiped it away. Just because I finally found someone who made my heart sing when he was near didn't mean I was supposed to be with him. In fact, as soon as we were done with keeping the vow Camden had made, I would teleport myself home.

The private plane was full of bodies by the time I arrived. Twelve stone-faced wolves sat in the back. Stephan sat in front with Cecil and Celia. Cecil was still in his chains. No one had bothered to free him, and Celia was tied up with rope. Both had duct tape on their mouths. It was for the best. Thanks to Kong, Cecil probably suffered from multiple concussions. Celia glared at me as I walked by. How anyone tied up like a pig at a barbeque could manage to still look condescending was beyond me.

Stephan was currently taking turns staring at each of the siblings while he ran his tongue over an elongated fang. I should probably intervene, but I wasn't feeling it. Kong sat on the floor in the middle of the plane—the only place the giant would fit. There were three seats left. I chose to sit next to one of the werewolves, so I didn't have to sit next to Camden. When he boarded the plane, his eyes searched for me and disappointment colored his face. He wanted to sit next to me, but he also wanted to keep me in a nice, tidy box that I couldn't step out of? No, thanks. I closed my eyes, so I wouldn't be tempted to look at him again.

I must have fallen asleep because Kong shook me awake right before we landed. "Time to go crush."

I patted his hand. "Yes, Kong. We can play crush the skulls if things go wrong."

"But not that one." He pointed to Cecil.

My brows scrunched together. "Did Ariana talk to you?" At his nod, I asked, "And what did she have to say?"

"No crush that one. Rest, I crush."

I held his hand as we exited the plane. How was I going to convince Kong to go back home with me? There was no way he would fit in our trailer, and no one from my town had probably ever seen an ogre. He would be miserable from all of their gawking and taunts. My heart sank even further. Kong would have to stay here.

He squeezed my hand. "Sad friend?"

I smiled just for him. "Not when you're around."

His gigantic face split into a grin showing chunky teeth with gaps between them. We walked behind the small group, until Camden stopped everyone at the gate. "We have the key now, and they will try to take it back from us. They can't but they'll try."

"Where is the key?" I asked.

He looked at me longingly for a minute before clearing his throat. "Stephan, could you take care of Cecil and Celia?"

I watched in fascination as the vampire barked a command and the siblings fell asleep. That vampire had some amazing skills for sure. I would siphon off of him more if it didn't hurt my head so damn bad. Plus, I could actually feel his bloodlust. That was a definite no thanks.

"Half of it is in a sealed vault, and the other half is in a lair behind my house," Camden said.

"I knew I smelled dragon on you," Stephan said.

"Whoa, you have dragons? Like real dragons." Wait until Jo heard about this, if she hadn't already seen it with her own eyes.

Camden gave me a smile. "Yes, and I'll show them to you when we get back."

"I'm leaving when I get back. I'll have to take a rain check."

He stopped walking and gave me his full attention. His fists clenched by his sides. "If you think that is wise."

"I do. I've done my part here, and I'm anxious to get back home to family and friends."

There was something he wanted to say, but when he noticed we had an avid audience, he nodded curtly and strolled to the guard at the gate. I could just read his mind to see what was on the tip of his tongue, but that felt like a violation of privacy, and I couldn't do it to him.

When the guard saw almost twenty people, two who were tied with chains and ropes, walking up the paved road, he grabbed for his walkie-talkie. Camden didn't say a word; instead, he grabbed the guard by the neck and banged his head on the station he was working at. He then reached over and hit a button, and the gate swung open. We all marched towards Merek's estate.

It was daylight, so any rogue vampires he had would be inside asleep, but one would think there would be some activity. There was nothing. His grounds were completely quiet. The air grew thick, and every step I took felt like I was treading through high-waisted mud. My legs grew heavy.

"He has cast a ward," Camden said. "There is a bubble around his property."

"Why would he do that?" I asked.

Stephan popped his neck. "This is like Vegas. Whatever happens in the bubble, stays in the bubble, and busybody Sharon two miles down won't be calling the cops."

"I guess he figured out that we stole his key and if he has his children back, then what's to stop him from killing us, huh?" I said out loud to no one in particular.

Merek came bounding out of his house. On the roof, men's heads popped out over the ledge, and they were all pointing guns at us. My guess was there were silver bullets in those guns. Merek clapped his hands. "Well done. CG, I knew that you would be able to accomplish the impossible. Come, kids."

The siblings walked to the best of their ability towards their dad, where he immediately started cutting the ropes off of Celia. Cecil's chains were magicked, so after a couple of attempts, he had to give up. He removed the duct tape from their mouths. That's when the whining began, this time from both of them instead of just one.

Kong took a step forward, but I squeezed his hand. "Sorry, friend. Maybe later." He looked defeated that he couldn't crush them.

Stephan clapped the ogre on the back. "Come on, big fella. I've got a job for you."

"Your children are delivered to you… alive," Camden said. "Let everyone here recognize that I have honored my vow."

"You have," Merek said, nodding, "but unfortunately, you have also stolen something from me, and I'm going to need it back." Merek noticed the vampire and the ogre strolling towards the house. "And where the hell do you think you're going?"

Stephan had his hands in his pockets. His signature move. "I'm here because that crazy soothsayer told me to be. The way she gives commands to everyone is deplorable. The woman thinks she's Beyoncé."

Stephan and Kong went in the side door to Merek's house while Merek just stood there with his mouth open. I heard something break. Stephan was laughing and someone was swearing. Kong must have finally got to crush someone.

Several guns cocked. My head tilted back to look at the men on the roof. I imagined Chron's aura as I concentrated on the weapons. Merek pointed at us while he shouted, "Fire!" But it was too late. I removed all of the guard's guns from them. They clattered to the ground, and Cecil stomped his foot as best as his shackled feet would allow and crossed his scrawny toothpick arms over his chest. Was he throwing a temper tantrum? When I thought he couldn't get any more disgusting, he went and surprised me. Ugh.

Merek flapped his flabby arms, making him look like a pterodactyl. "Carmen! I summon thee."

Smoke began to swirl around our legs and in our moment of shock, Merek and his kids made a run for the house. Good luck with that. The vampire was in there with Kong, and both were in a crushing mood.

Camden said, "I hate freaking demons."

Carmen came in the form of a twelve-year-old girl. What the hey? She had long, strawberry blonde pigtails with ribbons and baby blue eyes matching the dress she was wearing. "Once I get free of that fat arse, I'm going to melt his flesh from his bones."

Oh, wow. Obviously, she wasn't a kid. She noticed me looking at her. "What? Haven't you ever seen a kid before? My father—you know the self-righteous Demon King—got a little mad at the rumors circulating about my future powers and thought it would behoove me to lose my shell, so here I am, sporting this body. Do you know how hard it is to get laid like this? I look like that kid from the *Brady Bunch*." She studied the dead ends of one of her braids. "You summoned me, fatso, now what?"

Merek, the coward, stuck his head out from the door. "Summon as many as you can and kill them."

Carmen rolled her blue eyes and scrunched up her adorable face. "I'll be back in a flash, but this better not take too long. Stanley is getting flogged today, and I did want to witness it."

She disappeared in a swirl of smoke. Camden swore. "Son of a—"

"What are we going to do?" I demanded.

"Well, we really shouldn't kill Carmen. Since she is the Demon Princess, her father will come after us, and it's not that I can't defeat him, but if we could avoid that battle, that would be great. Carmen is brilliant; she knows that it doesn't matter how many demons she brings with her, she'll die if she goes up against me. My guess is she'll do her best to stay out of the way while we fight off her army and kill the summoner. Once Merek is dead, she is free of his command."

"Then we need to hurry." I walked towards the house when someone opened fire. I closed my eyes and waited for the sharp pain of the bullet to enter me but nothing happened. Camden had jumped in front of me and was riddled with holes. I found the guard who had shot him. Pulling the late Zander's aura to me, I made the guard turn the gun on himself. His eyes widened as he pulled the trigger. I felt no remorse. He had shot my wolf.

I knelt down next to Camden. "Are you okay?"

He grunted. "Been better." I watched in amazement as the bullets popped out of him.

He stood while I studied his black shirt hosting at least ten holes in it now. Crazy. I would have been dead, but here he stood just moments later.

"There are about a hundred guards or soldiers—whatever you want to call them—inside his home. They are made up of rogue werewolves, vampires, and witches. He has invited a lot of Degenerates here today, and soon we will be dealing with demons, too. I'm sure Carmen will probably stall for as long as she's able."

"She's a good demon? I mean, those exist?"

"I wouldn't go that far, but she hates Merek more than us, and she can beat him. Plus, you either have to be a powerful witch to summon a demon, which he is not, or you have to have something on them. She has probably been waiting impatiently for someone to kill him. Either way, we need to hurry."

I nodded. "The vampires will rise soon. We need to handle them now, and I can do that by myself. Go deal with the wolves." He hesitated for a moment before he took off towards the back of the house. I tapped into Zander's aura once again and called all vampires to come outside. Reaching out to one at a time would've been more effective, and if we had time I would have, but we didn't, so I concentrated on them all. Lumping them together, I told them to rise and come outside. Some were strong and fought my persuasion, but others were eager to please me. My legs began to shake, and something warm trickled down my chin. I wiped the blood away. Slowly but surely, they all tumbled out onto the yard where smoke rose from their skin. They began to scream and thrash around on the ground as the sun did its part. I just had to convince them to stay out in the rays a while longer. My knees buckled. The smell of burnt flesh filled me until I felt nauseated.

Stephan's shoes came into view. How he always seemed to dress so immaculately and keep everything so pristine and clean was beyond me. "I know that you did not try to tap into my mind and ask me to come out here," he said, helping me stand.

"I did, but I couldn't figure out how to not call you when I was calling all of your kind."

"At least you took care of all of the vampires in one fell swoop." He looked around at the piles of ash. "You're forgiven. Now let's go and—" His body tensed. "Oh, hell. She's back."

"From hell, actually." Carmen sneered. "It's good to see you again, Stephan. Let's see. When was the last time

I saw you? Oh yes, now I remember. It was when you wined and dined me then snuck out of my hotel room that morning."

"Aww, yes, the walk of shame. I remember it but not fondly." The vampire glanced at me and in a mock whisper said, "Full disclosure, she did not look like Barbie's little toddler sister that night. Don't judge me."

Carmen glared, and I had no words. "Ugh. Please. We did not sleep together."

She had brought an army of demons with her, and thanks to Stephan, she appeared ready to fight. At least forty demons were fanning out behind her, making a semi-circle.

Stephan whistled. "Look. They are all big, red, and horny. They came to party!"

"Stephan, please." The vampire was going to get us killed. I looked at the little girl in front of us. "Carmen, you must hate being summoned. Wouldn't it be nice if Merek was eliminated? You would never be summoned again."

Carmen studied me. "I want a new body."

"Um…" I looked to Stephan for help.

He dusted a spec of imaginary dust off of his suit. "Tired of attracting pedophiles?" At her glare, he sighed. "What if there was a body here that you could have?"

Pigtails swung as her head turned towards me. "That would be terrific."

"Nope, sorry, not this one," he said. "But there is a red-headed witch in there that is all yours—if you can get to her before the ogre kills her. While CG and his wolves are taking out most of the rogue werewolves, the ogre has taken a strong dislike to witches. There are very few left."

I knew the reasoning behind that. It was witches that took him to the portal and tossed him on a plane he didn't deserve.

"You will not fight me on this?" Carmen asked, and we both shook our heads. "I've run out of time. I have to obey his command. Try not to kill my father's demons but if you must, aim for the heart."

Wait. What? I thought we had worked out a deal. Carmen sat on a bench, swinging her legs as the rest of the demons ambled towards us.

Stephan let out a dramatic sigh. "With my strength, speed, and just overall greatness, I'll come out of this alive, but the last time I checked, you're not immortal, correct?" When I didn't answer, he said, "Just try to stay out of my way."

I watched him flash in front of one demon. He grabbed his horns and broke them off, causing the demon to fall to the ground. There was no way he was going to be able to stop all forty demons. I could run and hide, or I could stay and fight to the best of my abilities. As they were closing in on me, I made my decision. I let my wall down. Completely. Something Ariana had suggested I not do, but it was my best option right now. I gathered Camden's aura to me. I was going to taste the rainbow and pray it didn't kill me.

A demon wielding a sword tried to sneak up behind me. I turned to face him, dodging his sword at the same time. Using Camden's power, I jumped into the air and kicked him on the right side of his face. He hit the ground. Without thinking, I relieved him of his sword and stabbed him through the heart.

I looked at the bloody sword and remembered when I had accidentally tapped into Jo. This was the very scene that I had foreseen. But like she had said, it could always be worse. At least I wasn't dead. Yet. That thought spurred me into motion. There were more demons to take care of. I glanced at the sword in my hand and channeled Chron's ability to control objects. I imagined the sword cleaving the demon in front of me and then returning back to my waiting hand. His top half separated from his torso, both pieces hitting the ground.

The demons were smarter than they looked. They had just realized maybe I was more powerful than they initially gave me credit for. I didn't have the option of a fair fight. They were about to ambush me. I needed to do something fast. Stephan was breaking horns from one demon just to flash in front of a different demon, stabbing them through the heart with their comrade's horns. The vampire was completely savage. Just as we were helping to dwindle the demon population, more smoke swirled off to the right of Merek's house. More demons were coming. This was not good. Stephan uttered a four-letter curse word then yelled at me to run, but I couldn't leave him. At the same time, he was having a hard time fighting the huge demons because he was worried about me. If the cool, level-headed vampire was flustered, then we were in trouble. With Camden's hearing, I knew that between him and Kong, they were about to bring the house down. I could hear Camden grunting as he fought multiple supernaturals. I couldn't call him for help. It would distract him. I wiped my nose. I'd been steadily bleeding for the last five minutes. If I tried to control all the demons at once, it would kill me. We had run out of time.

Chapter twenty seven

I teleported in front of Stephan, who fought two demons at once. Grabbing him, I teleported him into the house, where the battle appeared like it was winding down. Body parts were strewn everywhere. I took a moment I didn't have to calm my breathing. I could have a panic attack later.

Stephan glanced around with a half-smile on his handsome face. "Please tell me that a girl did not just rescue me."

"I just delayed the inevitable. Those demons will be in this house within seconds. We need to find Merek and fast."

We stepped over bodies as we ran through Merek's estate. He had been building quite the army. My feet tripped as I recognized one of the bodies. It was Garren. Bile rose to my throat.

Stephan gripped my elbow. "The dead don't need your sympathy. We need to save the living by finding Merek."

"He has locked himself along with his children in a steel bunker." Camden came around a corner, bloody and bruised. "It's in the basement. You can manipulate

the steel door. Use Chron's abilities and bend it to your will, Sadie. You can make the door open." He finally made eye contact with me and let out a curse. "You're already bleeding."

"Yeah, I might have borrowed your powers. Right now is not the time for a lecture. Let's finish this, so I can finally get some rest and heal."

I could tell he wanted to argue. He warred with his emotions as one hand cradled his ribs. He was obviously in some pain as well. Finally, he turned his back on me and started moving down the hall. "Follow me."

We heard a crash. "The demons are in the house," I said.

"We will deal with them when we have to. All seventy-five witches are dead. Kong obviously had some issues there."

I kept quiet. It wasn't my place to tell them what I had witnessed. "The werewolves?"

"All are dead, except for the few that keep running from me. They won't be able to get out because of the demons, so eventually they will have to face me."

After we ran down the steps and into the basement, the three of us halted in front of a door that looked like it belonged to a bank vault. Carmen had somehow managed to beat us down here and was biting on one of her nails as she paced in front of the door. Her braids swung with every step she took.

"I'm supposed to kill you. It is taking everything I have not to try," she said without glancing at any of us.

"Get out of the way, and let Sadie try to open this door," Camden said. "Then you will be free of his power."

She moved, and I began concentrating on manipulating the steel. There had to be a way to keep my walls up partially as Ariana suggested. Too bad she didn't just come right out and tell me how to do that. No, that would have been way too easy. I dropped my walls and peeled the door back with my mind. Blood flowed freely. Camden shouted at me to stop. He promised we would find another way, but like him, I could hear the demons coming for us. The door flew open the same time my body sagged. He grabbed me from behind, preventing me from collapsing.

He placed a kiss on top of my head. "You did it."

Five shocked faces glared at us. Like rats trapped in a corner, they ran out of the safe room that was anything but safe. Carmen pounced on Celia. The girl shrieked as Carmen took over her body. Celia's body started convulsing. Her eyes rolled back in her head and drool covered her chin. Taking over one's body was not a pretty sight.

There was a commotion to the right of us. Merek made a run for it. He almost reached the bottom of the steps when Camden set me on my feet and went after him. Merek didn't have a chance. Camden grabbed him by the throat and pinned him to the wall. With one squeeze he broke the chubby man's neck just as the demons came down the stairs.

As if their mission had been aborted, they looked at their princess. Carmen, in her new body, gave them all an eerie smile. "Go back to Hell. We are done here."

Stephan had quickly disarmed and killed the two werewolves who were in the safe room with Merek.

When he stepped out, his pristine shirt was covered with blood. I would wager that none of it was his own. Cecil was crouched low to the ground. His arms covered his head and he whimpered.

Stephan took two long strides towards the coward but Camden intercepted him. "We have been ordered not to harm him. Ariana said it's not his time."

This gave Cecil hope. He bent down and picked up one of the dead wolves' guns and took aim at my chest. As the gun sounded, a blurry image appeared before me, wrapping me up in their arms as we both hit the cold cement floor. Everything that followed seemed to happen in slow motion. Stephan removed the gun from Cecil, smacking him in the head with the butt of it. Cecil crumpled to the ground, still alive but motionless. I rolled Camden over. Why wasn't he moving? The bullet had gone through his heart.

Stephan voiced what I already knew. "His heart is not beating."

I laid my forehead against his, as I cradled his upper body in my lap. Then I remembered Ariana's words about what I would see that wasn't so. He wasn't dead. He couldn't be. Even Camden told me the only thing that would temporarily kill him was leaving the bullet to penetrate his heart. I ripped his T-shirt in half, so I could get a better look at his chest.

"This has been fun," Carmen said. "But I really should be getting back before blondie here goes all crazy and starts carving her name is his flesh."

"Rot in hell." Stephan smirked, as she began to disappear in a cloud of smoke.

"Stephan, I need you to go upstairs and check on Kong. Camden is not dead, and I'll wait here with him until he wakes up."

He ran a hand down the back of his neck. "I hate to break it to you, but—"

"Leave us!"

He looked like he wanted to say more but decided against it. I waited until his vampire hearing would no longer reach us. No one could know Camden's secret.

As I placed my palms on either side of the hole in his chest, I concentrated. Tears fell from me as I imagined the bullet moving upward. After what seemed like an hour, but was only seconds, the bullet exited his body and floated in front of my face. I reached out and grabbed it. Why I wanted to keep it was beyond me, but that's exactly what I did. I pocketed the silver bullet in my jeans. Then I waited.

Blue-green eyes met mine with confusion. A calloused hand gently reached up to my face, wiping the last of the tears away. "Why are you crying?"

Still cradling him in my lap, I said, "Happy tears."

He rubbed his chest and then looked around him. "That weasel hit me in my sweet spot?"

"Yeah. Another bone I have to pick with Ariana. If she hadn't told you to keep him alive, you would have never gotten shot trying to protect me."

"I would die for you," he said. At his admission, a look of horror washed over his face. He rolled off my lap and climbed to his feet. My heart clenched. He loved me. It was written all over his face, but he didn't want to admit to it.

The moment was over. I ignored the extended hand he held out for me. My heart squeezed like it was in a vise. No matter how much he wanted me, he would never choose me. He was so caught up in the past, in what had happened to him and his brother, he wouldn't give love a chance. I stood up and dusted off my pants.

"Thank you," he said, his voice quiet.

I shrugged his gratitude off. "What do we do about him?" I pointed at an unconscious Cecil.

"Leave him."

"He tried to kill me and shot you, and we're going to leave him?" My feelings were hurt, and I was spoiling for a fight.

"Ariana said—"

I threw my hands up. "Ariana said this and Ariana said that. Ugh. I'm so over it. You've got your key. You've upheld your vow to Merek and your promise to Ariana. You won't harm the precious Cecil. I think we're done here."

As I was marching up the steps, I heard him softly say, "Ariana never said that Cecil wouldn't die; she just needs him to set someone else on their correct path."

I turned on the top step. "And what is your story, Camden? To live in the past?"

I didn't wait for him to respond. I stormed through the house searching for Kong. He ended up being outside with Stephan. The ogre I had grown so attached to appeared forlorn.

"Kong, what is it, buddy?"

He held up his gigantic hands for me to see the blood on them. "Kong crushed."

"I know and it's okay." I held both of his hands in mine. "You saved us. Don't ever regret saving your friends." When he finally made eye contact with me, I said, "Listen, buddy, I have to go and where I'm going, there isn't any ogres. If you come with me, life isn't going to be easy for you."

Camden had exited the house, but I pretended not to notice. There were only four of his men left, and they all gathered outside, looking battered.

Stephan said, "I can look after him."

"Or he can stay with me," Camden said from behind me. "I have plenty of acres where he can run through the woods."

Kong shook his head. "I go with friend."

"Are you sure?" *Please say yes*. I selfishly wanted him to come with me. "You would probably be happier here."

"You go. I go," Kong said.

I gave him a big smile. Glancing around at the men, I said, "Boys, you'll have to excuse us." Trying to act like my heart wasn't breaking in two, I winked at Stephan. "Take care, vamp." He hugged me.

With a deep breath, I turned to face Camden. "Please tell Lil I said goodbye."

"Don't go," he begged.

"Why would I stay?" When he didn't reply, I had my answer. I would use my powers one last time for the night. Then I would pass the hell out. Turning back to the ogre, I held onto him tightly as I pictured the shabby, little pink trailer I had lovingly called home. Even though I felt like I would break from my decision, it was the right one. Camden had issues. Ones that he needed to work on without me.

chapter twenty eight

The moment our feet touched down in front of the trailer, Jo was waiting outside on the porch with a smile. "Dude, I'm loving the new pet. I mean, I was all for a cat, but this is so much better."

"Do you know who this is?" I asked her as she bounded down the steps.

She nodded. "I get little blips here and there. The scenes play out like a movie reel in my head, and since I don't get to pick and choose what comes to me, there are some deleted scenes. But yeah, I saw enough to know you were coming here with him."

Kong walked over to her and patted her head so hard I thought he was going to drill her in the ground. "Friend."

Her short black hair, always so artfully arranged, was now a mess. "Dude. Control your pet."

I laughed. "Kong, be easy, buddy."

Kong nodded. "Pretty."

Her blue eyes roamed his gigantic body. "Anatomically speaking, that could never work." She studied him in a calculating way. Her hand stroked her chin. "You know, though, I will allow you to be my bodyguard. Anytime I say the word, 'Timmy,' I want you to growl."

Kong tilted his square face to the side. "Timmy not friend."

"Good Lord, no," she said as she turned to me. "How are we going to fit him in the trailer?"

"We can't. But we will have to think of something."

We both watched as Kong went over to the flower beds and did three circles before lying down in the mulch. He closed his eyes and murmured, "Sleep."

I followed my best friend up the steps to our little trailer where I spent the next three hours laughing and then crying. I was a rollercoaster of emotions. I built my walls before she hugged me because now more than ever, I realized what a burden my friend carried. The last thing I wanted was any visions of the future. I would never search for her aura because that was one gift I did not want.

She caught me up on what had happened the last week of school and how life had been treating her while I had been away. She tried at first to stay away from anything concerning Camden, but he had been a considerable part of my life since I started on this adventure; we might as well not talk about anything if we avoided talking about him. So, I told her everything she didn't already know, until I had cried every tear from my body. Then I went to bed utterly exhausted.

Someone was in my bedroom. I pretended to be still asleep. There was a creak in the floorboards right next to my bed, and my eyes shot open. A scream tore from me as I gazed up into the weathered face an inch from mine.

Jo flipped the lights on as I pressed myself into the mattress to get away from the creature hunched over me.

It took me several more seconds before I realized the creature was Ariana.

"Dude, is she trying to give you the kiss of death?" Jo asked.

"Hellifiknow!" I shrieked. "Either kill me or give me some room, woman."

Ariana slowly straightened up as much as her curved back would allow. She shrugged a bony shoulder. "I was trying to read her."

"Read me?" I pulled the covers to my chin. "I'm not a book. What are you doing here, Ariana? Aren't your powers so vast that you don't need to show up uninvited to my humble home to see the future?"

Ariana's wrinkled face lifted into a smile. Obviously, I hadn't tried hard enough to insult her. "Child, I know that you don't like me."

"Of course, I don't like you. You use all of us as pawns. To be honest with you, I'm not sure that you're on the Lux side."

Ariana nodded. "This is about Cecil? Try to understand that if Camden hadn't rescued him, or worse, if Cecil were to die right now, then Death wouldn't be spurred into action, and Stephan's life would end very differently and not for the better. Cecil is a vital part of everyone staying on the correct path."

Jo walked into the room. "Death?"

"The Undertaker." Ariana's head turned to the side. "You've seen him, no?"

"Oh, now I got you," Jo said. "Dude, I have had so many fantasies about that morsel. He is one fine piece of—"

"Jo! Focus." I scooted up in the bed. "Ariana, I get what you're saying, but I think if you are here to help us, then you would be upfront with us instead of shady."

"Shady?" she asked. "I like shade. It's hot in the South." At my eye roll, she smirked. "What if I were to tell you that you needed to go back to Camden? That is the place you will be safe. Would you go?"

Point for the freaky soothsayer. "No, I wouldn't."

She sat on the edge of my bed, and it took everything I had not to cringe. If she knew of my discomfort, she didn't let on. Jo walked over to the only chair in my tiny room. In typical Jo fashion, she raked all of the clothes in the chair onto the floor before she took a seat.

Ariana patted my knee. "I see all. When I deal with the most stubborn of supernaturals, sometimes I have to do some meddling. You might not understand it right then, and I don't expect you to."

Jo's brow was furrowed. "I didn't see you coming. Why are you here?"

"You didn't see me coming because you are not using your powers correctly. You are like an open line. You let anything and everything come through. Once you learn control, you won't stay up most nights from seeing complete nonsense. There is nothing you can do about cheating Dan or Susan's addiction to chocolate. Nonsense, I tell you."

I looked over at Jo. "Dan? The guy that owns the gas station? Who is also Timmy's dad? He's cheating on his sweet wife who volunteers at the elementary school?"

"Yep," Jo said.

Um. Well, that might be nonsense to Ariana, but as soon as the soothsayer left, I was going to figure out why my bestie didn't tell me about that golden nugget.

"I'm here because of Sadie. Her mind frame is in a different place when she is away from her mate, and now there's a fifty percent chance that she will go down a different path than the one I previously foresaw. I can't have that. The Lux can't afford that. I came to ask permission to show you something."

I still didn't trust this woman. "What?"

"I would like to show you a vision," she said. "One that will give you a better understanding. I need you to be patient."

I looked to Jo for guidance. She shrugged. "Dude, I'm not going to lie. I'm getting nothing off of her. Your guess is as good as mine. If she's as good as everybody says, then she knows that if she hurts you, I'll stab her in the eye."

To my astonishment, Ariana tilted her head back and laughed, a beautiful sound. "I do like you, Jolene. A lot. I can't wait until that Fae Prince stumbles upon you. You will show him who's boss."

Jo's blue eyes rounded. "Want to elaborate?"

Ariana shook her head. "Sorry, I can't. Now, ladies, I have got to go make sure that handsome, arrogant, and slightly crazy vampire stays on the path that I need him to. Before I go, may I please show you the vision?"

Why the hell not. "Sure."

She scooted up on the bed and placed each of her hands on either side of my head. At first nothing happened, but then my world changed. I was no longer in my homey pink trailer. I was transported to a time when cars didn't exist, and there were no paved roads. A house that appeared vaguely familiar came into view. After studying it for a few minutes, I recognized it as Camden's family estate. It was smaller, someone had added to the house over time, and it didn't look as luxurious as it did now. Two little boys tumbled in the yard as their parents lovingly watched from a blanket on the grass. One child had fair hair and one had dark hair. One had pale skin, and one looked like his skin was bronzed from the sun. The fair one with his bright blue eyes the color of the sky favored his mother, and the dark one shared his father's coloring. The oldest brother—the dark-haired one—laughed, causing both parents to smile. He looked over to where his parents were, and his blue-green eyes twinkled. My heart squeezed as I recognized Camden as a small boy. He was the cutest child. One memory after another flooded me, and each time I saw the same family. One thing never changed—the amount of love they had for one another.

Then a vision came riddled with pain. A group of rogue werewolves approached Camden's mother. She was out in her garden when she heard them. Her husband was at a council meeting, and she was alone with her small boys. She knew what the rogue werewolves were there to do, so she led them into the woods far from the house, where she didn't fear her sons would hear the commotion and come out to investigate. She died with honor by protecting the ones she loved.

The next image had me sobbing. Camden's father cradled her mauled body and wept. The guilt of not being there to protect her consumed him, for Ariana had warned them both that his mate was in danger. He'd refused to listen because his pride got in the way. Who would go against a king? Everyone feared him and with Ariana's powers, his sons would be even more powerful. More feared. No one would touch his family. He hadn't listened to the soothsayer's warnings, and now he had to pay the ultimate sacrifice. He had lost his mate.

Ariana had known the king would take his own life in his grief, but she hadn't stopped him. It was eleven-year-old Camden who stumbled upon his father's body. It was also Camden who shielded his brother from the ugly truth. Vision after vision and memory after memory showed how Camden struggled to hold his own against grown wolves wanting the title of king, and how he had to be strong not only to survive for himself, but for his brother. His life was anything but easy, and my heart wept for the boy who hadn't had a childhood.

Ariana lifted her hands and the memories stopped. I opened my eyes. Jo was pacing by my bed, chewing on her already short nails.

Ariana gave me a sad smile. "You've seen everything that Camden went through, and you know that I could have stopped it. Would you like to know why I didn't?" At my nod, she said, "Because when Camden's father,

Jacoby, lost his mate, he lost his mind. I saw he also had a fifty-fifty chance of living, and that path showed me more death. I would have lost Camden and Jamison. They would have been with their father one night somewhere they should have never been. My boys would have died trying to protect their father from a mass of rogue werewolves. A father riddled with guilt who didn't care if he lived or died. I love my boys, and I wasn't going to lose them."

Maybe I misunderstood her intentions, but I still didn't understand why she was showing me any of this. She stood up from the bed. "Patience. Please remember to be patient." She turned to Jo. "You've seen what you must do?"

Jo nodded. "Yes, but I can't see my outcome."

"You'll live. I've already told you that you will go up against the Fae Prince. Whether you will be the victor or not is totally up to you." She gave each of us a nod before fog swirled around her and she disappeared. I didn't know she could do that. It seemed like I didn't know a whole lot about Ariana.

"Was she talking about the Fae Prince who betrayed his grandfather? The one that stole the key from him?"

"One and the same," she said. Her face was pale against her midnight hair. Even paler than normal. She stood to leave my bedroom.

"What have you seen that you must do?"

"Sorry, dude. You'll have to file that under need to know, and you don't need to know." She gave me a saucy wink. "Maybe one day I'll let you sit at the cool kids' table. But not today."

"Just answer this, are you okay?"

"Dude, when have I ever been less than exceedingly magnificent? 'Okay' is too generic of a word for me. It's not even in my vocabulary."

I chuckled as she left my small bedroom. I had no clue what the two paths were that Ariana said that I might take, but I felt hopeful she wouldn't have left here if she didn't think it would have been the right path. Maybe her impromptu visit helped me in some way, and if that were the case, then I would thank her. That was if our paths ever crossed again. I might not be psychic, but I had a feeling I would see Ariana again.

chapter twenty nIne

The second visitor of the night was just as unwelcome as the first. Apparently, no one believed in calling or had any sense of personal space. A beautiful girl sat in the same chair Jo had cleared out earlier. Her black dreadlocks hung to her lower back. Her nose was a little long and sported a nose ring, and her mouth a bit too wide, but it still didn't detract from her beauty. Her caramel eyes lit up when she saw that I was awake.

"It's about damn time," she said.

"I'm sorry that I was sleeping. At night. In my bedroom. Welcome to Grand Central Station. How can I help you?"

"Cheeky. I like it." That voice… I recognized that voice. Warm and sultry.

Aww hell. I sat up in bed, pushing my messy blonde hair behind me. "Carmen?"

"And smart. Good for you." She did a slow clap. "So, here's the thing, precious, like all beautiful princesses in every other fairytale, I have an evil stepmother. My father, the Demon King, has always been a douchecanoe, so it's not like I can blame that on her, but she has helped him up his game when it comes to pure evilness."

Why was she telling me this? Did it look like I needed a bedtime story? I rubbed the sleep out of my eyes. "Carmen, why are you in this body? What happened to Celia's body?"

She gave a laugh that died prematurely. "Yeah, so this is where the story gets funny. My body is kept in a concealed lava pit. It's the only way my father can control me. We have some serious dysfunction in my family. That's still not the funny part. Wait for it. It'll come in a second. I've had to resort to stealing bodies. The poor kid I inhabited was being pulled off of life support when I claimed her body. Then, of course, there was Celia. Normally, I don't take over someone's body unless they're dead, but I was desperate, and her life expectancy wasn't going to be long if that wolf of yours had anything to say about it. So, I went home to daddy dearest in Celia's body. After a demon inhabits a body for twenty-four hours, the source dies. Not a big deal, right?"

"Um. I'm guessing it was, or you wouldn't be here in another body."

She waved a hand over her body. "This one was overdosing in a club. Ask me where Celia's body is."

"Where is—"

"I'll tell you where! My father, that asshat, commanded me to exit her body. Apparently, he knows Celia and has been jonesing after her. So here I am, tracking down another body because my father won't let me have mine, and now Celia is planning to kill me."

My head spun. "Why does she want you dead? Because you took control of her body?"

She tossed a braid behind her shoulder and looked at her silver nail polish, which was chipping. "Oh, precious! Did I leave out that part? Celia is my new mommy."

"What?" I croaked.

"Yeah, maybe it wasn't so funny. Father married her, and now she's my new stepmother. Honestly, he goes through women faster than I go through underwear but still. Now that she's in an authoritative position, she wants revenge on you and your wolf because you killed her father. She also wants me dead because I took over her body, or it could be because once I released her, she was rude to me, so I threw a fork at her head. Or it might have been a dagger. Honestly, it's a toss up at this point. Your guess is as good as mine."

"Without trying to sound rude, why are you here?"

"Come to think of it, this part isn't funny either. Sorry I misled you. I'm here to warn you that they are on their way to kill you and your wolf. Who they will go after first, I haven't a clue."

I jumped up and started throwing on clothes, not caring that I had an audience. "Why come here and tell me anything?"

"Would you believe me if I said some creepy woman told me that if I didn't, I would die? The thing with my powers is I can tell when someone is lying. So either she believed what she was saying, or she was telling the truth. Plus, she promised that if I had your back when you needed me the most, then she would send the power eliminator to help me rescue my body."

"Power eliminator?"

She rolled her eyes. "Precious, you've been sheltered for way too long. There is only one known power eliminator. He's like a silencer, but he can drain supernaturals' power, well, except for the Undertaker's. No one can take his power." She waved a hand in front of her. "Look, I don't have time for a history lesson. You should know all of this, considering it's your brother. Besides, we have company."

My brother? I thought the coolest power my brother had was teleporting. Whenever he got back home, I would be having a long talk with him. How could he hide this from me and why? Carmen jumped up from the chair and withdrew a dagger. It was so unexpected that I just stood there, hating myself for misjudging her. The knife went sailing an inch past my head and through the only window I had in my room. The window was open because in the summer, our air conditioning never worked, and the trailer became a sauna. The dagger hit a demon in the eye. He wasn't dead, but it stopped him from grabbing me and pulling me through the window. Kong was outside roaring. He was my primary concern at the moment as I ran barefoot through the tiny trailer.

Outside in my small flower garden, he wrestled two demons. He grabbed both by their heads and rammed them together. Their heads thumped against each other like ripe watermelons. He did this over and over until they stopped moving.

Carmen stood beside me on the porch. She let out a loud whistle and gave the ogre a little shimmy. "You go, you big lug. There is another one that's missing an eye around here somewhere. I'll go find him."

She skipped off the porch and was whistling as she rounded the other side of the trailer. "Marco? Can I get a Polo? Little demon. Come out, come out wherever you are."

Kong looked at me. His massive head tilted to the side. "Friend, yet?"

I looked at where the Demon Princess had gone. "Still not sure, buddy."

Where was Jo? It wasn't like her to let all the entertainment go by without her commentary. "Kong, have you seen Jo?"

He nodded. "Gone."

"Gone where?"

He picked up one of the demons by his horns. "Gone with these."

"They took her?" I screamed in panic.

"No. She let them take."

I came down the porch steps just as Carmen was dragging a dead demon by his foot behind her. That wasn't possible. "Why would she leave with one of them without putting up a fight? She knows demons are sadistic, especially the king." Looking over at Carmen, I said, "No offense."

"It is what it is, precious."

The trailer phone rang, and I took off at a dead run. I knew it had to be Jo. What was she up to? This was somehow Ariana's doing. What was her game this time? Whatever path she needed me on, if she thought she could use Jo to get me there, she was dead wrong. Or maybe she was completely right.

"Hello?" I half screamed, as I picked up the phone.

A voice I had missed greeted me. "Sadie, I need you to come home."

"I am home, Camden."

I could almost hear him clenching his teeth. "Fine, I need you to come to my estate. Can you teleport here?" When I didn't say a word, he added, "It's about your friend."

"I'll be right there, and I'm bringing two with me." Before he could ask any questions, I hung up the phone. I would rather not ask him for permission to bring a Demon Princess to his home.

The first thing I did before I left was reach out to my father, telling him he needed to be aware that there could be a threat coming to town. How did those demons break through the town's wards? Unless Jo helped them. He promised to hold a council meeting. I didn't tell him that I had gotten back home earlier because I didn't want to hurt his feelings by not coming by to see him. The truth was I thought I was home for good and could visit with him and Granny soon. I had wanted to take the day to mope around, so I could put on a happy face for my family tomorrow. I took today for granted, and now I didn't know when I would get to see my family again.

After I teleported Kong and then Carmen to Camden's foyer, I went to search for the wolf. I found him coming out of the elevator.

Instead of exiting, he held the door. "I knew you were here. I was coming for you. Let's go upstairs to talk, okay?" I nodded, not knowing what else to do. My emotions were all over the place. I had been away from him for one day, and I had missed him so much the pain was surreal.

He was even more handsome than I remembered, and that was a difficult feat. I followed him to his upstairs haven where he led me to a couch. He took the armchair and turned it, so he was facing me. My heart pounded with fear. Just by his body language alone, I knew something was wrong. Jo had to be okay. Didn't Ariana say something about her battling a Fae Prince? My friend had a part in this war, too, and she couldn't do it if she were dead.

"You said you have information about Jo?"

He reached out and grabbed my hand. "Yes, and for right now, she's alive, and Ariana has sworn to me she'll be fine. There is something I want to discuss with you. Can you give me that?"

Everyone was all chatty Kathy all of a sudden. "I'm listening." I watched his Adam's apple bob as he tried to find his words. This Camden I wasn't used to. The unsure Camden. I reached up to brush some stray hair off his forehead. "Just tell me."

He sighed. "You need to go through a ceremony with Ariana and me."

I raised my eyebrows. "What kind of ceremony?"

"I know that you are powerful, and the more different kinds of supernaturals you come across will make you stronger. However, if a Degenerate was to catch you unaware, all they would have to do is kill you. You are not immortal."

"You didn't answer my question."

He let out a sigh. "It's a marriage vow."

I jerked my hands from his. "What?"

"There was a reason Celia wanted to be my wife, other than me being a powerful king and my wealth. It was because she wanted to be immortal as well. Whoever I marry, our spirits become as one. She will be as hard to kill as I am. The same goes for Jamison and whoever his mate is. You can still be killed, but it makes their job harder."

"You have tried to keep me at arm's length since the moment I met you because of your past, and now you are willing to go one above and talk about marriage?" I made a motion with my hands, waving at him then myself. "Are you on crack? Let me guess, Ariana told you to do this, so now you're willing to take the bullet; in this case, it comes in the form of taking a vow to me just because she said so?"

"Actually, no. Ariana told me about your friend, Jo, and how she intentionally got kidnapped, but she did not suggest us taking a vow. What she did say to me left me almost broken."

Livid? No, I was pissed. "Why the turnabout, Camden?" Part of me didn't even want to have this conversation. He'd had his chance. He'd missed the opportunity for happiness. But the other part of me needed to understand fully. "And why broken?"

"When you left, I felt like I couldn't breathe." His hair was a mess, and his clothes were rumpled. Did he not sleep last night? "After the first hour of your absence, I realized you'd already snared me. While you were gone, all I could think about was, were you safe? Fed? Happy? I can't live the rest of my life without you." He got down on his knees in front of me and grabbed both of my hands.

"I drove you away with my reluctance to let go of the past. The thought of losing you for good almost broke me. Never seeing your radiant smile or hearing your laughter again. The way you smell like vanilla and home or hearing my name roll off your tongue. I can't lose you. Sadie, you're my mate, but more than that, I want you to be my mate because the thought of not having you in my life is unbearable. I choose you, and I want you to choose me more than anything."

My heart swelled with love. Just as I was about to give him my answer, his cell phone rang. He gave me a quick apology before answering it.

If he was frustrated with his quick phone conversation, he didn't show it. As soon as he hung up, he said, "That was the vampire. He wanted to know what Ogres eat. Before I could answer, he screamed 'No! Not that. Put it down.' We should probably go and check on them."

"I agree."

He stood up while never releasing my hand. "You don't know why Jo went with the demons, do you?"

"No, but she was acting a little strange after we were woken up by Ariana's midnight visit."

His eyes that reminded me of a sea green ocean pierced mine. "She told me about that. Ariana also said we wouldn't have to wait long before we have the information we need to get your friend back. Celia is many things, but stupid isn't one of them. Even if I didn't want to admit how much you meant to me, I'm sure she knew. She can kill two birds with one stone if they kill you. They are going to demand your life for Jo's. The only way for them to win this battle is for you to be dead."

"I held my ground at Merek's estate. What were the odds again? And yet, I'm still alive."

"True, but you weren't fighting a band of the Demon King's finest either." He stood and helped me to my feet. "This is his second attempt to get you, but he will never have you. Let's go downstairs and see if word has come yet."

Before we got onto the elevator, he pulled me in for a kiss that was anything but gentle, but had the same effect on me as his tender kisses. He pushed a strand of white-blonde hair behind my ear. "I'm yours, Sadie Grey, and I'll tell you that every single day until you realize that you're mine, too."

I stepped from the elevator to go search for our group of misfit friends with my stomach in knots. All during the high school years, I'd avoided any excessive emotions when it came to boys, and now I was a rollercoaster of feelings when it came to Camden. He had my stomach going from loop to loop to free falling. I had a feeling my heart was going along for the ride, too.

chapter thirty

We found everyone in the living room. Kong sat on the Oriental rug in the middle of everyone. Lil rested on his shoulder. Stephan was reading a book on the opposite couch, where he ignored Carmen. She was equally ignoring him as she picked at her nail polish, sitting on the armrest of a wingback chair facing an unlit fireplace. I smiled as Lil flew over to me, talking ninety miles per hour like it had been months since I'd seen her instead of twenty-four hours. After cupping her fondly in my hand, I sat on the couch closest to Kong. I looked around to the people that I thought of as friends. I told them of my best friend and how she was missing, and then I told them what Carmen had shared with me. Celia was alive and married to another king. One who planned our death.

Stephan mumbled, "Get in line."

Ariana glided into the living room. Her eyes glazed over. Camden jumped up to help her sit in the other wingback chair. "Has it been a long night, noni?"

I smiled at the nickname. I could picture Ariana as many things, but noni? Nope. Not happening.

She sighed when she finally sat. "So long. So many things are coming through the lines these days. Your brother is on his own adventure. He will lose something but gain something." She gave a pointed look to the vampire who was still pretending to read. "And of course, I see a stubborn vampire who has trust issues. Then there is Jo."

"What have you seen?" I asked.

"They said you are to meet them tomorrow at midnight, alone in one of Savannah's famous graveyards. They said they would release your friend as soon as you arrive and after they make sure you have not brought reinforcements."

My hands started to shake. I was scared for Jo and me. This sounded like a trap. I would go through with it, even if there were no way for me to win. I couldn't leave Jo hanging.

The coward in me was relieved when Camden said, "They have midnight carriage tours in the downtown district, where they tell visitors all kinds of haunting stories. Fortunately for us, the tour goes right by the graveyard. I'm going to be guiding the tour tomorrow with a few allies dressed up as tourists. If you can stay alive long enough to free your friend, then we will come in and rescue you."

"Tourists?" Stephan turned a page in his book. "Yay! I've always wanted to wear a fanny pack."

"I'll do my best to stay alive," I said.

"Please do." Camden looked at each one of us. "Kong will have to stay here because we can't hide him."

Kong said, "I go."

Camden shook his head. "Sorry, bud. It could harm Sadie if you did, but we could use you here. I'll be leaving Ariana here by herself. Do you think you could stay and protect her?"

Kong's chest puffed out. "Yes. Ariana friend."

Ariana surprised me by getting up from her chair and kissing Kong on top of his head. "And you are mine."

"Do you think you could mask our scent?" Camden asked, and Ariana gave him a nod. "Thank you. That will help us from being detected."

"We're leaving in eight hours," Camden said. "Everyone prepare, however you need to." He held out his hand to me. "Come. I want to show you something before we leave."

I followed behind Camden as we left the house and took a path to the backyard. When the stonework ran out, we kept going. I didn't question where our destination was as we entered the forest. He held branches for me as I walked through the trees, helping me to step over fallen logs. Who said chivalry was dead?

The wildlife, including the crickets, became eerily quiet. Maybe they sensed Camden, a more significant predator than themselves invading their territory. The foliage started to open a little right before we stepped into a big clearing. I followed him through the dandelions and down a small hill. What awaited us took my breath away. There was a cascading waterfall dropping into a lagoon. Shiny rocks jutted out all around the bank, signifying the shallow areas. It was completely magnificent.

We hopped from stone to stone until we reached a dry, flat rock in the middle of the lagoon.

"Sit with me a minute?" Camden asked.

"I would love to."

"I thought my little mermaid would enjoy this. You are the first person other than family that I have ever brought here. It's wonderful here and instead of sitting and worrying for the next few hours about your friend, I thought this would help take your mind off things."

"And you believe Ariana when she said that Jo will be fine?"

"Absolutely."

We stretched out our legs side by side and sat in companionable silence, just watching the beautiful nature around us. I had no clue what tonight would bring, but I would forever hold this moment close to my heart.

"I'm sorry." He didn't look at me as he said those words, and at first, I thought I misunderstood. "The things I feel for you can't be measured. I think of you when you're right beside me and when you left, I couldn't think of anything but you returning. I was going to give you one more day before I went to get you. It's not fair of me to say we can't see where this thing between us goes when I can't let you leave me, so I'm sorry. Sorry that I have been giving you mixed signals."

I tried to tuck an unruly curl behind his ear but it bounced back. "I get it. I understand why you would be hesitant to travel a path you think would lead you down the same road as your father."

"It's more than that," he said, as he picked up a small pebble, skipping it over the water. "I have lost uncles, cousins, and friends all because my father couldn't hold onto the key. So many people tried to step in and protect my brother and me from the Degenerates, and they all ended up dying. If my father would have finished raising his children and protected the key like he had vowed to do, I wouldn't feel like this. Like this second chance of saving the world rests squarely on my shoulders."

"You shouldn't feel that way, though."

He brought my knuckles to his lips and gave them a light kiss. "But I do, and yet the whole world can go to hell if I can't have you by my side. I am asking two promises from you. The first is that after this is all said and done and we rescue your friend, you will come back here. Give me a month to win you over."

I thought about his words. I honestly didn't want to be any place other than here with him. The day away from him made me miserable. I was actually ready to be his mate, but I found myself asking, "What's the second promise?"

"After the first month, if I haven't won you over, you will give me a second and a third. Until I get it right."

I burst out laughing. "You know what? I think I can make that promise. In fact I think I can do you one better Camden Grant. I want to go all in."

I swear he stopped breathing. "You mean… you mean that you want to be my mate?"

I gave him a shy nod. "More than anything."

He was talking so fast that I almost couldn't understand him. His words spilled out of him in an excited rush. "Since you're not a werewolf, our mating bond will be a little different. For us to become one, we have to vow to except each other as mates, mix blood, and the werewolf in me has to bite you right here." His finger lightly trailed above my shoulder blade. "It's the way we mark our mates. Are you ready?"

I held up a hand. "Wait. You want to do this right now?"

"There is no reason not to. Not if you're sure—"

Was there a reason not to become his mate? I couldn't imagine life without him and as hard as he had tried to push me away, he was unsuccessful. He needed me just as much as I needed him.

"Tell me what we need to do."

His grin was megawatt bright. "We'll say our vows, we mix our blood, and I'll mark you. Our bond will grow stronger, and I can show you every day here forward how much I love you."

"Let's swap some blood then."

He laughed with joy before he stood up, bringing me with him. He pulled out a small knife from his back pocket. He made a cut on his palm before passing me the blade. I looked at the blood glistening on his hand and gathered my courage. Wincing a little, I made a similar cut.

He clasped my hand in his, mixing our blood. He said, "Sadie Grey, I vow to be your mate now and forever." After he gave me an encouraging nod, I repeated the words back to him.

I could feel my hand healing from whatever powers he was using. As soon as he released my hand, he grabbed the bottom of my T-shirt. "Arms up, love. I've got to remove this before the next part."

I obeyed him. Then I said, "Wait a minute. You couldn't just pull my shirt to the side?"

He dropped my shirt beside us on the rock we stood on. "Sorry, I didn't think of that."

Yeah, right. His gaze dropped, and he stared at me for so long that I became self-conscious. I started to cover myself, but he let out a growl. "Don't ever hide from me, Sadie Grey. You are beautiful."

I watched in fascination as he morphed in front of my eyes. His features became sharper, and his body elongated and widened. In whatever form he donned, he was so incredibly handsome. Definitely swoon-worthy. He twirled me around, pulling my back into his massive chest. He draped all of my hair over my left shoulder before nuzzling the right side of my neck. I rested the back of my head onto his chest as I closed my eyes and tried not to moan. This was definitely more interesting than reciting vows.

"I'm going to mark you now." His hands rubbed circles on my stomach. His five o'clock shadow tickled my sensitive skin as he tilted my head farther away from my shoulder. Sliding my bra strap down my arm, he left a trail of kisses from my neck down to the place he was about to mark. "Usually, this is done when mating, but this will have to work for now."

There was a slight pain before complete bliss as his teeth sunk into my shoulder. His grip on me tightened as my shoulder heated. After a few moments, he gave me several more kisses over the skin he just marked.

"It's done now. All other werewolves will recognize you as my mate and know that you are mine."

"And you are mine."

"I have been since day one."

He pulled me in for a kiss that ended way too soon for my liking.

"I can't," he said almost breathlessly. "Not after just marking you. Everything in me wants to mate with you." He turned his back. His fist was clenched, and he was taking deep breaths. He was trying to calm the beast inside of him, and it looked as if he was struggling.

"Maybe I want you to mate with me."

Another growl. "No. You need a couple of hours of rest before we go find your friend."

I fumbled with my shirt as I quickly tried to put it back on. I had a friend who needed me to come and rescue her, even if she did plan her own kidnapping, and here I was lusting after a man so hard my eyes were crossing.

I announced when I had my shirt back on. He gave me a nod before he swept me up into his arms and carried me back over the stones. I thought he would put me back down once we got to the bank, but he held me all the way back to his home. I laid my head on his chest, listening to his heartbeat while I let the exotic smell of him wash over me.

He put me down when we reached the paved stones making up the pathway back to his house. We entered through the side door leading to the kitchen. Ariana was there, waiting on us. She was half sitting on a barstool. I knew she was delighted with what just took place without her saying a word.

A single tear strolled down her check as her crinkled face lit up with a gigantic grin. "I came to see you both off before I go lay down for a bit." She hugged me before she embraced Camden.

"You have been so tired here recently. I worry about you."

She sighed heavily. "There is just so much information coming through it's almost impossible to keep track of all of it. I worry about the vampire. I could save his mate but if I did, she wouldn't be his mate, now would she?" She obviously didn't expect us to answer. "And that Vampire Queen! I've always hated her. Could I send someone to take that crown from her? Of course, I could, but then poor Stephan would never be who he is meant to be. There is your brother—"

"Jamison is fine, isn't he?"

"Would I let anything happen to him?" I swear she rolled her eyes. "But he's blunt when he shouldn't be and hides things when he should be honest. It will cost him his mate, if he's not careful."

"His mate?" Camden asked.

"Yes, do try and keep up. And Death, he stalks his prey like she's an adversary, when she could be his biggest ally, but try telling him that. The Undertaker thinks he knows all because he is all." The lines in her face deepened as she glanced at me. It was like she forgot I was there for a second. "Oh, and Austin—did you know that I knew your brother?" She didn't wait for me to answer. "He has gone silent on me. Very frustrating. Especially when I promised him you wouldn't be mad because you are one of the most logical of the bunch."

She was wigging out. "Um, mad about what?"

A long, gnarly finger tapped her chin. "Yes, I might have forgotten to tell you. Your brother was the one who silenced your powers for you. It needed to be done, or you would have suffered. The Vampire Queen would have come for you. Then she would have kept you her prisoner. You would have eventually met Stephan, but Camden… well, not in time. It would have—"

"Let me guess. It would have put me on the wrong path?"

She patted me on the head. "See? Logical. You've already calculated that your brother who adores you wouldn't have done something he thought would have harmed you, and you know that masking your powers kept you safe." She headed towards the servant steps leading to the second floor. "Now, things are coming through about that scoundrel." She said the term like it was an endearment and not a slight. "If I have to think of the Fae Prince and his shenanigans, I might as well be lying down while I do it. At least with Jo in training, she will be able to help me with the switchboard. After all she got you two together, didn't she? But the poor girl doesn't know it yet. She has got to learn how to use her powers better."

We both were quiet as we watched her climb the steps, all while mumbling to herself about some girl named Charlie and her insecurities. Logical or not, I was a little upset with my brother. As soon as I saw him, we'd be having a little chat.

"I don't know if I could take all of those visions and different scenarios coming through daily," I said. "I would go insane."

Camden chuckled. "And yet, she is probably the sanest of us all."

Well, wasn't that a scary thought. I followed him into the living room where Stephan and Carmen were still ignoring each other. Lil was babying Kong, which was hilarious, considering she was the size of my palm, and Kong was a giant. Thankfully, Camden had high vaulted ceilings, and Kong seemed to be comfortable. I listened to everyone talk like they didn't have a care in the world and wondered if it would ever truly be easy. Would there come a day when we wouldn't be fighting for our lives or the lives of someone we loved? Or should I be grateful that if we were fighting, we were still alive? I rested my head on my mate's shoulder as I drifted off to sleep, worried life would never be easier. But with work, it could be very enjoyable.

chapter thirty one

avannah, Georgia was different from the small coastal town that I was born and raised in, but it held its own magical beauty. Magnificent trees covered in moss lined the cobblestone roads. Most of the downtown area was made up of big plantation houses that were relatively close to one another. Musicians played on the corners, and when the wind blew, I smelled a hint of jasmine.

The scenery almost made me forget about the doom and dismay waiting for me. Almost.

Camden had brought fifteen werewolves. It was a risk to bring just one, but it was a risk he insisted on. Ten of them were spread all over downtown Savannah, pretending to be homeless beggars. I walked alone up an uneven, narrow street when I saw Stephan. He was playing the violin. Huh. Go figure. Whatever the song was, it made me want to weep. It was beautiful and sad at the same time. That vampire was such a mystery.

Camden was giving a fake tour to his remaining five werewolves. Three men and two women sat in the back of the horse-drawn carriage as Camden held the reins. He looked dashing in his top hat and coat. It was hard not to stare at him, but I somehow managed to avert my eyes. The whole way here he had reiterated a hundred times the importance of me ignoring them. I didn't want to let anyone know that I had brought reinforcements; it could cost Jo her life.

My steps slowed as I neared my destination. I crossed the street corner where Stephan was playing. He had a hat full of money and a handful of admirers. Total shocker, most of them were women.

My feet felt heavy as I came to the gate of the graveyard. It was locked, so after I made sure that no one was watching, I jumped the fence and headed towards the marble angel that stood in the center of the graveyard. I had pulled Camden's aura, which was now my new aura also, letting it wrap around me like a glove, so I already had a clue where the demons and the witch were. I was a little surprised when I saw fog snaking up around my legs. Somebody was wasting energy to produce that. They had the whole fear factor thing going on. Little did they know, I didn't need the fog or the creepy graveyard to be scared. Or maybe they were making sure no tourists could see into the cemetery. That wasn't a thrilling thought.

The fog parted around me, allowing my eyes to see what my mind already knew. At least twenty demons and Celia surrounded me. She was like a severe case of gonorrhea. She kept flaring up when you least expected her. The biggest demon stood nearly seven feet tall with eyes the color of blood and wore a black crown that appeared as if it was made out of bones. A very mad Celia stood beside him, glaring at me. She must have missed me. Her hand reached up and squeezed his bicep. Yep, this must be the king.

Not one to waste time, I directed my question towards him. "Where is my friend?"

The king nodded to a stout demon standing slightly off to the side. The smaller demon took his cue and started walking over to an above-ground grave. I saw red as he peeled the heavy cement lid off. How long had Jo been in there? The smaller demon reached in and grabbed an unconscious Jo out of the grave. Her eyes fluttered open, and she let out a scream, causing me to take two steps towards her.

The one who I assumed was the king held up a hand. "Take another step, and I will have Blaken kill your friend."

I glared at the enormous demon, who was number one on my "people I would like to die" list, but first I had to get my hands on my friend. Then I could teleport her out of here, and the rest of the gang would come in and clean house.

"Where are my manners? I am Dimitris, King of the Demons. I have been trying to secure this meeting with you." He inclined his head towards Celia. "I guess I have you and my daughter to thank for sending me my new wife. I do hope she's sturdier than the last." I glanced over at Celia, noticing she had bruises marring her pale skin. "So far, she's been a fascinating toy."

Eww. Gross. I refused to feel sorry for Celia. She brought this on herself. "Yes, my condolences are in order. Moving on. You've kidnapped my friend to bring me here. I'm here. Now what?"

"Actually," the Demon King said, studying me first then Jo, "that was something I've been meaning to ask your friend about. Rumor has it that if she doesn't go crazy first, your friend here will be as powerful as Ariana one day. Could someone tell me why a powerful psychic didn't see the Demon King coming?"

I looked over at Jo, and she winked at me. I couldn't believe it. She was becoming as bad as Ariana. Purposely getting kidnapped by demons, and now she looked as if she was perfectly content with the way things were going. I silently wondered if she was going to micromanage the rest of my life for me.

"You know," the Demon King purred, "I could give you anything your heart desires if you would join us."

"That's going to be a hard no from me, but thanks for the invite."

He flashed a set of sharp teeth as he leered at me. "Of course. Blaken, release the soothsayer."

This was my moment. I lunged for Jo as she jumped to the side, avoiding my grasp. What the hell? Didn't she get the memo? This was a rescue attempt, and she was blotching the whole thing. The demons moved in on us, but the king gave them a command in some foreign language, and they all stopped. Jo rolled on the ground as I tried again to get my hands on her. I barely managed to grab her jacket when she twisted and maneuvered herself, so she came out of her coat, and I stood there holding it in my hands. My mouth dropped open in shock. She was going to get us both killed.

The Demon King stood there with a confused look on his face. Yeah, well, welcome to the party. Jo now hid behind a demon. She mouthed the word "sorry" to me, but I wasn't having it. I screamed at the king, "What have you done to her?"

"Nothing. But this is very interesting." The Demon King observed both my friend and me. "Why were you trying to get to her? Where could you have possibly gone, and why didn't the soothsayer want you to touch her?"

Celia's eyes rounded before she smirked at me. It was official; she was number two on my list of people to hate. "Husband, I believe the power manipulator was going to teleport her to somewhere safe. My father had a teleporter in his employ, and I've seen her take others' powers."

"Is this true?" he asked. When I refused to answer, he asked Jo, "And why didn't you want to go with her?"

She didn't answer, either. At least we were on the same page about some things.

The Demon King was stumped, and I took perverse pleasure that I wasn't the only one grasping for straws. "Word is that the King of Werewolves is your mate. We planned to lure you here, and if you refused to join forces with us, we were going to wait for your mate to try and rescue you. Then kill you in front of him, watch the king crumble, and take his key, but it seems as if that plan isn't going to work now. If you can teleport, why are you still here?"

Wasn't that the million-dollar question? The closest demon to me was a good seven feet away. I could be gone in a split second, but thanks to my crazy friend, I found myself shrugging. The plan was to grab Jo and teleport her to where Camden was. That would give him and the others the green light to come slay some demons. Then I was to teleport Jo back to Camden's estate. No one knew I was going to return to the graveyard to help fight, but it didn't matter now since none of that would be happening thanks to Jo. Soon, though, my friends would figure out something went wrong.

The Demon King narrowed his black eyes at me. "I feel as if I'm being played."

Again, there was a club. One I was unwillingly a part of. Everyone should join. It was loads of non-fun.

The Demon King's flat nose twitched. "There are others in the area. Grab the soothsayer." The demon Jo was hiding behind snaked out a thick arm and pinned her to his chest. "If the power manipulator teleports, kill the girl. The only reason she has stayed this long is for the soothsayer. Why the soothsayer didn't want to go with her friend, though, is beyond me. This changes things."

Damn it, Jo! The Demon King started speaking in that foreign tongue of his again, and one didn't have to be a behavioral analyst to know he just commanded his demons to kill me.

Celia flipped her long, red hair behind her shoulders and sneered. "I've never liked you."

I glared right back at her. "Really? No way. I would've never guessed. Your acting skills are superb."

The Demon King said, "That'll be enough, Celia. Go stand over there before I get tired of your mouth and end you for good."

I gave her a wink and then made a shooing motion with my hand. She was obviously scared of her new hubs because she didn't say a word to me as she headed to the opposite end of the cemetery.

The Demon King said, "Brando. Now please."

One demon came towards me while the rest formed a tight circle around me. I was guessing this was Brando. He took out a long blade that curved at the end, and they all started snickering. Acting fast, I tapped into my ability to control minds. Stiffly, Brando pivoted to the demon on his right side. The blade swung at the shocked demon. Brando took off his compadre's head before pivoting to his left. The next demon was ready for the attack. Unfortunately for Brando, he was a lot smaller than the other demon. The large demon snatched the blade and Brando died quickly.

The Demon King started clapping. "You get more and more interesting. I think I'll keep you, train you, and by the end of the calendar year, you will be my best weapon."

"Um, not likely. You'd have to sleep with one eye open for as long as I was held prisoner."

"You're right. It'd be too much effort." He made eye contact with the closest demon to me. "Kill her."

The demons advanced and I panicked. I might not be able to teleport, but no one said anything about floating. So that was how I got to the other side of the graveyard. I Peter Pan-ed my way across. It would be humiliating, but my pride was the least of my problems right now. As soon as my feet touched the ground, I focused on making the demons nearest to me kill each other. I stood back and watched as four of them ripped each others' hearts out. Then I concentrated on the Demon King but nothing happened.

"I can feel you tampering, but mind control doesn't work on me."

The remaining demons fanned out. "Can't blame a girl for trying."

I heard them before I saw them. My grin was so big it almost split my face in two. They came in from all different angles. Camden strolled right through the front gates. Every eye was on him while Stephan flashed in front of a demon, grabbing him by the throat. Carmen jumped the side wall and the ground vibrated where she landed. Her braids were swinging about her as she attacked one of her own, causing the Demon King to sigh dramatically. "Why such disrespect for your father? Is it because I wouldn't let you keep Celia's body? Or is it because I won't give you back your original shell?"

"Oh, Daddy dearest. When have I ever respected you?" Carmen sneered. "You killed my mother when she tried to save me from your beatings, drowned my very first friend, killed my pet, and tortured me for telling a boy I loved him before you killed him as well. All because you're terrified that I'll be more powerful than you ever were. I think it's safe to say I'm not a fan of yours."

The Demon King looked bored. "You're not getting your shell back."

"Oh, but I have a feeling I'll be walking away with your crown tonight," she said.

"Not if I kill you first."

Carmen shrugged with indifference, but I was left speechless. The Demon King definitely wouldn't be getting the father of the year award anytime soon.

The fighting began in full force. Camden had morphed into his larger, more impressive version. He was clearing a path towards me. I almost felt bad for the demons.

Stephan was precise with his movements, and Lil was flying over the demons, shouting out commands to the rest of us. Her fairy dust didn't work on demons, but that didn't stop her from shouting out warnings. Camden's werewolves were helping clear a path so that Camden could get to me faster. I was now immortal, but his need to be by my side was endearing.

There was a chance if we killed the Demon King, the rest of his army would cease fighting. I focused my energy on him. Mind control? Maybe not, but I did have other talents that might work on him. I gathered Camden's aura that was very much a part of me, too, now and threw out a hand towards the Demon King. His large body lifted several feet off the ground, flying into one of the many statues in the graveyard. The marble busted into tiny smithereens. He wasn't dead, but I felt hope one of us could make that dream a reality soon. I saw Jo running through the graves with a demon on her heels. How did she escape? I teleported to the last place I saw her. Unfortunately, that took me farther away from the wolf that was hell bent on getting to me, and my actions had pissed him off if his shouts were any indication. The Demon King ran so fast it was almost too hard to track. His fist went flying into a statue above my head. I covered myself as marble rained down on me, and I barely had time to register he was in front of me before he shoved a shard of marble through my stomach. My knees buckled. He laughed. "Don't start something you can't finish, girly."

Somewhere close by, I heard Camden roaring my name. The Demon King crouched, so he was on my level.

He smiled at the hunk of marble protruding through my stomach. "Here, let me help you with that."

He grabbed a hold of the shard and slowly pulled it out of me. I screamed. This could have been fatal—if I was mortal. The moment the piece of marble was free, he reared back to stab me again. There was one small problem with his plan. He had made me mad. I let my walls down, and with my new aura, stopped the marble from going into my chest again. Then I turned the object with my mind, thanks to Chron, and thanks to my mate's strength, I rammed the marble into the Demon King's heart. I had no time to celebrate before I sensed someone appear behind me. The last sound I heard was my neck snapping.

chapter thirty two

woke to wounded werewolves and dead demons.

Score one for the home team. I rolled my head to the side to see Camden holding a heart in his hands. Considering that the dead Demon King had a hole in his chest the size of Mississippi, I guessed the organ belonged to him.

"Hey beautiful. Welcome back."

"I so need a vacation. This week has been a doozy."

He laughed and continued to hold me. "This is your first time healing yourself. It can be draining."

I was one hundred percent okay with that. I was in need of some old-fashioned TLC.

Carmen stepped over her father's dead body. She leaned down and removed the solid black crown from the Demon King's head. "Looks like there is a new sheriff in town." She wiped the blood off the tips of the crown and then placed it on her head. Talk about a cold-hearted biatch. But I couldn't help but admire her. She was wicked—wicked cool. The crown was way too big, so it slanted to the right. She gave us a finger wave. "I've got to go find your brother, Austin, so I can get my banging body back, and according to Ariana, he's just the man for the job. Sayonara, suckers."

She disappeared in a cloud of smoke. If I weren't exhausted, I would almost feel sympathetic for my brother. He was going to have his hands full with that one. I could give him a heads up that she was on her way, but considering he was secretive about his talents, I thought I'd leave him in the dark. Then maybe we'd call it even.

As the exhaustion of my body healing itself began to fade, the battle was rushing back to me. "Where's Jo? A demon was chasing her the last time I saw her."

Sweat beaded Camden's upper lip. "Can you sense her? If she's close, you should be able to read her mind."

My body wanted to hibernate, but I closed my eyes and tried. "She's in a tunnel. It's underground. Not too far from here. There is also water. Can you hear it flowing?"

"I'll find it," he said.

"Good because that's all I got. I'm all tapped out."

"That's normal. The first time I healed myself I slept for three days straight. I'm shocked you woke up so soon after that demon broke your neck. He died a slow, painful death by the way." He stood with me in his arms. "I'm not letting you out of my sight. Hold on tight."

"Where did Stephan go?"

"Too much blood. He was scared he would hurt my werewolves. Lil left to check on Kong and to prepare for the hurt wolves. They all heal at a fast rate, but some might need medical attention to help the healing process go quicker. All the demons are dead but Celia is missing."

Every step he took jostled me, and I couldn't help but wish sleep would claim me. "Thank you for watching over me while I was—what was I? Not dead, but what?"

"Healing. That's what you were doing, and I would do anything for you," he said, as we went down some narrow steps. My eyes closed until I heard a door squeaking open. We were in a tunnel. I couldn't lift my head off of his chest, but I could hear him wading through water. He stopped walking after a few minutes.

"Up ahead the tunnel branches off, and I've lost her scent." His blue-green eyes peered down at me. "Should we go left or right?"

"Left." I remembered what Jo had said about my birthday present. It was for me to go left. She got her own self kidnapped, refused my attempt at rescuing her, and then gave me the birthday gift of how to find her. Next time, I was going to ask her for some cookware.

We finally caught up to the demon who was playing a cat and mouse game with Jo.

She was barely evading him. She cocked a hip out. "Jeez, guys, it's about time. I was scared the both of you stopped for a make-out session along the way."

I wished I could stand, so I could knuckle punch her. "I'm assuming you saw me injured?"

"Dude, that was so twenty minutes ago." She ducked, just as the demon took a swing at her. "Do you think it's possible we could focus on the threat at hand?"

Camden placed me on my feet. I grabbed hold of a wrought iron ladder leading up to whatever street was above us. Once he made sure I wasn't going to crumble, he let go of me. Jo dodged the demon once again.

The demon must have been young because he didn't understand what kind of threat Camden was and that was his mistake. Camden quickly came up behind the demon and grabbed him by his neck, ramming the demon's face multiple times into the stone wall. In his signature move, he punched his hand through the demon's chest, coming away with a heart.

Jo wrinkled up her nose in disgust. "Yeah, so I've had visions of him doing that before, but in person, it is way more intense. Do you have hand wipes?" Camden just stared at her without blinking as he wiped his hands on his pants' legs. "Yeah, okay, that's not sanitary, but it looks like we're in a sewer, so who am I to judge?"

Camden glared at Jo. "You risked her life with your stunt!"

She waved a hand at him like he was being dramatic. "No, I didn't. I would know if she was going to die. Duh! Plus, I had to do this."

I rested my head against one of the rungs of the ladder. "You're always so sympathetic to Ariana and all of her meddling. I think the least you can do is hear Jo out."

"Aww. Thanks, bestie." She batted her long, black eyelashes at me. "So, this had to happen because one, this forced you lovebirds back together. Which, by the way, you still haven't fully committed to this bond. Shall we? I'm ordained."

I snorted. "No, you're not."

Camden looked at me and I shrugged. Should we tell her? Maybe but I was willing to see where this went. She really needed to get a better hold on these visions. Especially if she was going to be meddling like Ariana.

She nodded. "You're right. I'm not. Plus, it's not the time and sure as hell not the place. Can you imagine telling the grandkids about this? It would go like, 'So we were in this rat-infested tunnel that smelled like the back end of a donkey, and we took our vows right then and there beside a heartless demon and a hot ass witch.'"

"Funny. So, what's the second reason?" Camden asked.

"Did I say I had more reasons?" At Camden's glare, she said, "Whoa kidding. Kidding. Easy, big fellow. So secondly, the Demon King had to lose his crown, and he had to lose it to his daughter. Why? Sorry folks, that has to remain a cliffhanger. You might—"

"Set Carmen on a different path," I groaned. I was really starting to hate that saying.

"Dude, you're so getting it. Another reason is Celia would have remained in Hell with the Demon King until he tired of her, and that was not to be her fate. Also, I would like to point out at this time that if the Demon King hadn't kidnapped me, he would have joined forces with someone that I cannot mention, and dude, let me tell you," she said, pointing at Camden, "you would have lost so many werewolves. Like totally tragic. So that red-horned freak had to die and quickly. You don't have to thank me with words. I take gift cards and wine in the box because I'm classy like that."

Camden scowled again, and I was terrified that he was going to harm my best friend. "Camden, let's go home."

Jo winced. "Yeah, about that. We should get out of the tunnel, but the night is not quite over."

"Okay, Miss Riddles, but you should know something. We're mates."

Jo's face was priceless. "You're kidding me."

"Why would she kid about that?" Camden said.

Obviously, he was still angry over her endangering me. "Man," Jo said, "this sucks. You would think I would have seen that tidbit. I so need to watch some training videos or something. Oh well. The rest still had to happen, so whatever."

Camden mumbled something under his breath as we climbed up the ladder to exit the tunnel. I was pretty sure he was plotting ways to kill Jo. My friend, being the awesome psychic she was, had a fifty percent chance of knowing that, so I wasn't too worried. And by the way she was humming, I would say she wasn't too concerned either. As soon as we were clear of the tunnel, I realized this night would never end.

he street we were on was completely void of any humans. Cecil had wrapped the whole block in magic, repelling tourists. He stood there with a cocky grin splitting his freckled face. His red hair had recently been trimmed, and it was gelled back from his forehead. Behind him stood ten supernaturals, including Celia. According to their auras, they were mostly witches. Wait, why was Celia smirking? We'd defeated the Demon King, and she was standing there bruised and dirty and smirking. What was I missing?

"Welcome to the party," Cecil said. "I'm not sure if you know Fredrick?" A tall, muscular man stepped forward. His buzz cut and blank stare made him look like ex-military. His hands were clasped in front of him. "Fredrick here used to be in your father's pack before he defected. I will be assisting him with leading your pack after we kill you tonight. He is the one that will take your throne and wear your crown."

Camden laughed. "Is that right? You and what army?"

"Funny you should ask. Celia? If you don't mind. Give me the object that I've had hidden away for some time now."

Celia gave us both an evil smile before she procured a black key from behind her back. She held it up to a thin piece of shimmering air. Oh, great. Just what we needed. The portal was open, and there was no telling what would come over first.

"Go, teleport you and Jo to somewhere safe," Camden said.

"Yeah, you probably don't need a psychic to tell you that she's not going to leave you high and dry," Jo said. "Besides, she's immortal now."

Camden let out a growl as he morphed into his larger version. Jo was in her custom head to toe black leather. Her heavy boot tapped on the ground like she was impatient for the so-called party to begin. I wouldn't trade places with my bestie for all the gold in the world. I didn't want to see the future. Hell, at this very moment I didn't like the present too much. But with that being said, it irritated me to no end that she knew exactly how this was going to go down. I was so tired of the damn fighting. At least I would be getting no more nosebleeds, but I still wanted to rest for at least twenty-four hours. Was that too much to ask?

Jo sighed. "Pay attention, it begins in five, four, three, two—"

A witch threw a magic ball at us, but thanks to Jo, she knew it was coming and easily maneuvered both of us around it. The ball hit the ground and exploded. The way the concrete sizzled it was clear the ball held acid.

Another ball flew at us, and we barely had time to get out of the way. Embarrassment colored her face. "Sorry. Didn't see that one."

We both watched as Camden engaged with Fredrick.

I started to join the fray but Jo stopped me.

"Dude! This is a portal for witches gone bad. We've got this, let those walls down, baby. Let them crash and go kick some butt."

"Got it."

I ran across the uneven stones when Celia appeared in front of me. She tossed the key to her brother. He sneered at his sibling. "What are you waiting for? Kill her!" Such a sweet family!

"There is nothing I would rather do than watch the breath leave your body," she said.

"It seems like you might have some anger issues you should probably work out." I dodged a ball of fire she sent at my face. "There are definitely some unresolved feelings you should talk to someone about. Just not me because I have things to do."

Her hands heated with another ball. "I will kill you." The first of the Degenerates came through the portal; they looked confused but ecstatic. I had no time to waste. Calling Stephan's aura to me, I flashed behind Celia and used his vampire strength to throw her against the ground. She rolled over on her stomach and hurled something. A small, golden dagger. I used my mind to stop the blade just before it entered my chest. Karma happened as I made Celia fly backwards with a wave of my hand thanks to Lil's powers. She stopped when a street sign impaled her body. The metal buried itself in her chest. The same spot she'd initially intended for me. Blood seeped through her shirt as she took her last breath. Her brother let out a scream, as he made his way to his fallen sister.

I flashed behind someone else but not before I saw Jo whispering something to Cecil. After I had fought two more witches, I noticed Cecil was gone. Ugh. This whole keeping the slimeball alive was going to be my undoing. Camden elbowed one of Fredrick's werewolves in the face while he kicked the witch in front of him in the chest. Hmm. He must have already disposed of Fredrick. That was my boy.

"I have to close the portal!" His bellow carried out over all of the fighting. "I can use our key, but we need to hurry."

He fought his way to the open portal. He took out the black key as several supernaturals ran towards him. He was trying to close the portal with the key that now had all fifty or so supernaturals' attention. Someone knocked the key out of Camden's hand, and I watched in horror as a witch picked it up and took off. Someone attacked her, and then it was a free for all. We had lost the key, the portal was still open, and there was a possibility we wouldn't make it out of this alive.

"Watch out!" Jo screamed as a male witch grabbed me by my throat and started squeezing. I teleported to the other end of the magically contained space with him in tow. As he was trying not to get sick, I used Camden's strength to throw him into a parked car that, unfortunately for the owner, was also trapped in the magical bubble. Jo's heavy boots clomped towards me, as she dodged fiery balls aimed at her.

She halted mid-step and shouted at the witch, "You can take your balls and shove them! Today isn't my day to die, freak."

I used mind control on the witch she was yelling at, convincing him to throw her fireballs at the witches behind him.

A fireball smacked me in my middle. I rolled to all fours. "Seriously, Jo! You have got to get better at your visions."

Jo stood over me, fighting every witch that came towards us the only way she knew how. By knowing where they were going to attack and moving us like chess pieces on a board game. "Shh. I'm concentrating."

I looked across the bubble to where Camden should be but couldn't see him. But my body recognized that my mate was fine. I could hear his heartbeat as if it was mine. Thanks to my mate, my vision was better than it had ever been, along with my hearing. I felt invincible. As I climbed to my feet, I felt victorious. With a flick of my wrist, I sent the witch hitting Jo into the side of a tree.

My walls came crashing down. The power resting inside of me was no longer hard to control. It was as if everything had clicked into place. Now, my power was so easy to wield. I needed to move an object. One in particular. Using my mind, I called the key to me. It came soaring out from underneath a haystack of witches all scrambling for the it. The key landed in my palm. My mind quickly separated the witches and rogue werewolves from Camden and Jo. I gathered the Degenerates up and had each and every one of them floating in the air before I dribbled them like basketballs on the road. It was almost comical. Now, I had their attention. They were no longer in charge of their bodies. Their mouths gaped open as I lined them up like little ducks.

I teleported to the portal. "Thanks for visiting, but now it is time to go back. I understand that sometimes we can be misjudged. I have a friend that didn't deserve to be sent through a portal. If you feel as if you have been misjudged for your crimes, please speak up." Before anyone could speak, I held up a hand. "Know that I can and will read your mind. If you lie to me, I will personally redeposit you to portal forty-nine." The expressions on their faces were pure horror. Good. They knew I wasn't playing. No one said a word and after a moment, I moved every single one through the open portal and quickly sealed it after the last one crossed over. I had controlled multiple beings at once while crossing powers. I wasn't bleeding or dizzy. In fact, I felt energized.

Jo clapped, and Camden smiled as he walked towards me. I tossed him the key, and he snatched it in midair. When he stood right in front of me, he grabbed me by the back of the neck and kissed me so hard, Jo let out catcalls. His lips pulled back from mine. "Hello, my queen."

"Oh, I do like the sound of that."

"You did good, real good." His turquoise eyes glinted with happiness. "Shall we go home?"

Home. That sounded unbelievably good. But there was something I needed to do first. "I have to go to portal forty-two before we go back home. There are some ogres I need to free. Then we can finally rest."

"Dude, you're like indestructible now," Jo said. "We can rule the world, and I do mean we because you're going to need a sidekick. I know you have the ogre, but my vocabulary is better. I say we go to the beach. You can use your mind control on everyone. Convince them they need to clear the area, and then we will have the whole place to ourselves. Or maybe you can convince Timmy that he needs to relieve his bladder every time he goes out into public? Oh, dude, think of the things we can do with your fantastic powers. This is going to be epic."

I laughed at her ramblings. Camden swooped me up and twirled me around, and then he was kissing me again. Somewhere in the distance, I could still hear Jo planning out the things we were going to do.

We had the key. I had my mate and he had me. My friends and family were safe, and my powers were steady, true, and strong. Indestructible? Maybe. Grateful? More than anything. I was where I needed to be and with the person I was meant for.

chapter thirty four

I woke up in Camden's huge bed, wearing nothing but one of his T-shirts. I would never get tired of his scent. Who needed an exotic island when your mate smelled of ocean, wind, and the promise of tomorrow? I threw the covers off of me and padded barefoot to the kitchen where I heard noises. A disheveled, bare-chested Camden was making breakfast. Another thing I would never get used to... waking up next to my mate. It had been four months since I had become Camden's mate. My granny and father were coming for a visit today, and I was so excited to see them. No one had been able to get a hold of my brother, but I had it on good authority that he was fine, if not a little perturbed he'd been forced to work with a demon. My brother was stubborn and Carmen was bossy. Their teamwork had to be less than ideal.

Cecil was still missing, but apparently that was all part of the big plan. I wanted to see his head on a spike, but whatever. We had found all of Kong's family. Just remembering the portal we had to go into gave me the willies. I hoped to never revisit that portal again. Jo insisted I retrieve the missing ogres while wearing all black, because it was authoritative and total badass. Camden insisted I wear the family crown, so others would know it was the Werewolf Queen that was all powerful, so I had to teleport home before we could go collect his family, but it was worth it. I rocked that crown. It took us hours, but we finally brought over the ogres who'd been misjudged.

Now, at least twenty ogres inhabited Camden's woods. I thought Camden would object, but he just smiled and said he would do whatever made me happy. I didn't tell him this, but I was hoping I would see baby ogres running around one day.

Ariana was training Jo, and my best friend seemed to be able to control her powers better now. Stephan had left months ago. I missed that vampire, but I had a feeling I would be seeing him again. Well, mainly because Jo said so.

I sat at one of the barstools as Camden loaded me up a plate with fresh eggs. "Good morning, beautiful."

"I'm so excited about my family coming to visit. I'm sorry about the call with Granny."

He was trying hard not to smile. "Oh, the one where she said, 'Look dawg, you hella cool, and I'm crunked about you and my girl, Sadie, but we're going to need a for-real wedding. You feelin' me?'"

Once she started watching *Empire*, her vocabulary took on a whole new life. I felt blood rush to my face in embarrassment. "Sorry. I know that she insisted on a wedding, but we don't have to go through with it. I could just tell her—"

"Stop right there." He leaned over the counter and tilted my chin up, so I would meet his eyes. "In the werewolf community, the mating bond is stronger than any wedding ceremony that could take place, but if your family needs a wedding, I'm all for it. Saying you're mine in two different ways couldn't make me happier." He gave me a wink. "Besides, this way you get a ring."

I turned my face to kiss his hand. This was why I loved him. He would do anything to make the ones I loved happy. "What kind of ring are we talking about?"

He let out a laugh, making my heart smile. "Are you happy?" he asked.

I stood up and walked around the counter. I started placing kisses all over his face. "I am so incredibly happy." He chuckled as I wrapped my legs around his waist. I kissed him with all my heart, letting him know what my words could never convey.

Camden started walking in the direction of our bedroom. "We have a couple of hours before your father and Granny B get here. Let's put the time to good use."

"Granny B?"

His lips trailed over the mark he had given me. "Hmm. Yeah. She's totally into someone called Cardi B, and she told me today to just 'roll with it.'"

I laughed as he threw me back onto the bed. Since the last week of high school, I had been on some crazy adventures, but it was all worth it because I found exactly where I belonged. With my king.

about the author

Brandi Elledge lives in the South, where even the simplest words are at least four syllables.

She has a husband that she refuses to upgrade...because let's face it he is pretty awesome, and two beautiful children that are the light of her life.

23340389R00182

Printed in Great Britain
by Amazon